Mates at Billabong

Mary Grant Bruce

Mates at Billabong

The present edition is a reproduction of previous publication of this classic work. Minor typographical errors may have been corrected without note; however, for an authentic reading experience the spelling, punctuation, and capitalization have been retained from the original text.

ISBN: 978-1-63637-018-7

CONTENTS

CONTENTS

CHAPTER I

NORAH'S HOME

The grey old dwelling, rambling and wide,
With the homestead paddocks on either side,
And the deep verandahs and porches tall
Where the vine climbs high on the trellised wall.

G. Essex Evans.

Billabong homestead lay calm and peaceful in the slanting rays of the sum that crept down the western sky. The red roofs were half hidden in the surrounding trees—pine and box and mighty blue gums towering above the tenderer green of the orchard, and the wide-flung tendrils of the Virginia creeper that was pushing slender fingers over the old walls. If you came nearer, you found how the garden rioted in colour under the touch of early summer, from the crimson rambler round the eastern bay window to the "Bonfire" salvia blazing in masses on the lawn; but from the paddocks all that could be seen was the mass of green, and the mellow red of the roof glimpsing through. Further back came a glance of rippled silver, where the breeze caught the surface of the lagoon—too lazy a breeze to do more than faintly stir the reed-fringed water. Towards it a flight of black swans winged slowly, with outstretched necks, across a sky of perfect blue. Their leader's note floated down, as if in answer to the magpies that carolled in the pine trees by the stables. The sound seemed to hang in the still air.

Beyond the tennis-court, in the farther recesses of the garden, a hammock swung between two grevillea trees, whose orange flowers made a gay canopy overhead; and in the hammock Norah swayed gently, and knitted, and pondered. The shining needles flashed in and out of the dark blue silk sock. Outsiders—mothers of prim daughters,whom Norah pictured as finding their wildest excitement in "patting a doll"—were wont to deplore that the only daughter of David Linton of Billabong was brought up in an eccentric fashion, less girl than boy; but outsiders are apt to cherish delusions, and Norah was not without her share of gentle accomplishments. Knitting was one; the sock grew quickly in the capable brown fingers that could grip a stock-whip as easily as they handled the needles. All the while, she was listening.

1

About her the coo of invisible doves fell gently, mingling with the happy droning of bees in the overhead blossoms. Somewhere, not far off, a sheep bell tinkled monotonously, the only outside sound in the afternoon stillness. It was very peaceful. To Norah, who knew that the world held no place like Billabong, it only lacked one person for the final seal of perfection.

"Wish Dad would come," she said aloud, puckering her brow over a knot in the silk. "He's late–and it is jolly dull without him." The knot came free, and the needles raced as though making up for lost time.

Two dogs lay on the grass: a big sleepy collie that only moved occasionally to snap at a worrying fly; and an Irish terrier, plainly showing by his restlessness that he despised a lazy life, and longed for action. He caught his mistress's eye at last, and jumped up with a little whine.

"If you had the heel of a sock to turn, Puck," said Norah, "you'd be more steady. Lie down, old man."

Puck lay down again discontentedly, put his nose on his paws, and feigned slumber, one restless eyelid betraying the hollowness of the pretence. Presently he rolled over–and chancing to roll on a spiky twig, rose with a wild yelp of annoyance. Across Norah's laugh came a stock-whip crack; and the collie came to life suddenly, and sprang up, as impatient as the terrier. Norah slipped out of the hammock.

"There's Dad!" she said. "Come along!"

She was tall for her fourteen years, and very slender–"scraggy," Jim was wont to say, with the cheerful frankness of brothers. Norah bore the epithet meekly–she held the view that it was better to be dead than fat. There was something boyish in the straight, slim figure in the blue linen frock–perhaps the quality was also to be found in a frank manner that was the product of years of the Bush and open-air life. The grey eyes were steady, and met those of others with a straight level glance; the mouth was a little firm-set for her years, but the child was revealed when it broke into smiles–and Norah was rarely grave. No human power had yet been discovered to keep in order the brown curls. Their distressed owner tied them back firmly with a wide ribbon each morning; but the ribbon generally was missing early in the day, and might be replaced with anything that came handy–possibly a fragment of red tape from the office, or a bit of a New Zealand flax leaf, or haply even a scrap of green hide. Anything, said Norah, decidedly, was better than your hair all over your face. For the rest, a nondescript nose, somewhat freckled, and a square chin, completed a face no one would have dreamed of calling pretty. In his own mind her father referred to it

2

as something better. But then there was tremendous friendship between the master of Billabong and his small daughter.

The stock-whip cracked again, nearer home this time; and Norah crammed the blue silk sock hastily into a little work-bag, and raced away over the lawn, her slim black legs making great time across the buffalo grass. Beside her tore the collie and Puck, each a vision of embodied delight. They flashed round the corner of the house, scattered the gravel on the path leading to the back, and came out into the yard as a big black horse pulled up at the gate, and the tall man on his back swung himself lightly to the ground. From some unseen region a black boy appeared silently and led the horse away. Norah, her father, and the dogs arrived at the gate simultaneously.

"I thought you were never coming, Daddy," said the mistress of Billabong, incoherently. "Did you have a good trip?–and how did Monarch go?–and did you buy the cattle?–and have you had any dinner?" She punctuated each query with a hug, and paused only for lack of breath.

"Steady!" said David Linton, laughing. "I'm not a ready reckoner! I've bought the bullocks, and Monarch went quite remarkably well, and yes, I've had dinner, thank you. And how have you been getting on, Norah?"

"Oh, all right," said his daughter. "It was pretty slow, of course–it always is when you go away, Daddy. I worked, and pottered round with Brownie, and went out for rides. And oh, Dad! ever so many letters–and Jim's coming home next week!" She executed an irrepressible pirouette. "And he's got the cup for the best average at the sports–best all-around athlete that means, doesn't it? Isn't it lovely?"

"That's splendid!" Mr. Linton said, looking as pleased as his daughter. "And any school prizes?"

"He didn't mention," Norah answered. "I don't suppose so, bless him! But there's one thing pretty sickening–the boys can't come with him. Wally may come later, but Harry has to go to Tasmania with his father–isn't it unreasonable?"

"I'm sorry he can't come, but on the whole I've a fellow feeling for the father," said Jim's parent. "A man wants to see something of his son occasionally, I suppose. And any news from Mrs. Stephenson?"

"She's better," Norah answered, her face growing graver. "Dick wrote. And there's a letter for you from Mrs. Stephenson, too. She says she's brighter, and the sea-voyage was evidently the thing for her, 'cause she's more like herself than at any time since–since my dear old Hermit died." Norah's voice shook a little. "They expect to be in Wellington all the summer, and perhaps longer."

"It was certainly a good prescription, that voyage." Mr. Linton

3

said. "I don't think she would have been long in following her husband—poor old chap!—if they had remained here. But one misses them, Norah."

"Horrid," said Norah, with emphasis. "I miss her all the time—and it's quite rum, Dad, but I do believe I miss lessons. Over five weeks since I had any! Are you going to get me another tutor?"

"We'll see," said her father. They were in the big dining-room by this time, and he was turning over the pile of letters that had come during his three days' absence from the station. "Any chance of tea, Norah?"

"Well, rather!" said Norah. "You read your letters, and I'll go and tell Sarah. And Brownie'll be wanting to see you. I won't be long, Daddy." She vanished.

A few minutes later Mr. Linton looked up from a letter that had put a crease into his brow. A firm, flat step sounded in the hall, and Mrs. Brown came in—cook and housekeeper to the homestead, the guide, philosopher and friend of everyone, and the special protector of the little motherless girl about whom David Linton's life centred. "Brownie" was not a person lightly to be reckoned with, and her master was wont to turn to her whenever any question arose affecting Norah. He greeted her warmly now.

"We're all glad to welkim you back, sirr," said Brownie. "As for that blessed child, she's not like the same 'uman bein' when you're off the place. Passed me jus' now in the passige, goin' full bat, an' turned 'ead over 'eels, she did—I didn't need to be told you'd got 'ome!" She hesitated: "You heard from Mrs. Stephenson, sir?"

"Yes," said Mr. Linton, glancing at the letter in his hand. "As I thought—she confirms our opinion. I'm afraid there's no help for it."

"I knew she would," said Mrs. Brown, heavily, a shadow falling onto her broad. pleasant face. "Oh, I know there's no 'elp, sir—it has to be. But—but—" She put her apron to her eyes.

"We're really very lucky, I suppose," Mr. Linton said, in tones distinctly unappreciative, at the moment, of any luck. "Mrs. Stephenson has been a second mother to Norah, these two years—between you and her I can't see that the child needed anything; and with Dick as tutor she has made remarkable progress. Personally, I'd have let the arrangement go on indefinitely. Now that they've had to leave us, however—" He paused, folding up the letter slowly.

"She couldn't stay 'ere, poor lady," Mrs. Brown said; " 'tain't in reason she'd be able to after the old gentleman's death, with the place full of memories an' all. An', of course, she'd want Mr. Dick along with her. Anyway, the precious lamb's getting a big girl to be taught only by a young gentleman—" and Brownie pursed up her lips, looking such a model of all the proprieties that Mr. Linton smiled involuntarily.

"She's all right," he said shortly. "Of course, her aunt has been at me for ever so long to send her to school."

"Beggin' your pardon, sir, Mrs. Geoffrey don't know everythink," said Mrs. Brown, bridling. "Her not havin' any daughters of 'er own, 'ow can it be expected that she'd understand? An' town ladies can't never compre'end country children, any'ow. Our little maid's jus' grown up like a bush flower, an' all the better she is for it."

"But the time comes for change, Brownie, old friend," said Mr. Linton.

"Yes," said Mrs. Brown, "it do. But what the station'll do is more'n I can see just at present—an' as for you, sir—an' let alone me—" Her comfortable, fat voice died away, and the apron was at her eyes again. "What'll Billabong be, with its little girl at school?"

"At—where? " asked Norah.

She had come in with the tea-tray in her hands—a little flushed from the fire, and her brown face alight with all the hundred-and-one things she had yet to tell Daddy. On the threshold she paused, struck motionless by that amazing speech. She looked a little helplessly from one face to the other; and the two who loved her felt the same helplessness as they looked back. It was not an easy thing to pass sentence of exile from Billabong on Norah.

"I—" said her father. "You see, dear—Dick having gone—you know, your aunt—" He stopped, his tongue tied by the look in Norah's eyes.

Brownie slipped into the breach.

"You're so big now, dearie," she said, "so, big—and—and—" With this lucid effort at enlightenment she put her apron fairly over her head and turned away to the open window.

But Norah's eyes were on her father. Just for a moment the sick sense of bewilderment and despair seemed to crush her altogether. She had realized her sentence in a flash—that the home that meant all the world to her, and from which Heaven only differed in that Mother was there, was to be changed for a new, strange world that would be empty of all that she knew and loved. Vaguely she had always known that the blow hung over her—now that it had fallen, for a moment there was no room for any other thought. Her look, wide with grief and appeal, met her father's.

And then she realized slowly that he was suffering too—that he was looking to her for the response that had never failed him yet. His silence told her that this thing was unavoidable, and that he needed her help. Mates such as they must stand by one another— that was part of the creed that had grown up in Norah's heart.

5

Daddy had always said that no matter what happened he could rely upon her. She could not fail him now.

So, just as the silence in the room became oppressive, Norah smiled into her father's eyes, and carefully put the tea-tray upon the table.

"If you say it's got to be, well, that's all about it, Daddy," she said. The voice was low, but it did not quiver. "Don't worry, darling; it's all right. Sarah was out, and Mary goodness knows where, so I made tea myself; I hope it's drinkable." She brought her father's cup to his side and smiled at him again.

"My blessed lamb!" said Mrs. Brown, hastily—and fled from the room.

David Linton did not take the cup; instead he slipped his arm round the childish body.

"You think we can stand it, then?" he asked. "It's not you alone, little mate; your old Dad's under sentence too."

"I think that makes things a lot easier," said Norah, " 'cause you and I always do things together, don't we, Daddy? And—and—" Just for a moment her lips trembled. "Must we, Dad?"

He tightened his arm.

"Yes, dear."

There was a pause.

"After Christmas?"

"Yes—in February."

"Then I've got nine weeks," said Norah, practically. "We won't talk about it more than we can help, I think, don't you? Have your tea, Daddy, or it'll be cold and horrid." She brought her own cup and sat down on the arm of his chair. "How many bullocks did you buy?"

CHAPTER II

TOGETHER

And you and I were faithful mates.

Henry Lawson.

Afterwards–when the blow was a little less heavy as Norah grew accustomed to it–they talked it over thoroughly.

Norah's education, in the strict sense of the term, had only been carried on for about two years. In reality it had gone on all her life, spent mostly at her father's side; but that was the kind of education that does not live between the covers of books. Together, David Linton and his daughter had worked, and played and talked–much more of the former condition than of either of the latter. All that the bush could teach her Norah knew, and in most of the work of the station–Billabong was a noted cattle-run–she was as handy as any of the men. Her father's constant mate, every day shared with him was a delight to her. They rode together, fished, camped and explored together; it was the rarest occurrence for Mr. Linton's movements not to include Norah as a matter of course.

Yet there was something in the quiet man that had effectually prevented any development of roughness in Norah. Boyish and offhand to a certain extent, the solid foundation of womanliness in her nature was never far below the surface. She was perfectly aware that while Daddy wanted a mate he also wanted a daughter; and there was never any real danger of her losing that gentler attribute– there was too much in her of the little dead mother for that. Brownie, the ever watchful, had seen to it that she did not lack housewifely accomplishments, and Mr. Linton was wont to say proudly that Norah's scones were as light as her hand on the horse's mouth. There was no doubt that the irregular side of her education was highly practical.

Two years before Fate had taken a new interest in Norah's development, bringing as inmates of the homestead an old friend of her father's, with his wife and son. The latter acted as Norah's tutor, and found his task an easy one, for the untrodden ground of the little girl's brain yielded remarkable results. To Mrs. Stephenson fell the work of gently moulding her to womanly ways–less easy this, for while Norah had no desire to be a tomboy, she was firmly of the opinion that once lessons were over, she had simply no time to stay inside the house and be proper. Still, the gentle influence told, imperceptibly softening and toning her character, and giving her a standard by which to adapt herself; and Norah was nothing if not adaptable. Then, six months previously, the old man they all loved had quietly faded out of life; and after he had gone his widow could no longer remain in the place where he had died. She pined slowly, until Dick Stephenson, the son, had taken her almost forcibly away. The unspoken fear that the parting was not merely temporary had merged into certainty. Billabong would know them no more. The question remaining was what to do with Norah.

"I want you to have the school training," Mr. Linton said, when they talked the matter over. "You must mix with other girls—learn to see things from their point of view, and realize how many points of view there are outside Billabong. Oh, I don't want you to think there are any better "—he laughed at the vigorous shake of the brown curls—"but the world has wider boundaries, and you must find them out. There are other things, too"—vaguely—"dancing and deportment, and—er—the use of the globes, and I think there's a thing called a blackboard, but I'm not sure. Dick didn't know. In fact, there's a regulation mill, and I suppose you must go through it—I don't feel afraid that they'll spoil my little girl's individuality in the process."

"Is it a big school, Daddy?"

"Yes, I believe so. Several people I know send their girls there. And it's a great place for sports, Norah. You'll like that. They're keen on hockey and cricket and all sorts of things girls never dreamed about when I was young. Possibly I may live to see you a slow bowler yet, and playing in a match! Honestly, Norah, I believe you'll be very happy at school."

"And what'll you do, Daddy?"

"I don't know," he said, heavily. "I told you I was under sentence."

They sat awhile in silence. It was evening, and they were on the verandah; Mr. Linton in a big basket chair, and Norah curled up at his feet in the way she loved. She could not see his face—just then she did not want to. She said nothing. The moon climbed up slowly, and the frogs were merry in the lagoon. Far off the cry of a bittern boomed across the flats.

"Well, at least we've got nine weeks," Norah said at length. "Nine weeks to be mates—and Jim'll be home next week, and he'll be mates, too. Don't let's get blue about it, Daddy. It'll be so horrid when the time comes, that it's no good letting it spoil these nine weeks. Can't we try to forget it?"

"We can try," said David Linton.

"Course, we won't do it," Norah said. "But don't let's talk about it. I'm going to put it out of my head as much as ever I can, and have this time for just Billabong and us. Will you, Daddy?"

"I'll do all I can, my girlie," said her father. "You mustn't start off with any bad memories; we'll have the most crowded nine weeks of our lives, and make a solemn resolve to 'buck up.' I'd like to plan something for this week, but, upon my word, I'm too busy to play, Norah. There's any amount to be done."

"But I don't want to play," Norah said. "Work's good enough for me, Daddy, if I can work with you. Can't I come, too?"

"I'll be exceedingly glad of your help," said her father—which was exactly what Norah wanted him to say, and went far to cheer her. She put the dismal future resolutely from her, and set out upon the present with a heart as light as possible.

It was never dull at Billabong. Always there were pets of all kinds to be seen to. Mr. Linton laid no restriction on pets if they were properly tended, and Norah had a collection as wide as it was beloved. Household duties there were, too; but these could be left if necessary—two adoring housemaids were always ready to step into the breach if "business on the run" claimed Norah's attention. And beyond the range of the homestead altogether there lay an enchanted region that only she and Daddy shared—the wide and stretching plains of Billabong dotted with cattle, seamed with creeks and the river, and merging at the boundary into a long low line of hills. Norah used to gaze at them from her window—sometimes purple, sometimes blue, and sometimes misty grey, but always beautiful to the child who loved them. Others might know Billabong—visit it, ride over it, exclaim at its beauties; but Norah always felt that there were only two who really understood and cared—Daddy and herself.

Of course there was Jim—the big brother who was seventeen now, and just about to leave school. Norah was immensely proud of him, and the affection between them was a thing that never wavered. Jim loved Billabong, too; but it was only to be expected that six years of school in Melbourne would make something of a difference. He knew, in the words of the old Roman, "There is a world elsewhere." But Norah knew no world beyond Billabong.

For all that, Jim was distinctly desirable as a brother. He had always made a tremendous chum of Norah, and the friends he brought home found they were expected to do the same. This might cause them surprise at first, but they very soon found that "the kiddie" was quite excellent as a mate, and could put them up to a good deal more than they usually knew about the Bush. Norah was

9

invariably Jim's first thought. He was a big, quiet fellow, very like his father; not over-brilliant at books, but a first-rate sport, and without a trace of meanness in his generous nature. At school he was worshipped by the boys—was not he captain of the football team, stroke of the eight, and best all-round athlete?—and liked by the masters, who found him inclined to be careless over work but absolutely reliable in every other way. Such a fellow does not win scholarships, but he is a tower of strength to his school.

For the week preceding Jim's return Norah and her father worked hard, clearing up various odd jobs so that their time might be free when the boy arrived. There was a quaint side to this, in that Jim would without doubt have been delighted to help in any station work, which always presented itself to him as "no end of a lark" after the strenuous life at school. But it was a point of honour with those at home to leave none of their work until the holidays and the last week was invariably the scene of many labours.

Not that there were not plenty of hands on the station. It was a big run, and gave employment in one way or another to quite a band of men. But Mr. Linton preferred to keep a very close watch over everything, and he had long realized that the best way of seeing that your business is done is to take a hand yourself. The men said, "The boss was everywhere," and they respected him the more in that he was no kid-glove employer, but was willing to share in any work that was going forward. Especially he insisted on working among the cattle, and—Norah was nearly always with him on his rides—they had a more or less accurate knowledge of every beast on the place. Outside the boundary fences they went very seldom; the nearest township, seventeen miles away, Norah regarded as merely a place where you called for the mail, and save that it meant a ride or drive with her father, she had never the slightest desire to go there.

Summer was very late that year, and "burning-off" operations on the rougher parts of the run had been carried on much longer than was generally possible. Norah always regarded "burning-off" as an immense picnic, and used to beg her father to take her out. Night after night found them down on the flats, getting rid of old dead trees, which up to the present had refused obstinately to burn. It was picturesque work, and Norah loved it, though she would have been somewhat embarrassed had you hinted that the picturesqueness had anything to do with its attractions.

One after another, they would light the stumps, some squat and solid, others rising thirty or forty feet into the air. Once the fires were lit, it was necessary to keep them going; moving backwards and forwards among the trees, stoking, picking up fallen bits of burning timber and adding them to the fires, coaxing sullen embers

10

into a blaze, edging the fire round a tree, so that the wind might do its utmost in helping the work—there were no idle moments for the "burners-off." Sometimes it would be necessary to enlarge a crack or hole in a tough stump, to gain a hold for the fire. Norah always carried a light iron bar, specially made for her at the station forge, which she called her poker, and which answered half a dozen purposes equally well, and though not an ideal weapon for killing a snake, being too stiff and straight, had been known to act in that capacity also. Every scrap of loose timber on the ground would be picked up and added to the flames. Some stumps were very obstinate and resisted all blandishments to burn; but careful handling generally ensured the fate of the majority.

There are few sights more weird, or more typically Australian, than a paddock at night with burning-off in process. Low and high, the red columns of fire stand in a darkness made blacker by their lurid glow. Where the fire has taken hold fairly the flames are fierce, and showers of sparks fall like streams of gold. Sometimes a dull crack gives warning of the fall of a long-dead giant; and the burning mass leans slowly over, and then comes down with a crash, while the curious bullocks, which have poked as near as they dare to the strange scene, fling round and lumber off in a heavy gallop, heads down and tails up. From stump to stump flit the little black figures of the workers, standing out clearly sometimes, by the light of a blaze so fierce that to face it is scarcely possible; or half seen in the dull glow of a smouldering tree poking vigorously—seeming as ants attacking living monsters infinitely beyond their strength. Perhaps it is there that the fascination of the work comes in—the triumph of conquering tons of inanimate matter by efforts so small. At any rate it is always hard to leave the scene of action, and certainly the first glance next morning is to see "which are down."

Then there were days spent among the cattle—days that always meant the high-water mark of bliss to Norah. She road astride, and her special pony, Bobs, to whom years but added perfection, loved the work as much as she did. They understood each other perfectly; if Norah carried a hunting-crop, it was merely for assistance in opening gates, for Bobs never felt its touch. A hint from her heel, or a quick word, conveyed all the big bay pony ever needed to supplement his own common sense, of which Mr. Linton used to say he possessed more than most men. The new bullocks arrived, and had to be drafted and branded—during which latter operation Norah retired dismally to the house and the socks that had to be finished in time to be Jim's Christmas present. Then, after the branding, came a most cheerful time, putting the cattle into their various paddocks.

One day was spent in mustering sheep, an employment not at all

11

to Norah's taste. She was frankly glad that Billabong devoted most of its energies to cattle, and only put up with the sheep work because, since Daddy was there, it never occurred to her to do anything else but go. But she hated the slow, dusty ride, and hailed with delight a gallop that came in their way towards the end of the day, when a hare jumped up under Bob's nose as they rode homewards from the yards. The dogs promptly gave chase; and, almost without knowing it, Norah and Bobs were in hot pursuit, with Monarch shaking the earth behind them. The average sheep dog is no match for a hare, and the quarry easily escaped into the next paddock, after a merry run. Norah pulled up, her eyes dancing.

"Don't you know it's useless to try to get a hare with those fellows?" asked Mr. Linton, checking the reeking Monarch, and indicating with a nod the dogs, which were highly aggrieved at their defeat.

"But I never wanted to get it," said his daughter, in surprise. "It's perfectly awful to get a hare; they cry just like a baby, and it makes you feel horrid."

"Then why did you go after it?"

"Why?" asked Norah, opening her eyes. "Well, I knew the dogs couldn't catch it—and I believe you wanted a gallop nearly as much as I did, Daddy!" They laughed at each other, and let the impatient horses have their heads across the cleared paddock to the homestead.

There a letter awaited them.

Norah, coming in to dinner in a white frock, with her curls unusually tidy, found her father looking anything but pleased over a closely covered sheet of thin notepaper.

"I wish to goodness women would write legibly," he said, with some heat. "No one on earth has any right to write on both sides of paper as thin as this—and then across it! No one but your Aunt Eva would do it—she always had a passion for small economies, together with one for large extravagances. Amazing woman! Well, I can't read half of it, but what she wants is unhappily clear."

"She isn't coming here, Daddy?"

"Saints forbid!" ejaculated Mr. Linton, who had a lively dread of his sister—a lady of much social eminence, who disapproved strongly of his upbringing of Norah. "No, she doesn't mention such an extreme course, but there's something almost as alarming. She wants to send Cecil here for Christmas."

"Cecil! Oh, Daddy!" Norah's tone was eloquent.

"Says he's been ill," said her father, glancing at the letter in a vain effort to decipher a message written along one edge. "He's better, but needs change, and she seems to think Billabong will prove a

12

sanatorium." He looked at Norah with an expression of dismay that was comical. "I shouldn't have thought we'd agree with that young man a bit, Norah!"

"I've never seen him, of course," Norah said unhappily, "but Jim says he's pretty awful. And you didn't like him yourself, did you, Daddy?"

"On the rare occasions that I've had the pleasure of meeting my nephew I've always thought him an unlicked cub," Mr. Linton answered. "Of course it's eighteen months since I saw him; possibly he may have changed for the better, but at that time his bumptiousness certainly appeared to be on the increase. He had just left school then—he must be nearly twenty now."

"Oh—quite old," said Norah. "What is he like?"

"Pretty!" said Mr. Linton, wrinkling his nose. "As pretty as his name—Cecil—great Scott! I wonder if he'd let me call him Bill for short! Bit of a whipper-snapper, he seemed; but I didn't take very much notice of him—saw he was plainly bored by his uncle from the Bush, so I didn't worry him. Well, now he's ours for a time your aunt doesn't limit—more that that, if I can make a guess at these hieroglyphics, I've got to send a telegram to say we'll have him on Saturday."

"And this is Wednesday—oh, Dad! expostulated Norah.

"Can't be helped," her father said. "We've got to go through with it; if the boy has been ill he must certainly have all the change we can give him. But I'm doubtful. Eva says he's had a 'nervous breakdown,' and I rather think it's a complaint I don't believe in for boys of twenty."

The dinner gong sounded. Amid its echoes Norah might have been heard murmuring something about "nervous grandmother."

"H'm," said her father, laughing; "I don't think he'll find much sympathy with his more fragile symptoms in Billabong—we must try to brace him up, Norah. But whatever will Jim say, I wonder!"

"He'll be too disgusted for words," Norah answered. "Poor old Jimmy! I wonder how they'll get on. D'you suppose Cecil ever played football?"

"From Cecil's appearance I should say he devoted his time to wool-work," said Mr. Linton. "However, it may not turn out as badly as we think, and it's no use meeting trouble halfway, is it? Also, we've to remember that he'll be our guest."

"But that's the trouble," said Norah, laughing. "It wouldn't be half so bad if you could laugh at him. I'll have to be so hugely polite!"

"You'll probably shock him considerably in any case," said her

13

father. "Cecil's accustomed to very prim young ladies, and it's not at all unlikely that he'll try to reform you!"

"I wish him luck!" said Norah. But there was a glint in her eyes which boded ill for Cecil's reformatory efforts

CHAPTER III

A BATH—AND AN INTRODUCTION

Quiet and shy, as the Bush girls are,
But ready-witted and plucky, too.

A. B. Paterson.

The telegram assuring a welcome to Cecil Linton was duly dispatched, and the fact of his impending arrival broken to Mrs. Brown, who sniffed portentously, and gave without enthusiasm directions for the preparation of his room. "Mrs. Geoffrey" was rather a bugbear to Brownie, who had unpleasant recollections of a visit in the past from that majestic lady. During her stay of a week, she had attempted to alter every existing arrangement at Billabong— and when she finally departed, in a state of profound disapproval, the relief of the homestead was immense. Brownie was unable to feel any delight at the idea of entertaining her son.

Norah and her father made the utmost of their remaining time together. Thursday was devoted to a great muster of calves, which meant unlimited galloping and any amount of excitement; for the sturdy youngsters were running with their mothers in one of the bush paddocks, and it was no easy matter to cut them out and work them away from the friendly shelter and refuge of the trees. A bush-reared calf is an irresponsible being, with a great fund of energy and spirits—and, while Norah loved her day, she was thoroughly tired as they rode home in the late evening, the last straggler yarded in readiness for the branding next day. Mr. Linton sent her to bed early, and she did not wake in the morning until the dressing gong boomed its cheerful summons through the house.

Mr. Linton was already at breakfast when swift footsteps were heard in the hall above; a momentary silence indicated that his daughter was coming downstairs by way of the banisters, and the next moment she arrived hastily.

"I'm so sorry, Dad," Norah said, greeting him. "But I did sleep ! Let me pour out your coffee."

She brought the cup to him, investigated a dish of bacon, and slipped into her place behind the tall silver coffee pot.

"What are we going to do to-day, Dad?"

"I really don't quite know," Mr. Linton said, smiling at her.

15

"There aren't any very pressing jobs on hand—we must cut out cattle to-morrow for trucking, but to-day seems fairly free. Have you any ideas on the subject of how you'd like to spend it? I've letters to write for a couple of hours, but after that I'm at your disposal."

Norah wrinkled her brows.

"There are about fifty things I want to do," she said. "But most of them ought to wait until Jim comes home." She thought for a moment. "I don't want to miss any more time with Bobs than I have to—could we ride over to the backwater, Dad, and muster up the cattle there? You know you said you were going to do so, pretty soon.

"I'd nearly forgotten that I had to see them," Mr. Linton said, hastily. "Glad you reminded me, Norah. We'll have lunch early, and go across."

Norah's morning was spent in helping Mrs. Brown to compound Christmas cakes—large quantities of which were always made and stored well before Christmas, with due reference to the appetites of Jim and his friends. Then a somewhat heated and floury damsel donned a neat divided riding skirt of dark-blue drill, with a white-linen coat, and the collar and tie which Norah regarded as the only reasonable neck gear, and joined her father in the office.

"Ready? That's right," said he, casting an approving glance at the trim figure. "I've just finished writing, and the horses are in."

"So's lunch," Norah responded. "It's a perfectly beautiful day for a ride, Daddy—hurry up!"

The day merited Norah's epithet, as they rode over the paddocks in the afternoon. As yet the grass had not dried up, thanks to the late rains, and everywhere a green sea rippled to the fences. Soon it would be dull and yellow; but this day there was nothing to mar the perfection of the carpet that gave softly under the horses' hoofs. The dogs raced wildly before them, chasing swallows and ground-larks in the cheerfully idiotic manner of dogs, with always a wary ear for Mr. Linton's whistle: but as yet they were not on duty, and were allowed to run riot.

An old log fence stretched before them. It was the only one on Billabong, where all station details were strictly up-to-date. This one had been left, partly because it was picturesque, and partly at the request of Jim and Norah, because it gave such splendid opportunities for jumping. There were not many places on that old fence that Bobs did not know, and he began to reef and pull as they came nearer to it.

"I don't believe I'll be able to hold him in, Daddy!" said Norah, with mock anxiety.

"Not afraid, I hope?" asked her father, laughing.

16

"Very—that you won't want to jump! I'd hate to disappoint him, Daddy—may I?"

"Oh, go on!" said Mr. Linton. "If I said 'no' the savage animal would probably bolt!" He held Monarch back as Norah gave the bay pony his head, and they raced for the fence; watching with a smile in his eyes the straight little form in the white coat, the firm seat in the saddle, the steady hand on the rein. Bobs flew the big log like a bird, and Norah twisted in her saddle to watch the black horse follow. Her eyes were glowing as her father came up.

"I do think he loves it as much as I do!" she said, patting the pony's neck.

"He's certainly as keen a pony as I ever saw," Mr. Linton said. "How are you going to manage without him, Norah?"

Norah looked up, her eyes wide with astonishment.

"Do without Bobs! " she exclaimed. "But I simply couldn't—he's one of the family." Then her face fell suddenly, and the life died out of her voice. "Oh—school," she said.

The change was rather pitiful, and Mr. Linton mentally abused himself for his question.

"He'll always be waiting for you when you come home, dear," he said. "Plenty of holidays—and think how fit he'll be! We'll have great rides, Norah."

"I guess I'll want them," she said. Silence fell between them.

The scrub at the backwater was fairly thick, and the cattle had sought its shade when the noonday sun struck hot. Well fed and sleek, they lay about under the trees or on the little grassy flats formed by the bends of the stream. Norah and her father separated, each taking a dog, and beat through the bush, routing out stragglers as they went. The echoes of the stock-whips rang along the water. Norah's was only a light whip, half the length and weight of the one her father carried. It was beautifully plaited—a special piece of work, out of a special hide; while the handle was a triumph of the stockman's art. It had been a gift to Norah from an old boundary rider whose whips were famous, and she valued it more than most of her possessions, while long practice and expert tuition had given her no little skill in its use,

She worked through the scrub, keeping her eyes in every direction, for the cattle were lazy and did not stir readily, and it was easy to miss a motionless beast hidden behind a clump of dogwood or Christmas bush—the scrub tree that greets December with its exquisite white blossoms. When at length she came to the end of her division and drove her cattle out of the shelter she had quite a respectable little mob to add to those with which her father was already waiting.

17

It was only to be a rough muster; rather, a general inspection to see how the bullocks were doing, for the nearest stockyards were at the homestead, and Mr. Linton did not desire to drive them far. He managed to get a rough count along a fence—Norah in the rear, bringing the bullocks along slowly, so that they strung out under their owner's eye. Occasionally one would break out and try to race past him on the wrong side. Bobs was as quick as his rider to watch for these vagrants, and at the first hint of a breakaway he would be off in pursuit. It was work the pair loved.

"Hundred and thirty," said Mr. Linton, as the last lumbering beast trotted past him, and, finding the way clear, with no harrowing creatures to annoy him and head him back to his mates, kicked up his heels and made off across the paddock.

"Did any get behind me, Norah?"

"No, Daddy."

"That's a good girl. They look well, don't they?"

Norah assented. "Did you notice how that big poley bullock had come on, Dad?"

"Yes, he's three parts fat," said Mr. Linton. "All very satisfactory, and the count is only two short—not bad for a rough muster."

They turned homewards, cantering quickly over the paddocks; the going was too good, Norah said, to waste on walking; and it was a delight to feel the long, even stride under one, and the gentle wind blowing upon one's cheeks. As he rode, Mr. Linton watched the eager, vivid little face, alight with the joy of motion. If Bobs were keen, there was no doubt that his mistress was even keener.

They crossed the log fence again by what Norah termed "the direct route," traversed the home paddock, and drew up with a clatter of hoofs at the stable yard. Billy, a black youth of some fame concerning horses, came forward as they dismounted and took the bridles. But Norah preferred to unsaddle Bobs herself and let him go; she held it only civil after he had carried her well. She was leading him off when the dusky retainer muttered something to her father.

"Oh, all right, Billy," said Mr. Linton. "Norah, those fellows from Cunjee have come to see me about buying sheep. I expect I shall have to take them out to the paddock I don't think you'd better come."

"All right, Dad." Sheep did not interest Norah very much. "I think I'll go down to the lagoon."

"Very well, don't distinguish yourself by falling in," said her father, with a laugh over his shoulder as he hurried away towards the house.

Left to herself, Norah paid a visit to Brownie in the kitchen, which resulted in afternoon tea—there was never a bush home where tea did not make its appearance on the smallest possible pretext. Then she slipped off her linen jacket and brown leather leggings and, having beguiled black Billy into digging her some worms, found some fishing tackle and strolled down to the lagoon.

It was a broad sheet of water, at one end thickly fringed with trees, while in the shallower parts a forest of green, feathery reeds bordered it, swaying and rustling all day, no matter how soft the breeze. The deeper end had been artificially hollowed out, and a bathing box had been built, with a springboard jutting out over the water. Under the raised floor of the bathing box a boat was moored. Norah pulled it out and dropped down into it, stowing her tin of worms carefully in the stern. Then she paddled slowly into the deepest part of the lagoon, baited her line scientifically, and began to fish.

Only eels rewarded her efforts; and while eels are not bad fun to pull out, Norah regarded them as great waste of time, since no one at Billabong cared to eat them, and in any case she would not let them come into the boat—for a good-sized eel can make a boat unpleasantly slimy in a very short time. So each capture had to be carefully released at the stern—not a very easy task. Before long Norah's white blouse showed various marks of conflict; and being by nature a clean person, she was rather disgusted with things in general. When at length a large silver eel, on being pulled up, was found to have swallowed the hook altogether, she fairly lost patience.

"Well, you'll have to keep it," she said, cutting her line; whereupon the eel dropped back into the water thankfully, and made off as though he had formed a habit of dining on hooks, and, in fact, preferred them as an article of diet. "I'm sure you'll have shocking indigestion," Norah said, watching the swirl of bubbles.

The boat had drifted some way down the lagoon, and a rustle told Norah that they were near one of the reedy islands dotted here and there in the shallows. There was very little foothold on them, but they made excellent nesting places for the ducks that came to the station each year. The boat grounded its nose in the soft mud, and Norah jumped up to push it off. Planting the blade of the oar among the reeds, she leant her weight upon it and shoved steadily.

The next events happened swiftly. The mud gave way suddenly with a suck, and the oar promptly slithered, burying itself for half its length; and Norah, taken altogether by surprise, executed a graceful header over the bow of the boat. The mud received her softly, and clung to her with affection; and for a moment, face downward among the reeds, Norah clawed for support, like a crab suddenly

19

beached. Then, somehow, she scrambled to a sitting position, up to her waist in mud and water—and rocked with laughter. A little way off, the boat swayed gently on the ruffled surface of the water.

"Well—of all the duffers!" Norah said. She tried to stand, and forthwith went up to one knee in the mud. Then, seeing that there was no help for it, she managed to slip into deeper water—not very easy, for the mud showed a deep attachment to her—and swam to the boat. To get into it proved beyond her, but, fortunately, the bank was not far off, and, though her clothes hampered her badly—a riding skirt is the most inconvenient of swimming suits—she was as much at home as a duck in the water, and soon got ashore.

Then she inspected herself, standing on the grass, while a pool of water rapidly widened round her. Alas, for the trim maiden of the morning! soaked to the skin, her lank hair clinging round her face, her collar a limp rag, the dye from her red silk tie spreading in artistic patches on her white blouse! Over all was the rich black mud of the lagoon, from brow to boot soles. Her hat, once white felt, was a sodden black-streaked mass; even her hands and face were stiff with mud.

"Thank goodness, Daddy's out!" said the soaked one, returning knee-deep in the water to try and cleanse herself as much as might be—which was no great amount, for lagoon mud defies ordinary efforts. She waded out, still laughing; cast an apprehensive glance at the quarter from which her father might be expected to return, and set out on her journey to the house, the water squelching dismally in her boots at every step.

In the garden at Billabong walked a slim youth in most correct attire. His exquisitely tailored suit of palest grey flannel was set off by a lavender-striped shirt, with a tie that matched the stripe. Patent leather shoes with wide ribbon bows shod him; above them, and below the turned-up trousers, lavender silk socks with purple circles made a very glory of his ankles. On his sleek head he balanced a straw hat with an infinitesimal brim, a crown tall enough to resemble a monument, and a very wide hat band. His pale, well-featured face betrayed unuttered depths of boredom.

The click of the gate made him turn. Coming up the path was a figure that might have been plaintive but that Norah was so immensely amused at herself; and the stranger opened his pale eyes widely, for such apparitions had not come his way. She did not see him for a moment. When she did, he was directly in her path, and Norah pulled up short.

"Oh !" she said weakly; and then—"I didn't know anyone was here."

The strange youth looked somewhat disgusted.

"I should think you'd—ah—better go round to the back," he said condescendingly. "You'll find the housekeeper there."

This time it was Norah's turn to be open-eyed.

"Thanks," she said a little shortly. "Were you waiting to see anyone?"

The boy's eyebrows went up. "I am—ah—staying here."

"Oh, are you?" Norah said. "I didn't know. I'm Norah Linton."

"You!" said the stranger. There was such a world of expression in his tone that Norah flushed scarlet, suddenly painfully conscious of her extraordinary appearance. Then—it was unusual for her—she became angry.

"Did you never see anyone wet?" she asked, in trenchant tones. "And didn't you ever learn to take your hat off?"

"By Jove!" said the boy, looking at the truculent and mud-streaked figure. Then he did an unwise thing, for he burst out laughing.

"I don't know who you are," Norah said, looking at him steadily. "But I think you're the rudest, worst-mannered boy that ever came here!"

She flashed past him with her head in the air. Cecil Linton, staring after her with amazement, saw her cross the red-tiled verandah hurriedly and disappear within a side door, a trail of wet marks behind her.

"By Jove!" he said again. "The bush cousin!"

21

CHAPTER IV

CUTTING OUT

And the loony bullock snorted when you first came into view,
Well, you know, it's not so often that he sees a swell like you.

A. B. Paterson.

Norah did not encounter the newcomer again until dinner-time.

She was in the drawing-room, waiting for the gong to sound, when Cecil came in with her father. For a moment he did not recognize the soaked waif of the garden whom he had recommended "to go round to the back."

A hot bath and a change of raiment had restored Norah to her usual self; had helped her also to laugh at her meeting with her cousin, although she was still ruffled at the memory of the sneer in his laugh. Perhaps because of that she had dressed more carefully than usual. Cecil might have been excused for failing to recognize the grave-faced maiden, very dainty in her simple frock of soft white silk, with her still-moist curls tied back with a broad white ribbon.

"As you two have already met, there's no need to introduce you," said Mr. Linton, a twinkle in his eye. "Sorry your reception was so informal, Cecil—you took us by surprise."

"I suppose the mater mixed things up, as usual," Cecil said, in a bored way. "I certainly intended all along to get here to-day, but she's fearfully vague, don't you know. I was lucky in getting a lift out."

"You certainly were," his uncle said, dryly. "However, I'm glad you didn't have to wait in the township. You'd have found it slow."

"I'd probably have gone back," said Cecil.

"Ah—would you?" Mr. Linton looked for a moment very much as though he wished he had done so. There was an uncomfortable pause, to which the summons to dinner formed a welcome break.

Dinner was very different from the usual cheery meal. Cecil was not shy, and supplied most of the conversation as a matter of course; and his conversation was of a kind new to Norah. She remained unusually silent, being, indeed, fully occupied in taking stock of this novel variety of boy. She wondered were all city boys different from those she knew. Jim was not like this; neither were the friends he was accustomed to bring home with him. They were not a bit grown up, and they talked of ordinary, wholesome things like cricket and football, and horses, and dormitory "larks," and were altogether sensible and companionable. But Cecil's talk was of theatres and bridge parties, and—actually—clothes! Horses he only mentioned in connexion with racing, and when Mr. Linton inquired mildly if he were fond of dances, he was met by raised eyebrows and a bored disclaimer of caring to do anything so energetic. Altogether this product of city culture was an eye-opener to the simple folks of Billabong.

Of Norah, Cecil took very little notice. She was evidently a being quite beneath his attention—he was secretly amused at the way in which she presided at her end of the table, and decided in his own mind that his mother's views had been correct, and that this small girl would be all the better for a little judicious snubbing. So he ignored her in his conversation, and if she made a remark contrived to infuse a faint shade of patronage into his reply. It is possible that his amazement would have been great had he known how profoundly his uncle longed to kick him.

Dinner over, Norah fled to Brownie, and to that sympathetic soul unburdened her woes. Mr. Linton and his nephew retired to the verandah, where the former preferred to smoke in summer. He smiled a little at the elaborate cigarette case Cecil drew out, but lit his pipe without comment, reflecting inwardly that although cigarettes were scarcely the treatment, though they might be the cause, of a pasty face and a "nervous breakdown," it was none of his business to interfere with a young gentleman who evidently considered himself a man of the world. So they smoked and talked, and, when, after a little while, Cecil confessed himself tired, and went off to bed, he left behind him a completely bored and rather annoyed squatter.

"Well, Norah, what do you think of him?"

Norah, sitting meekly knitting in the drawing-room, looked up and laughed as her father came in.

"Think? Why, I don't think much, Daddy."

"No more do I," said Mr. Linton, casting his long form into an armchair. "Of all the spoilt young cubs!—and that's all it is, I should say: clearly a case of spoiling. The boy isn't bad at heart, but he's never been checked in his life. Well, I'm told it's risky for a father to bring up his daughter unaided, but I'm positive the result is worse when an adoring mother rears a fatherless boy! Possibly I've made rather a boy of you—but Cecil's neither one thing nor the other. Why didn't you come out, my lass?"

"Felt too bad tempered!" said Norah; "he makes me mad when he speaks to you in that condescending way of his, Daddy. I'll be calmer to-morrow." She smiled up at her father. "Have a game of chess?"

"It would be soothing, I think," Mr. Linton answered. He laughed. "It's really pathetic—our Darby and Joan existence to be ruffled like this! Thank goodness, he's in bed, for to-night, at any rate!" They got out the chessmen, and played very happily until Norah's bedtime.

"Do you ride, Cecil?" Mr. Linton asked next morning at breakfast.

"Ride? Oh, certainly," Cecil answered. "I suppose you're all very keen on that sort of thing up here?"

"Well, that's how we earn our living," his uncle remarked. "Norah is my right-hand man on the run."

"Ah, how nice! Do you find it hard to get labour here?"

"Oh, we get them," said Mr. Linton, his eyes twinkling. "But I prefer to catch 'em young. We're cutting out cattle for trucking to-day. Would you care to come out?"

"Delighted," said the nephew, glancing without enthusiasm at his flannels. "But I didn't dress for riding."

"Oh, we're not absolute sticklers for costume here," Mr. Linton said, laughing outright. "Wear what you like—in any case, we shan't start for an hour."

It was more than that before they finally got away. The delay was due to waiting for the visitor, whose toilet was a lengthy proceeding. When at length he sauntered out, in blissful ignorance of the fact that he had been keeping them waiting, no one could have found fault with his clothes—a riding suit of very English cut, with immensely baggy breeches, topped by an immaculately folded stock, and a smart tweed cap.

"That feller plenty new," said black Billy, gazing at him with astonishment.

Mr. Linton chuckled as he swung Norah to her saddle.

"Let's hope his horsemanship is equal to his attire!"

Norah smiled in answer. Bobs was dancing with impatience, and she walked him round and round, keeping an eye on her cousin.

A steady brown mare had been saddled for Cecil—one of the "general utility" horses to be found on every station. He cast a critical eye over her as he approached, glancing from her to the horses of his uncle and cousin. Brown Betty was a thoroughly good stamp of a stock horse, with plenty of quality; while not, perhaps, of the class of Monarch and Bobs, she was by no means a mount to be despised. That Cecil disapproved of her, however, was evident. There was a distinct curl on his lip as he gathered up the reins. However, he mounted without a word, and they set off in pursuit of

24

Murty O'Toole, the head stockman, who was already halfway to the cutting-out paddock.

The Clover Paddock of Billabong was famous—a splendid stretch of perfect green, where the cattle moved knee-deep in fragrant blossoming clovers, with pink and white flowers starring the wide expanse. At one end it was gently undulating plain, towards the other it came down in a gradual slope to the river, where tall gums gave an evergreen shelter from winter gales or summer heat. The cattle were under them as the riders came up—great, splendid Shorthorns, the aristocracy of their kind, their roan sides sleek, their coats in perfect condition, and a sprinkling of smaller bullocks whose inferiority in size was compensated by their amazing fatness. It was evident that this week there would be no difficulty in making up the draft for the Melbourne market.

The cattle were mustered into one herd; no racing or hastening now, but with the gentle consideration one should extend to the dignified and portly. They moved lazily, as if conscious of their own value. Cecil, hurrying a red-and-white bullock across a little flat, was met by a glare from Murty O'Toole, and a muttered injunction to "go aisy wid 'em," followed by a remark that "clo'es like thim was only fit to go mustherin' turkeykins in!" Luckily the latter part of the outbreak was unheard by Cecil, who was quite sufficiently injured at the first, and favoured Murty with a lofty stare that had the effect of throwing the Irishman and black Billy into secret convulsions of mirth.

Norah rode not far from her father as they brought the cattle out into the open and to the cutting-out camp—a spot where the beaten ground showed that very often before such scenes had been enacted. The bullocks knew it, and huddled there contentedly enough in a compact body, while slowly Mr. Linton and Murty rode about them, singling out the primest. Once marked down, O'Toole would slip between the bullock and his mates and edge him away, where Billy took charge of him, preventing his returning to the mob. With the first two or three this was not quite easy: but once a few were together they gave little trouble, feeding about calmly: and generally a bullock cut out from the main body would trot quite readily across to the others.

Privately, Cecil Linton thought it remarkably dull work. All that he had read of station life was unlike this. He had had visions of far more exciting doings—mad gallops and wild cattle, thoroughbred horses, kangaroo hunts and a score of other delights. Instead, all he had to do was to tail after a lot of sleepy bullocks and then watch them sorted out by some men whose easy-going ways were unlike anything he had imagined. He had no small opinion of his riding,

25

and he yearned for distinction. The very sight of Norah, leaning a little forward, keenness on every line of her face, was an offence to him. He could see nothing whatever to be keen about. Yawning, he lit a cigarette.

Just then a bullock was cut out and pointed in the way he should go. He lumbered easily past black Billy, apparently quite contented with his fate; and Billy, seeing another following, gave a crack of his whip to speed him on his way, and turned to deal with the newcomer. The first bullock became immediately seized with a spirit of mischief. He flourished his heels in the air, turned at right angles and made off towards the river at a gallop.

Cecil, busy with his cigarette, saw Norah sit up suddenly and tighten her hand on the bridle. Simultaneously Bobs was off like a shot—tearing over the paddock a little wide of the fugitive. The race was a short one. Passing the bullock, the bay pony and his rider swung in sharply and the lash of Norah's whip shot out. The bullock stopped short, shaking his head; then, as the whip spoke again, he wheeled and trotted back meekly to the smaller mob. Behind him Norah cantered slowly. The work of cutting out had not paused and no one seemed to notice the incident. But Cecil saw his uncle smile across at the little girl, and caught the look in Norah's eyes as she smiled back. She and Bobs took up their station again, silently watchful.

Cecil was fired with ambition. Norah's small service had seemed to him ridiculously easy; still, insignificant though everyone appeared to regard it, it was better than doing nothing. He had not the faintest doubt of his own ability, and the idea that riding in a decorous suburb might not fit him for all equine emergencies he would have scouted. He gathered up his reins, and waited anxiously for another beast to break away.

One obliged him presently; a big shorthorn that decided he had stayed long enough in the mob, and suddenly made up his mind to seek another scene. Norah had already started in pursuit when she saw her cousin send his spurs home in Betty, and charge forward. So she pulled up the indignant Bobs, who danced, and left the field to Cecil.

Betty took charge of affairs from the outset. There was no move in all the cattle-game that she did not understand. Moreover, she was justly indignant at the spur-thrust, which attention only came her way in great emergencies; and the heavy hand on her mouth was gall and wormwood to her. But ahead was a flying bullock, and she was a stock horse, which was sufficient for Betty.

"That feller brown mare got it all her own way!" said Billy, in delight.

26

She had. Cecil, bumping a little in the saddle, had no very clear idea of how things were going. He had a moment of amazement that the quiet mare he had despised could make such a pace. Once he tried to steady her, but at that instant Betty was not to be steadied. She galloped on, and Cecil, recovering some of his self-possession, began to think that this was the thing whereof he had dreamed.

The bullock was fat and scant of breath. It did not take him very long to conclude that he had had enough, especially when he heard the hoofs behind him. It was sad, for close before him was the shade of the trees and the murmur of the river; but discretion is ever the better part of valour, particularly if one be not only valorous but fat. He pulled up short. Betty propped without a second's hesitation, and swung round.

To Cecil it seemed that the world had dropped from under him— and then risen to meet him. The brown mare turned, in the bush idiom, "on a sixpence," but Cecil did not turn. He went on. The onlookers had a vision of the mare chopping round, as duty bade her, to head off the bullock, while at right-angles a graceful form in correct English garments hurtled through the air in an elegant curve. When he came down, which seemed to be not for some time, it was into a shady clump of wild raspberries—and only those who know the Victorian wild raspberry know how clinging and intrusive are its hooked thorns. Two legs kicked wildly. There was no sound.

When the rescuing party extricated Cecil from his involuntary botanical researches he was a sorry sight. His clothes were torn in many places, and his face and hands badly scratched, while the red stains of the raspberries had turned his light tweeds into something resembling an impressionist sketch. It was perhaps excusable that he had altogether lost his temper. He burst out in angry abuse of the mare, the bullock, the raspberry clump, and the expedition in general—anger which the scarcely concealed grins of the stockmen only served to intensify. Norah, who had choked with laughter at first, but had become sympathetic as soon as she saw the boy's face, extracted numerous thorns from his person and clothing, and murmured words of regret, which fell on unheeding ears. Finally his uncle lost patience.

"That'll do Cecil," he said. "Everyone comes to grief occasionally— take your gruel like a man. Come on, Norah. Murty's waiting." Saying which, he put Norah up, and they rode off, while Billy held the brown mare's rein for Cecil, who mounted sulkily. Something in his uncle's face forbade his replying. But in his heart came the beginning of a grudge against the Bush, Billabong in general, and Norah in particular. Later on, he promised himself, there might come a chance to work it off.

For the present, however, there was nothing to be done but nurse his scratches and his grievance; so he sat sulkily on Betty, and took no further active part in the morning's work, the consciousness of acting like a spoilt child not tending to improve his temper. Nobody took any notice of him. One by one the bullocks were cut out, until between twenty and thirty were ready, and then the main mob was left to wander slowly back to the river, while O'Toole and Billy started with the others to the paddock at the end of the run, which was their first stage in the seventeen-mile journey to the trucking yards at Cunjee. They moved off peacefully through the blossoming clover.

"Luckily they don't be afther knowin' what's ahead av thim!" said Murty. He lifted his battered felt hat to Norah, as he rode away.

"We'll go down and see how high the river is before we go home," said Mr. Linton.

So they rode down to the river, commented on the unusual amount of water for so late in the year, inspected the drinking places, paid a visit to a beast in another paddock, which had been sick, but was now apparently in rude health, and finally cantered home to lunch. Brownie prudently refrained from comment on Cecil's scratched countenance, further than to supply him with large quantities of hot water in his room, together with a small pair of pliers, which she remarked were 'andy things for prickles. Under this varied treatment Cecil became more like himself, and recovered his spirits, though a soreness yet remained at the thought of the little girl who had done so easily what he had failed so ignominiously in trying to do. He decided definitely in his own mind that he did not like Norah.

CHAPTER V

TWO POINTS OF VIEW

You found the Bush was dismal, and a land of no delight—
Did you chance to hear a chorus in the shearers' nut at night?

A. B. Paterson.

"Dear Mater,—Arrived at Cunjee safely, and, thanks to the way you fixed up things, found no one to meet me, as Uncle David thought I would not arrive until next day. However, a friendly yokel gave me a lift out to Billabong in a very dirty and springless buggy, so that the mistake was not a fatal one, though it gave me a very uncomfortable drive.

"The place is certainly very nice, and the house comfortable, though, of course, it is old-fashioned. I prefer more modern furniture; but Uncle David seems to think his queer old chairs and table all that can be desired, and did not appear interested when I told him where we got our things. I have a large room, rather draughty, but otherwise pleasant, with plenty of space for clothes, which is a comfort. I do think it's intensely annoying to be expected to keep your clothes in your trunk. The view is nice.

"Uncle David seemed quite prepared to treat me as a small boy, but I fancy I have demonstrated to him that I know my way about— in fact, as far as city life goes, I should say he knew exceedingly little. I can't understand any man with money being content to live and die in a hole like this out-of-the-way place: but I suppose, as you say, Aunt Helen's death made a difference. Actually, they have not even one motor! and when I spoke of it Uncle David seemed almost indignant, and said horses were good enough for him. That is a specimen of the way they are content to live. He seems quite idiotically devoted to the small child, and she lives in his pocket. If she weren't so countrified in her ways she wouldn't be bad looking; but, of course, she is quite the bush youngster, and, I should think, would find her level pretty quickly when she goes to school among a lot of smart Melbourne girls. I should hope so, at any rate, for she is quite spoilt here. It is exactly as you said—everyone treats her like a sort of tin god, and she evidently thinks herself someone, and is inclined to regard those older than herself quite as equals. When I

29

first saw her she had just fallen into some mud hole, and her appearance would have given you a fit. But what can you expect?

"The fat old cook is still here, and asked after you. It's absolutely ridiculous to see the way she is treated—quite considers herself the mistress of the place, and when I told her one morning to let me have my shaving water she was almost rude. I think if there's one thing sillier than another it's the sort of superstition some people have about old servants.

"So far I find it exceedingly dull, and don't feel very hopeful that things will be much better when Jim comes home. Of course, he may be improved, but he appeared to me a great overgrown animal when I last saw him, without an idea in his head beyond cricket and football. I don't feel that he will be any companion to me. He will probably suffer badly from swelled head, too, as every one is making a fuss about his return. So quaint, to see the sort of mutual admiration that goes on here.

"I have had some riding, being given a horse much inferior to either Uncle David's or Norah's—the latter rides like a jockey, and, of course, astride, which I consider very ungraceful. She turns out well, however, and all her get-up is good—her habits come from a Melbourne tailor. I think I will get some clothes in Melbourne on my way back; they may not have newer ideas, but it may be useful for purposes of comparison with the Sydney cut. My riding clothes were evidently a source of much wonderment and admiration to the yokels. Unfortunately they have become badly stained with some confounded raspberry juice, and though I left them out for Mrs. Brown to clean, she has not done so yet.

"Well, there is no news to be got in a place like this; we never go out, except on the run, and there seems absolutely no society. The local doctor came out yesterday, in a prehistoric motor, but I found him very uninteresting. Of course, one has no ideas in common with these Bush people. Where the 'Charm of the Bush' comes in is more than I can see—I much prefer Town on a Saturday morning to all Billabong and its bullocks. They wanted me to go out one night and—fancy!—help burn down dead trees; but, really, I jibbed on that. There is no billiard room. Uncle David intends building one when Jim comes home for good, but that certainly won't be in my time here. I fancy a very few weeks will see me back in town.

"No bridge played here, of course! Have you had any luck that way?

"Your affectionate son,
"CECIL AUBREY LINTON."

Cecil blotted the final sheet of his letter home, and sat back with a sigh of satisfaction, as one who feels his duty nobly done. He stamped it, strolled across the hall to deposit it in the post box which stood on the great oak table, and then looked round for something to do.

It was afternoon, and all was very quiet. Mr. Linton had ridden off with a buyer to inspect cattle, Norah ruefully declining to accompany him.

"I'm awfully sorry, Dad," she had said, "But I'm too busy."

"Busy, are you? What at?"

"Oh, cooking and things," Norah had answered. "Brownie's not very well, and I said I'd help her—there's a lot to do just now, you know." She stood on tiptoe to kiss her father. "Good-bye, Dad—don't be too long, will you? And take care of yourself!"

Cecil also had declined to go out, giving "letters to write" as a reason. The truth was that several rides had told on the town youth, whose seat in the saddle was not easy enough to prevent his becoming stiff and sore. Bush people are used to this peculiarity in city visitors, and, while regarding the sufferers with sympathy, generally prescribe a "hair of the dog that bit them"—more riding—as the quickest cure; which Cecil would certainly have thought hard-hearted in the extreme. However, nothing would have induced him to say that he had felt the riding, since Cecil belonged to that class of boy that hates to admit inferiority to others. So he suffered in silence, creaked miserably at his uprising and down-sitting, and was happily unaware that everyone in Billabong knew perfectly well what was the matter with him.

Cecil and his mother were very good friends in the cool, polite way that was distinctive of them. They "fitted" together admirably, and as a general rule held the same views, the one on which they were most in accord being the belief in Cecil's own superior talents and characteristics. He wrote to her just as he would have talked, certain of her absolute agreement. When his letter was finished he felt much relieved at having, as Jim said, "got it off his chest." Not that Cecil would ever have said anything so inelegant.

Sarah crossed the hall at the moment, carrying a tray of silver to be cleaned, and he called to her—

"Where is Norah?"

"Miss Norah's in the kitchen," said the girl shortly. The Billabong maids were no less independent than modern maids generally are, but they had their views about the city gentleman's manner to the daughter of the house. "On'y a bit of a kid himself," Mary had said to Sarah, indignantly, "but any one'd think he owned the earth, an' Miss Norah was a bit of it." So they despised Cecil exceedingly, and refrained from shaking up his mattress when they made his bed.

"Er—you may tell her I want to speak to her."

"Can't, I'm afraid," Sarah said. "Miss Norah's very busy, 'elpin' Mrs. Brown. She don't care to be disturbed."

"Can't she spare me a moment?"

"Wouldn't ask her to." Sarah lifted her tray—and her nose—and marched out. Cecil looked black.

"Gad! I wish the mater had to deal with those girls!" he said viciously—Mrs. Geoffrey Linton was of the employers who "change their maids" with every new moon. "She'd make them sit up, I'll wager. Abominable impertinence!" He strolled to the door, and looked out across the garden discontentedly. "What on earth is there for a man to do? Well, I'll hunt up the important cousin."

At the moment, Norah was quite of importance. Mrs. Brown had succumbed to a headache earlier in the day. Norah had found her, white-faced and miserable, bending over a preserving pan full of jam, waiting for the mystical moment when it should "jell." Ordered to rest, poor Brownie had stoutly refused—was there not more baking to be done, impossible to put off, to say nothing of the jam? A brisk engagement had ensued, from which Norah had emerged victorious, the reins of government in her hands for the day. Brownie, still protesting, had been put on her bed with a handkerchief steeped in eau-de-Cologne on her throbbing forehead, and Norah had returned to the kitchen to varied occupations.

The jam had behaved beautifully; had "jelled" in the most satisfactory manner, just the right colour; now it stood in a neat array of jars on a side table, waiting to be sealed and labelled when cold. Then, after lunch, Norah had plunged into the mysteries of pastry, and was considerably relieved when her mince pies turned out very closely akin to those of Brownie, which were famous. Puddings for dinner had followed, and were now cooling in the dairy. Finally, the joint being in the oven, and vegetables prepared, the cook had compounded Jim's favourite cake, which was now baking; during which delicate operation, with a large dab of flour on her nose, the cook sat at the table, and wrote a letter.

"DEAR OLD JIM,—This must be in pencil, 'cause I'm watching a cake that's in the oven, and I'm awfully scared of it burning, so I don't dare to go for the ink. Dad said I was to write and tell you we would meet you on Wednesday, unless we heard from you again. We are all awfully glad and excited about you coming. I'm sure Tait and Puck understand, 'cause I told them to-day, and they barked like anything. Your room is all right, and we've put in another cupboard. We're all so sorry about Wally not coming, but we hope he will come later on. Do make him.

32

"Dad and I aren't talking about me going to school. It can't be helped, and it only makes you jolly blue to talk about it.

"Cecil's come, and he's the queerest specimen of a boy I ever saw. He's awfully grown up, but he's small and terribly swagger. His riding clothes are gorgeous, and you mustn't laugh at them. Dad did, but it was into Bobs' mane. He came with us cutting-out, and Betty was too good for him, swinging round, so he came a lovely cropper into some wild raspberries. It was so funny no one could have helped laughing, and he wasn't really hurt, only prickled and very wild. I am afraid he isn't enjoying himself very much, but of course he will be all right when you come. It's jolly hard to entertain him, 'cause he isn't a bit keen about anything. He has a tremendous array of shaving tackle. And he has a hand glass. Do you think he will lend it to you to see your back hair?

"Bobs is just lovelier than ever. I never knew him go so well as he is now, and he perfectly loves a jump. Dad has a new horse he calls Monarch, and he is a beauty, he is black with a star. Of course, don't say anything about Cecil's spill to anybody, he could not help it. And he had a much bigger laugh at me, 'cause I fell into the lagoon the day he came. I will tell you all about it when you come.

"The place is looking lovely, and hasn't dried up a bit–"

An unfamiliar step came along the passage, and Norah sat up abruptly from the labours of composition, and then with promptness concealed her letter under a cookery book.

"Why Cecil! How did you find your way here?"

"Oh–looked about me. I had finished my writing, and there was nothing to do."

"I'm so sorry," Norah said contritely. "You see, Brownie's sick, and I'm on duty here."

"You!" said Cecil, with a laugh. "And what can you do in a kitchen?"

Norah blushed at the laugh more than at the words.

"Oh, you'll get some sort of a dinner," she said. "Don't be too critical, that's all."

"What, you really can cook? Or do you play at it?"

"Well, there are mighty few girls in the Bush who can't cook a bit," Norah said. "Of course we're lucky, having Brownie–but you really never can tell as a rule when you may have to turn to in the kitchen. Dad says it's one of the beauties of Australia!"

"Can't say I like the idea of a lady in the kitchen," quoth Cecil loftily.

"Can't say I'd like to be one who was scared of it," Norah said. "And I guess you'd get very bored if you had to go without your dinner!" She seized a cloth and opened the oven door gingerly, and

33

made highly technical experiments with her cake, rising presently, somewhat flushed. "Ten minutes more," she said, with an air of satisfaction. "And, as Brownie would say, 'he's rose lovely.' Have some tea, Cecil?"

Cecil assented, and watched the small figure in the voluminous white apron as she flitted about the kitchen.

"I like having tea here," Norah confided to him. "Then I use Brownie's teapot, and don't you always think tea tastes miles better out of a brown pot? You won't get the proper afternoon cups either— I hope you don't mind?" She stopped short, with a sudden sense of talking a language altogether foreign to this bored young man in correct attire; and a rush of something like irritation to think how different Jim or Wally would have been—she could almost see Wally sitting on the edge of the table, with a huge cup of tea in one hand, a scone in the other, and his thin, eager face alight with cheerfulness. Cecil was certainly heavy in the hand. She sighed, but bent manfully to her task again.

"You take sugar, don't you? And cream? Yes, you ought to have cream, 'cause you've been ill." She dashed into the pantry, returning with a small jug. "The cake's not mine, so I can recommend it; but if you're not frightened you can have one of my mince pies."

"Thanks, I'd rather have cake," said Cecil., and again Norah flushed at his tone, but she laughed.

"It's certainly safer," she agreed, "I'm sure Brownie thought it was a hideous risk to leave the pies to me." She supplied her cousin with cake, and retreated to the oven.

"Why don't you let one of the girls do this?" he asked.

"Sarah or Mary? Oh, they're as busy as ever they can be," explained Norah. "We always do a lot of extra cleaning and rubbing up before Christmas, and they haven't a moment. Of course they'd do it in a minute, if I asked them, but I wouldn't—as it is, Sarah's going to dish up for me. They're the nicest girls; I'm going to take them tea as soon as I get my cake out!"

"You!" said Cecil. "You don't mean to say you're going to cart tea to the servants?"

"I'd be a perfect pig if I didn't," Norah said, shortly. "I'm afraid you don't understand the bush a bit, Cecil."

"Thank goodness I don't then," said Cecil, stiffly. "Who's that tray for?"

"Brownie, of course." Norah was getting a little ruffled—criticism like this had not come to her.

"Well, I think it's extraordinary—and so would my mother," Cecil said, with an air of finality.

"I suppose a town is different," said Norah, striving after

patience. "We like to look after everyone here—and I think it's grand when everyone's nice to everyone!" She paused; it was hard to be patient and grammatical, too.

"School will teach you a number of things," said her cousin loftily. He rose and put down his cup. "A lady shouldn't lower herself."

"Dad says a lady can't lower herself by work," retorted Norah. "Anyhow, if taking tea to dear old Brownie's going to lower me, it'll have to, that's all!"

"You don't understand," said Cecil. "A lady has her own place, and to get on terms of familiarity with the lower classes is bad for both her and them." He looked and felt instructive. "It isn't exactly the action that counts—it's the spirit it fosters—er—the feeling—that is, the—er, in short, it's a mistake to—"

"Oh, please be careful, Cecil, you're sitting in some dough!"

Norah sprang forward anxiously, and instructiveness fell from Cecil as one sheds a garment. He had sat down on the edge of the table in the flow of his eloquence; now he jumped up angrily, and, muttering unpleasant things, endeavored to remove dough from his person. Norah hovered round, deeply concerned. Pastry dough, however, is a clinging and a greasy product, and finally the wrathful lecturer beat a retreat towards the sanctuary of his own room, and the cook sat down and shook with laughter.

"My cake!" she gasped, in the midst of her mirth. She flew to the oven and rescued Jim's delicacy.

"Thank goodness, it's all right!" said she. Her mirth broke out afresh.

A shadow darkened the doorway.

"What—cooking and in hysterics?" said Mr. Linton. "May I have some tea? And what's the matter?"

"Cecil's begun the reforming process," said his daughter, becoming solemn with difficulty. "You've no idea how improved I am, Daddy! He seems to be certain that I'm not a lady, and he's very doubtful if I'm a cook, so could you tell me what I'm likely to be?"

"A better all-round man than Cecil, I should hope," said David Linton, with a sound like a snort of wrath. "Give me some tea, mate, and don't bother your head about the future. Your old Dad's not scared!"

35

CHAPTER VI

COMING HOME

The top of my desire
Is just to meet a mate o' mine.

Henry Lawson.

It had suddenly become hot—"truly Christmas" weather, Norah called it, as she stood waiting on the Cunjee platform for a train which, in accordance with all railway traditions at Christmas, was already over an hour late. Norah felt it hard that to-day, of all days in the year, it should be so—when Jim was actually coming home for good! At the thought of Jim's arrival she hopped cheerfully on one leg, completely oblivious of onlookers, and looked up the shining line of rails for the thousand-and-first time. Would the old train never come?

"Aren't you contriving to keep warm, with the mercury trying to break the thermometer? Or do you dance merely because you feel like it?" asked a friendly voice; and Norah turned with a little flush of pleasure to greet the Cunjee doctor. She and Dr. Anderson respected each other very highly.

"Because I feel like it, I expect," she said, laughing and shaking hands.

"Which my wide professional experience leads me to diagnose as the fact that you're probably waiting for Jim!" said the doctor, gravely. "There's a certain hectic flush, an intermittent pulse, which convinces me of your painful state, when coupled with the restlessness of the eye."

"Which eye?" asked Norah anxiously.

"Both," said the doctor. "Don't be flippant with your medical man. So he's really coming, Norah?"

"Yes," said Norah, "and I don't care if I am excited—so'd you be, doctor. Billy's outside with the horses, and he's just as excited as I am."

"Billy!" said the doctor. "But he'd never say more than 'Plenty!' no matter how excited he was."

"No, of course not, but then he finds it such a useful word," Norah said a little vaguely. She was peering up the rails. Suddenly she spun round, her face glowing. "There's the smoke—she's coming!"

Whatever additional remarks Dr. Anderson may have made fell on deaf ears, for Norah had no further ideas from that moment. The train came into view over the brow of the hill, and slid down the long slope into the station, pulling up with a mighty grinding of brakes. Almost as it stopped a door was flung open violently, and a very tall boy with the Grammar School colours on his hat jumped out, cast a hurried glance around, and then seized the small person in blue linen in an unashamed bear's hug.

"Oh, Jim!" said Norah. "Oh, Jimmy—boy!"

"Well, old kiddie," said Jim. "You all right? My word, I am glad to see you!"

"Me, too," said Norah. "It's been just ages, Jim."

"Hasn't it? Jim said. He started. "Oh, by Jove! There's someone else here!"

Norah wheeled round, and uttered a little cry of joy. Another boy with the dark-blue hat band was grinning at her in most friendly fashion—a thin, brown-faced boy, with especially merry dark eyes. Norah's hands went out.

"Wally! But, how lovely! I thought you couldn't come."

"So did I," said Wally Meadows, pumping her hands vigorously. "I was going home, but my aunt obligingly got measles. I'm awfully sorry for Aunt. But it's an ill-wind that blows nowhere—old Jim took pity on me, and here I am!"

"I should think so," Norah said. "We haven't felt a bit complete without you. Dad was saying only this morning how sorry he was you couldn't come. He'll get such a shock! Oh, it's so lovely to have you two—and isn't it getting like Christmas! I'm so happy!" She jigged on one foot, regardless of interested faces watching her from the train.

"You've grown about a foot," said Jim, patting her on the shoulder. "Pretty thin, too—sure you're all right?"

Norah reassured him, laughing.

"Well, you look awfully fit, if you are thin," was Jim's comment. "Doesn't she, Wally?"

"Never saw her look fitter," said Wally. "I'm glad as five bob Aunt got the measles! Oh, what a beast I am—but, you know what I mean! Jim, this train'll go on, and we've fifty million things in the carriage!"

"So we have!" Jim said, hurriedly, taking his hand from Norah's shoulder and diving after his chum into the compartment they had quitted. They emerged laden with suitcases, parcels, rackets, fishing rods, golf sticks and other miscellaneous impedimenta.

"Catch!" Jim said, tossing a big box into Norah's hands.

"Chocolates!" said Norah blissfully. "Jim, you're an angel!"

"Always knew that," her brother replied, dropping his load on the platform with a cheerful disregard of what might break. "Come on, Wally, we'll get the heavy things out of the van. You watch those, Nor. Who's in, by the way? And where's Dad?"

"Dad's in Cunjee; but he had business, and he couldn't wait at the station, the train was so late. Cecil's with him—they're both riding. I've got the light buggy with the ponies for you, and Billy's driving the express for your luggage and heaps of things that Brownie wants for the house." Norah spoke in one breath and finished with a gasp.

"Guess people must have thought you were a circus procession!" was Jim's comment. "All right, we'll cart the things out to Billy."

Out at the bid express-wagon drawn by a pair of greys, Billy stood, welcoming them with a smile on his dusky countenance that Wally likened to a slit in a coconut. The luggage was piled in with special injunctions to the black boy not to put the bags of flour on anything that looked delicate—whereat Billy's smile widened to a grin, and he murmured "Plenty!" delightedly.

"That's the lot," Jim said. "The buggy's at the hotel, I suppose, Norah?"

"Yes—and we're to have lunch there with Dad. And you've got to be awfully polite to Cecil!"

"Cecil!" said Jim, lifting his nose. "If Cecil's anything like what he used to be—" He did not finish the sentence.

"Do we play with Cecil?" Wally asked, grinning.

"The question is, if Cecil will condescend to play with you," Norah said. "He thinks me too much of a kid to look at—"

"Oh, does he?" asked Jim resentfully.

"But you're both ever so much bigger than he is, so perhaps he'll let you love him!" Norah finished.

"I'm relieved to my soul," said Wally, with gravity. "Visions of my unrequited affection poured out on Cecil have been troubling my rest for days. May I kiss him?"

"I'd wait a little while, I think," Norah answered. "He may be shy—not that we've found it out yet. Indeed, he's the unshyest person I ever met."

"Is he very awful, Nor?"

"Oh, he's a bit of a drawback," Norah said. "Dad says he's not bad at heart, only so spoilt—and he's just terribly bumptious, Jim, and thinks he can do everything; and his clothes are lovely! He isn't caring for me a bit to-day, 'cause he gave me a broad hint that he wanted to ride Bobs, and I didn't take it."

38

"Ride Bobs!" exclaimed Jim, in amazement. "Well, I should think you didn't!"

"Well, I felt rather a pig, considering he's our guest," Norah said, a little contritely. "If it were you or Wally, now—but he's really got an awful seat, Jim, and Murty says he's a hand like a ham on a horse's mouth! I didn't feel I could let him have Bobs."

"Bobs is your very special property—no one but an ass would ask for him, and I told Cecil last year you were the only person who ever rode him," said Jim indignantly. "Surely there are enough horses on the place without him wanting to collar your pony!"

"Well, he didn't get him," said Norah, tranquilly, "so that's all right and you needn't worry, Jimmy. I do think, if only one could get him off his high horse, he wouldn't be at all bad—perhaps he'll thaw now you boys are here. I hope he will, for his own sake, 'cause he'd have such a much better time."

"Well, if he's going to be patronizing—" Jim began.

"Ah, perhaps he won't—I don't believe he could try to patronize you!" Norah glanced lovingly at her tall brother. "You're nearly as big as Dad, Jimmy, aren't you? and Wally's going to be too."

"Ill weeds grow apace," quoted the latter gentleman solemnly. "Jim's a splendid example of that proverb."

"M'f!" said Norah. "How about yourself?"

"I'm coming up as a flower!" Wally replied modestly. "A Christmas lily, I should think!"—whereat Jim murmured something that sounded "More like an artichoke!" His exact remark, however, was lost, for at that moment they arrived at the hotel, just as Mr. Linton emerged from it, and Jim quickened his pace, his face alight.

"Dad!"

"Well, my boy!" They gripped hands, and David Linton's eye kindled as it dwelt on the big fellow. "Glad to have you back, old son. Why—Wally!"

"Turned up like a bad penny, sir," said Wally, having his hand pumped in turn. "Hope you'll forgive me—it's pretty cool to arrive without an invitation."

"As far as I know, you had invitations from all the family," said Mr. Linton, laughing. "We regard you as one of the oldest inhabitants now, you know. At any rate, I'm delighted to see you; the mistress of Billabong must answer for herself, but she doesn't look cast down!"

"She's been fairly polite," Wally said. "On the whole I don't feel as shy as I was afraid of feeling! I was horribly scared of having Christmas with my aunt—but she's chosen measles instead, so I expect she was just as scared as I was!"

"It's probable," said his host, laughing.

"You haven't grown up a bit, Wally, and it's such a comfort!" Norah said.

"I'm getting old and reverend," said Wally severely, "and it's up to you to treat me with respect, young Norah. Sixteen's an awful age to support with any cheerfulness." His brown face at the moment gave the impression of never having been serious during the sixteen years he lamented. "As for this ancient mariner"—indicating Jim—"you can see the signs of senile decay quite plainly!"

"Ass!" said Jim affectionately. He broke off. "How are you, Cecil?"

Cecil, coming out of the hotel, a dapper figure beside the two tall schoolboys, gave languid greetings. He cast at Jim a glance of something like envy. Height was the one thing he longed for, and it seemed to him hard that this seventeen-year-old youngster should be rapidly approaching six feet, while he, three years older, had stopped short six inches under that measurement. However, generally speaking, Cecil was uncommonly well satisfied with himself, and not even the contemplation of Jim's superior inches could worry him for long. He asked polite questions about the journey, and laughed at the freely expressed opinion that the day was hot "You should go to Sydney if you want to know what heat is," he said, with the superiority of the travelled man; "Victoria really has no heat to talk about!"

"Well, I'm a Queenslander," said Wally bluntly, "and we're supposed to know about heat there. And I do think to-day is beastly hot—look at my collar, it's like a concertina! Sydney heat is hot, and Brisbane heat is hotter, but Victorian heat has a hotness all of its own!" Whereat everybody laughed, and the discussion was adjourned for lunch.

It was a merry meal; and if the fare was no better than that of most township hotels, the spirits of the party were too high to trouble about such trifles as tough meat, watery puddings, and weary butter that bore out Wally's remarks about the heat by threatening to float away on a sea of its own oil. Everything was rose colour in Norah's estimation that day. She sat by Jim and beamed across the table at her father and Wally. Even Cecil found himself at times included in the beam, and took it meekly, for the happy face was infectious, while the frank delight of the boys in having her with them again was to a certain extent educational to the outsider. There was no lack of manliness in Jim's strong, handsome face. If he found it worth his while, Cecil reflected, to make such a fuss over a child, it might be possible that she was not altogether a person to be snubbed. So he was unusually affable to his small cousin, and lunch passed off very successfully.

40

Afterwards there was shopping to be done. A long list of groceries had been made out by Mrs. Brown, who professed herself far too busy with Christmas preparations to come in person, and had laid the responsibility on Norah, not without misgivings. It was, perhaps, fortunate that the storekeepers were able to rise to the contents of the list unaided, for Norah was scarcely in a condition to grapple with problems relating to anything so ordinary as groceries, and found it indeed difficult to read out her list coherently, with Jim standing sentinel in the doorway and Wally wandering about the shop sampling all he could find, from biscuits to brooms. On one occasion, when making a special effort to preserve her dignity, she came to the item "flaked oatmeal," and asked the shopman in rather frigid tones for "floked atemeal," which had a paralysing effect on the unoffending storekeeper, while Wally retired to the shelter of a pile of saucepans, and shrieked. Thus the business of necessary purchases passed off cheerfully; and then what Norah termed the more interesting shops—saddlers' and stationers'—were visited, with a view to Christmas. Finally Jim brought the buggy from the hotel, and they picked up their lighter parcels.

"Surely that's all?" Jim inquired, as Norah and Wally came out of the fruiterer's laden with bags of assorted sizes, which they dumped thankfully into the buggy, with the immediate result that a bag of peaches burst, and had to be rescued from all over the floor. "Nor., you'll not have a penny left, and we'll all be violently ill if we eat half you've bought. Come on home."

"Brownie's laid in large stocks of medicine, she says," Norah answered, tranquilly, climbing into the buggy. "So you needn't worry, need you? But we've truly finished now, Jim, I think. Ready, Wally?"

"Quite," said Wally cheerfully. "I've put these peaches in with the neatsfoot oil, and it seems a beautiful arrangement!" He hopped up nimbly. "Right oh, J immy, and pray remember I am nervous!"

"I will," Jim grinned. He laid the whip on the ponies' backs, and they shot forward with a bound, unused to such liberties. They went down the main street of Cunjee in a whirl of dust, and turned over the bridge spanning the river, where the ponies promptly rose on their hind legs at the sight of Dr. Anderson's motor, and betrayed a rooted disinclination to come down from that unusual altitude. Jim handled them steadily, and presently they were induced to face the snorting horror, wherein the doctor sat, waving his hand and calling cheery Christmas greetings as they shot past, to which the three responded enthusiastically. Cunjee sank into the distance behind them.

The miles flew past. On the metalled road the rubbered tyres

41

spun silently, and only the flying hoofs clattered and soon they had left the made road and turned on to the hard-beaten track that led to Billabong, where progress was even smoother. The tongues flew almost as swiftly as the wheels. The hot sun sank gradually, and the evening breeze sprang up. It was a time for quick questions and answers. Norah wanted details of the term just over, the sports, the prize-giving, and had to laugh over messages from those of Jim's boy friends whom she knew; and Jim had a hundred things to ask about home—the cattle, the fishing, his horses, his dogs, "Brownie," and the prospects of fun ahead. They roared over her ducking and subsequent encounter with Cecil, and chaffed her unmercifully.

"Such a mud-lark!" said Wally, with glee. "And that prim young man! Oh, Norah, you are a dream! I'd have given something to see your face."

"I was altogether worth seeing," Norah remarked modestly. "When I caught sight of myself in a glass I really didn't wonder at Cecil." But Jim glowered and referred to the absent Cecil as a "silly ass."

They turned in at last at the homestead gate, and the ponies fairly flew up the long paddock, something in the spirits of their drivers communicating itself to them. The house was not visible until the track had passed through a thick belt of trees, and as they came to this Jim fell silent, looking keenly ahead. Then the red roof came into view and the boy drew a long breath.

"There's the old place," he said. "My word, I am glad to be home!"

Under the dust-rug Norah slipped her hand on to his knee.

"It's just lovely to have you—both of you." she added. "You're glad, too, aren't you, Wally?"

"I could sing!" said Wally.

"Once," said Jim, "you could. But for some years—"

"Beast!" said Wally. "If you weren't driving—"

"And you weren't nervous—!" grinned his chum.

"There'd be wigs on the green," finished Norah, cheerfully. "I'll drive, if it would be any convenience to either of you."

"We'll postpone it," said Jim. "There's Brownie at the gate, bless her old heart!"

They shot up the last furlong of the drive. At the big gate of the yard—very few people, not even bishops, go to the front gate of a Bush homestead—Brownie stood, her broad face beaming. As they pulled up, Murty O'Toole came forward to take the horses—a marked compliment from Murty, who, like most head stockmen, was a free and independent soul.

42

Jim went over the wheel with a bound, and seized Brownie's hand.

"How are you, Brownie, dear?"

"The size of him!" said she. "The shoulders. No wonder they 'ad you for captin of the football eleven, then, my dear!" The boys grinned widely. "If not eleven, then it's four," said Brownie placidly. "Strange, I can't never remember which, an' it don't sinnerfy, any'ow. Welkim 'ome–an' you too, Master Wally."

"How are you, Murty?" Jim shook hands with the stockman, while Wally bowed low over Brownie's hand.

"I've lived for this moment," he said, fervently. "Brownie, you grow younger every time I go away!"

"Naturally!" said Norah from the buggy.

"Be silent, minx!" said Wally, over his shoulder. "Who are you to break in on a heart-to-heart talk, anyhow? At this present moment, Mrs. Brown, you look seventeen!"

"Get along with you, now, do!" said the delighted Brownie. "You're no better than you was, I'm afraid, Master Wally–alwuz ready for your joke!"

"Joke!" exclaimed he, indignantly. "Any one who'd make a joke of you, Brownie, would rob a church. Jim might, but I–"

"Perish the idea!" said Jim, tipping the orator's hat over his eyes. "Come and take things out of the buggy."

Across the yard came Mr. Linton, surrounded by a mixed assemblage of dogs. Puck and the collie had already hurled themselves upon Jim in a delirium of joy. Cecil strolled after his uncle, looking slightly amused at the scene by the gate.

"We're quite a family," Mr. Linton said. "I begin to feel like Mr. Pickwick at a Christmas gathering! Do you think Billabong will stand the crowd, Mrs. Brown?"

"It looks to me, sir," said Mrs. Brown contentedly, "as if Billabong's goin' to 'ave the time of its life!"

CHAPTER VII

JIM UNPACKS

Holler-days
Were made for boys to holler!

Jim's room was a rather vast place, with two long windows opening upon the balcony, two exceedingly plain iron bedsteads in different corners, and in the midst a wide, vacant space, where a punching-ball was fixed whenever the owner was at home. There was a very shabby old leather armchair by one window, and near the other an even shabbier leather couch, very wide and solid. Jim used to declare that they were the most comfortable in the house, and nothing would have induced him to have them altered in any way.

One wall held a medley of various articles: Jim's rifle, the sporting gun his father had given him when he was fifteen, a revolver that had been through two wars, and a cavalry sword his grandfather had carried, together with an assortment of native weapons from various countries—assegais, spears, boomerangs, throwing sticks, sjamboks and South Sea Island clubs and shields. A special nail held Jim's own stockwhip, to which Norah always attended after he had gone away, lest the supple thong should become harsh through disuse. Then there were weapons of peace—hockey sticks, rackets, cricket-bats—the latter an assortment of all Jim had used, from the tiny one he had begun with at the age of eight to the full sized beauty that had split honourably in an inter-State school match the preceding summer.

All over the other walls were plainly framed photographs. Mr. Linton and Norah were there, in many positions, with and without horses; then there were pictures of all the favourite horses and ponies and dogs on the place, and a big enlargement of Billabong house itself. The others were school photographs, mostly football and cricket teams, tennis fours, the school crew, and some large groups at the yearly sports. In nearly all you could find Jim himself—if you looked closely enough. Jim loathed being photographed, and always retired as far out of sight in a group as his inches would permit.

The room held many of Jim's own manufactured ideas—his "contraptions," Brownie used to call them. There was a telephone he had rigged up when he was twelve, communicating with Norah's room by the balcony; and outside was a sort of fire escape, by which he could—and generally did—descend without using the stairs. There were various pieces of bush carpentry—a table, a candlestick and a book-case of his own construction, which in Norah's eyes were better than beautiful. There was an arrangement by which he could open his door or his windows without getting out of bed—which was ingenious, but quaint, since Jim was never known to shut his windows, and very rarely his door. Altogether it was an interesting room, and very typical of Jim.

At present it resembled a maelstrom, for Wally and Jim were unpacking. Brownie, putting in her head, described it as "a perfick shambles," and affected great horror at the havoc occasioned by having boys in the house—beaming all the while in a manner calculated to destroy the effect of any lecture. Norah, perched on the end of the sofa, which was the only free spot in the room, looked on at the operations with deep interest. Occasionally, when some special parcel was unearthed, one of the boys diverted her attention laboriously, since it was near Christmas-time, which is ever a season of mysteries. The parcel stowed away hastily in a cupboard, Norah was permitted to gaze once more, unrestricted.

"What's that, Jim?" she asked, catching a glimpse of silver in the recesses of a suitcase.

"Oh, nothing."

"I believe it's your cup," said his sister excitedly. "Do make him show me, Wally!"

"The mug it is!" said Wally, diving in under Jim's nose, and snatching the article in question. "Don't be an ass, Jimmy—d'you expect to keep it always in your boot-bag?"

"Very nice place for it," Jim was understood to mutter.

"Ripping—but you'll want it for your boots. Catch, Norah!"

The big silver cup flew across the room, and was deftly fielded by the lady on the end of the sofa.

"Oh, isn't it a beauty!" she said delightedly. "Jimmy, I'm so proud to know you!"

"You ought to have seen him going up to get it," Wally said. "Lovely sight—he blushed so prettily!"

"Blush be hanged!" said the victim.

"Don't be ashamed, my child; it's a very nice thing to be able to blush," Wally grinned. "No one would ever dream you could, either, so it's a happy surprise as well!"

"There's not a blush about you, that's one thing," said Jim, from the depths of his big box.

"Wore out all my powers that way blushing over you!" was

45

Wally's prompt reply. "Norah, will you use that thing for cocoa, or what?"

"Don't be disrespectful—I'm admiring it," Norah answered, turning the cup round. "Dad will like it awfully."

"Has he shown you his prizes?"

"Prizes!" Norah exclaimed, falling off the arm of the sofa in amazement. "Jim, you horrid boy, you never told us. Show me at once!"

"Never thought about 'em," said the unhappy Jim, un-earthing two resplendent books. "Here you are, anyhow —and Wally needn't talk; he's got three!"

"I'm faint in the presence of so much learning!" Norah said, sitting down on a golf bag. "Who'd ever have suspected you? French and Prefect's Prize—oh, l'm so glad you got that one, Jim, dear." Her quick ear caught a step, and she called her father excitedly.

Mr. Linton entered, to be greeted by incoherent tidings of his son's success, to the meaning of which the two books lent aid.

"That's especially good news, old chap," he said quietly, whereat Jim grinned happily, blushed with fervour, and muttered something entirely inaudible. "The cup, too! that's a beauty, and no mistake!" He looked round the "perfick shambles," and laughed a little. "I don't think they're very safe here," he said. "With your permission, I'll take charge of them." He left the room, carrying the books and the cup with him.

At the door he paused.

"Don't forget Cecil," he said quietly, and was gone.

The trio looked blank.

"Cecil!" said Wally.

"Hang Cecil!" from Jim disgustedly.

"Oh, he's such a bore!" Norah said. "And he'd simply hate to be in here—he wouldn't see any fun in it. I—I really think I've had an overdose of Cecil."

"Poor old kid!" said Jim. "Well, we'll hurry up unpacking and then find him." They dismissed the "bit of a drawback" airily from their minds, and proceeded with the business in hand, hampered slightly by much energetic conversation. Jim's boxes were full of interesting things, the result of his six years at school; his packing, he said, with pained recollection, had been a "corker."

"Lucky I had that extra chest of drawers put in here," remarked Norah, stowing away numerous small articles. "Jim, how many boys gave you knives as farewell gifts?"

"Sorra a one of me knows," said her brother. "I lost count—and lost some of the knives, too. I've an idea Bill Beresford picked up one I dropped—the one Lance Western gave me; it's got a tortoiseshell handle, and a nick out of the big blade—and gave it to me for himself."

"It sounds the sort of economical thing Bill would do," Wally remarked.

"Then there are five magnifying glasses, seven pencil cases, and six pens," said Norah. "All tokens of affection, Jim? I'll put them in the middle drawer."

"What on earth I'm going to do with 'em all," said their harassed owner, "I'm sure I don't know. Does any one chap use five magnifiers in his life? Never used one yet! I wish the fellows hadn't been so kind—it was awfully brickish of them, though, wasn't it? And the Doctor gave me this." He held up a large and solemn—looking book.

"What is it?"

"'Self Help,' by a chap named Smiles. Shouldn't have thought there were many smiles about a book looking like that, but it shows you can't tell everything by the cover. And Mrs. Doctor gave me this tie—knitted it herself. It was jolly decent of her, wasn't it? She's always been awfully kind to me," said the big fellow, who had no idea of what "Mrs. Doctor" thought of his cheerful habit of picking up two or three of her babies and treating them to a wild ride round the school grounds on his back; and who had on one occasion sat up all night with a sick three-year-old who had cried unreasonably for "Yinton" to come and carry him. The boy had recovered, somewhat against expectations, and Jim had thought no more of the matter, except to drop gently and firmly into a gorse bush a fellow who had chaffed him for being a nursemaid. He had been amazed, and greatly embarrassed, by the tears in little "Mrs. Doctor's" eyes as she bade him good-bye. Nothing on earth would have induced him to mention them.

"If the Doctor ever gives me anything barring the length of his tongue, I'll have apoplexy!" remarked Wally. "We don't twin-soul a bit better than we did. He caught me beautifully the other day. Three or four of us were going to have a supper. I'd been into town to the dentist, and was bringing home a lobster. Coming out, that idiot Bob Greenfield was next me on the train, and he amused himself by rubbing the lobster gently until the thin brown paper they wrap 'em in had worn through in places. I was talking cricket for all I was worth, and never noticed him. I'd bought an evening paper, and given him my lobster to hold while I looked up some scores."

"Yes?" said Norah, happily.

"Well, we came to the school, and off I jumped, and just inside the gate I ran into the Doctor. He was very affable, and we walked

47

up together, and he asked me quite affectionately how I'd got on with the dentist, and altogether he might have been my long lost uncle! Presently he glanced down at my parcel, and said, 'Been getting a boot mended, Meadows?' I didn't know what to say for a moment. And while I was floundering in my mind the string broke, and down went my parcel with a clatter on the asphalt!"

"Why do I miss these things?" asked Jim, plaintively.

"I wish I'd missed it instead of you!" said his chum. "I picked it up in a hurry, and the paper had burst pretty well all over-and-well, you know, there's no disguising the colour of a lobster! I just held it, and looked a fool, and the Doctor put up his eyeglass and looked it and me all over. Then he said, 'Curious colour for a boot, Meadows'—and I promptly turned the same shade as the lobster."

"Did you get into a row?" Norah asked.

"No; I will say for the old chap that he was a perfect brick," Wally said. "He just grinned, and walked off, remarking that there was no need to push investigations too far. And I fled, and the lobster was tip-top, thank you."

"I don't see why you've any cause to grumble at the Doctor," was Norah's comment.

"That's you, feminine ignorance," returned Wally. "He made me feel small."

"Well, if I get a head mistress as easy-going–" said Norah, dolefully.

"Don't you get the idea into your mind that our revered Head's easy-going!" Wally retorted. "He thinks nothing of skinning a fellow on occasion–only he didn't happen to think a lobster was occasion–that night, anyhow. You see, it was near the end of term, and even Heads get soft!"

"Lots of em," said Jim; "look at your own!" He dodged a hairbrush neatly. "Have a little sense, young Wally; don't you see I'm busy? Norah, old chap, did you see my blazer?"

"I hung it in your wardrobe," said Norah promptly "Also your overcoat, also your straw hat, also your cadet uniform–what are you going to do with that, by the way, Jim?"

"Get photographed in it," said Wally, wickedly.

"I'm likely to!" Jim said, with fine scorn. "Goodness only knows–I may find some fellow it'll fit. It certainly wouldn't fit me much longer."

"It's been the anxiety of the whole battalion," said Wally. "It creaked and began to split whenever he drilled in it, and for the last six parades we've always taken out a blanket in case we should need to drape his tattered form on the way home! It's an uncommonly good thing he's left. Most demoralizing for a young corps to see its corpulent lieutenant bursting out of his uniform!"

"He's not corpulent," said Norah indignantly, whereat Jim, who personified leanness with breadth of shoulder, grinned even more widely than Wally, and patted her on the head as he passed with an armful of clothes, which he stowed into his wardrobe much as he might have dumped sacks of potatoes into a barn. Even Norah's wide and free views on the subject of garments were not proof against the sight.

"Are those your good suits, Jim?"

"Yes," said her brother, cheerfully. "They're used to it. Chuck me that coat, Wally."

Wally complied, and the coat–which happened to be the one belonging to its owner's evening suit–was added to the heap in the wardrobe.

"I'll sort 'em out some time or other," said Jim. "I'm so jolly sick of unpacking. Wally, you animal, you're not finished, are you?"

"Ages ago," said his chum. "Hadn't anything like your quantity, you see. My clothes are neat and trim, and my pyjamas have blue ribbon in them and I have put out my lace pin cushion and my tulle slippers, and all is well! Now I feel I can go and play with Cecil with a quiet mind!"

"I really don't know why I brought a lunatic home with me," Jim said, patiently. "Sorry, Nor.; but we'll take him out in the scrub and lose him. Meanwhile–" He closed the last drawer with a bang, and advanced with slow deliberation upon the hapless Mr. Meadows.

For the next few minutes the air in the room was murky with pillows, other missiles and ejaculations. Out of the turmoil came yelps, much energetic abuse, and shrieks to Norah for aid to which that maiden, who was enjoying herself hugely, lent a deaf ear. Finally, the combat restricted itself principally to Wally's bed, from which the bedclothes gradually disappeared, until they formed a tight bundle on the floor, with Wally in the centre. Jim piled the mattress on top, and retreated to the door.

"Beast!" said Wally, disentangling himself with difficulty, until he sat on the pile, considerably dishevelled, and wearing a broad grin. "It's only your vile brute force–some day I'll get even with you!" He rose, hurled the mattress upon the bed, and looked inquiringly at his blankets. "How do you imagine I'm going to sleep there to-night?"

"Oh, we'll fix it up when we come to bed," laughed Jim. "Come on–we ought to go down to Cecil."

"Hold on till I brush my hair," said Wally, attacking his disturbed locks, and settling his tie. "All right; lead on, Macduff!"

49

"Ready, Nor.?"

Norah hesitated.

"I'm going to my room for something," she said. "I'll be after you in a few minutes, boys."

She disappeared within her room, and the boys clattered downstairs. When they had gone, Norah slipped back noiselessly to Jim's apartment, which gave the impression of having recently been the scene of a cyclone. She laughed a little, looking at it from the doorway.

"It certainly is a 'perfick shambles'," she said. "Poor old chaps— and they'll be so tired when they come up to bed!"

Moving quietly, she sorted out the tangled bedclothes and made up the bed, and reduced to order some of the chaos in the room. Then she opened the wardrobe and took out the mass of clothes, sorting out the suits and putting them away carefully, with a shake to the coats to remove creases. The dress suit she laid in a drawer, running to her own room for a tiny lavender bag to keep away the moths. She was closing the drawer when she started at a step, and Jim came in.

"What on earth are you up to?" was his question. His eye travelled round the room, taking in the open door of the wardrobe, and the dress coat in the drawer, where stood his small sister, rather flushed.

"Well!" he said, and paused. "Weren't we beasts?"

"No, you weren't," said Norah indignantly.

"H'm," said Jim. "It's a jolly good thing when a fellow has a sister, anyhow." He came over to her and put his arm round her shoulders. "Dear old chap!" he said. They went down the stairs together.

CHAPTER VIII

A THUNDERSTORM

The Bush hath moods and changes, as the seasons rise and fall,
And the men who love the Bushland—they are loyal thro' it all.

A. B. Paterson.

"The day after to-morrow is the date of the men's dance," Mr. Linton said. "Norah mustn't go in for any wild exertion on that day, as she'll probably want to dance several hundred miles at night. So if you boys want to plan anything, you had better make your arrangements for to-morrow."

"I don't know that I've energy enough to plan anything," said Jim, lazily. He was lying full length on the lawn, his head on Norah. Wally was close by, and Cecil and Mr. Linton occupied basket chairs. Peace would have reigned supreme had not the mosquitoes kept every one busy.

"Any wishes, Cecil?"

"None whatever," said Cecil. "There are no people to go and see, I think you said, Uncle David?"

"No one that would interest you," Mr. Linton said; and Wally and Jim, who had groaned internally with fear of being taken "calling," felt their spirits return.

"My brain's not equal to planning, as I remarked," Jim said. "But if I go anywhere, I'd like to do so on a horse. I want to feel a horse under me again."

"Hear, hear," from Wally, softly.

"Well, I can't go out to-morrow," said the squatter. "I've letters to see to, and Anderson may be out; so you must look after yourselves—which I believe you to be entirely capable of doing. Norah, haven't you any ideas?"

"Loads," said Norah, promptly, "but they're all connected with mosquitoes!" She aimed a vicious blow into space as she spoke, and sighed, before rubbing the bite. "Well, suppose we ride out and boil the billy somewhere along the river? Cecil, would you care for that?"

"Very much," said Cecil, in the tones that always gave the impression that he despised the particular subject under discussion. Norah had quite withdrawn the opinion formed in the first five

51

minutes of their acquaintance, that he was ill mannered—now she bewailed the fact that he was so uniformly and painfully polite.

"Well, if you would—" she said, hesitatingly. "What do you boys think?"

"Grand idea," responded Wally. Norah loved Wally's way; he was always so pleased and interested over any plan that might be formed. Jim was wont to remark that if you arranged to clean out a pigsty, Wally would probably regard it as a gigantic picnic, and enjoy his day hugely. She smiled at him gratefully in the darkness.

"You too, Jim?"

"Rather—anything you like," said her brother. "What horse can I have, Dad?"

Jim had no special horse of his own. His two ponies, Sirdar and Mick, he had outgrown, although they were still up to anything of a lighter weight—the former only inferior to Norah's beloved Bobs. His absences from home were so long that it had not seemed worth while to procure him a special horse, and for several holidays he had been accustomed to ride any of the station mounts. Privately, Jim was not altogether satisfied with the arrangement, although quite admitting its common sense. Now that he had left school he intended to ask his father if he could buy a horse.

"You can try my new purchase, Monarch, if you like," Mr. Linton answered. "He's quite a decent mover—I think you'll like him."

Cecil bit his lip, under cover of the darkness. He coveted a ride on both Bobs and Monarch, and had given hints on the subject, but neither had been taken. Now Jim, nearly three years his junior, was lent Monarch without even having asked for him; while he was still, he presumed, to ride the steady-going Brown Betty, whom he thoroughly despised, in spite of the fact that she had once got rid of him. He registered another notch in his general grudge against Billabong.

Mr. Linton was absolutely ignorant of what passed in his nephew's mind. To give the city boy, with his uncertain seat and heavy hands, anything but a steady horse, never occurred to him; he would have regarded it as little short of inviting disaster to put him on Monarch, thoroughbred and newly broken in as he was; and, of course, no one but Norah ever rode Bobs.

"That's all right," he said, as Jim expressed his pleasure. "And what about you, Wally? You're too long now for Mick, I think."

"Oh, anything you like, sir," said Wally, easily. "I haven't met any bad 'uns on Billabong. Warder, or Brown Betty, or Nan—have you got them all still?"

"They're all here," the squatter said. "Cecil generally rides Betty,

52

and I believe Burton's using old Warder just now. But you can have Nan, if you like."

"Thanks very much," said Wally. "I'll take the shine out of you, young Norah!"

"I'd like to see you," returned Norah. Monarch might beat Bobs or yes, perhaps one other horse she knew of, in a small tree-grown paddock; at the thought of which she smiled happily to herself. But no other horse on Billabong could see the way Bobs went when he was in earnest.

"Well, that's all settled," Mr. Linton said. "I hope you'll have a good day—you're bound to have it hot, so I should advise you to get an early start. If you go as far as the Swamp Paddock, Norah, you might ride round the cattle there, and see if they're settling down—I put the new bullocks there, you know."

"All right, Dad, we'll do it. I like having an object for a ride."

"Same here," said Jim sleepily. "Picnics are asinine things!"

"I don't believe you know much about anything—you're three parts asleep!" said Wally, flinging a cushion at his chum, which Jim caught thankfully, and, remarking that Norah was uncommonly scraggy, adjusted under his head. The result was a vigorous upheaval by the indignant Norah, who declined to be a head-rest for such ingratitude any longer. At this point Mr. Linton discovered that it was time for supper; and the boys, tired after their long journey, were not long in saying goodnight.

Jim came up with Norah, and switched on her light. His eye travelled round the pretty room.

"I don't know what part of home's homiest," he said—"but I always reckon your room runs pretty near it! Blest if I know what it will be like when you're not here, little chap."

Norah rubbed her face against his coat sleeve.

"We don't talk of it," she said. "If we did, I'd—I'd be a horrid coward, Jimmy—boy, and you wouldn't like me a bit!"

"Wouldn't I?" Jim said. "Well, I can't imagine you a coward, anyhow." He bent and kissed her. "Good-night, old kiddie."

They set out in good time next morning, for the sun gave promise of a scorching day.

Billy had the horses ready under the shade of a huge pepper-tree; even there the flies were bad enough to set Monarch and Bobs fretting with irritation, while the two stock horses lashed unceasingly with their tails and stamped in the dust. Nan was a long, handsome brown mare, with two white feet—an old friend of Wally's, who came and patted her and let her rub her worried head against his coat. Cecil mounted Betty and looked on sourly, while Jim walked round Monarch and admired the big black.

53

"He ought to carry you like a bird, Dad."

"He does; a bit green yet, but he'll mend of that," his father answered. "Now, get away, all of you." He put Norah up and watched, with a silent look of approval, the way Jim handled his impatient steed, taking him quietly, as one treats a fractious baby, and mounting gently. Then he stood under the tree to see them ride down the paddock, valises containing necessaries for the "asinine picnic" strapped on Nan and Betty's saddles. Norah, as the lady of the party, was exempt from carrying burdens, and Monarch brooked no load but his rider.

They made good time across the shadeless paddocks, anxious for the pleasanter conditions along the river bank, where a cattle track wound in and out under the gum trees. It was one of Norah and Jim's favourite rides; they never failed to take it when holidays brought the boy back to Billabong. They pushed along it for some time, eventually finding the slip rails, through which they got into the Swamp Paddock—so called because of a wide marsh in one corner, where black duck and snipe used to come freely. The new cattle had taken to the paddock like old hands. Satisfied with their inspection, Norah and Jim led the way back to the river, where presently they came to an ideal place to camp; a bend thickly shaded, with the river bank shelving down to a sandy beach, where it was easy to get good water.

Wally volunteered to boil the billy, which he accomplished after much vigorous fanning with his hat at the fire. The job took some little time, and if the tea was eventually brewed with water that had not quite reached boiling point, that was a matter between Wally and his conscience—certainly the other members of the party were far too thirsty to be critical! Lunch was lazily discussed close to the water, after which they lay about on the bank and talked of many things. Nobody was inclined to move, for the heat, even at the river, was very great; a still, thunderous day, on which no shade could keep out the moist heat, that seemed, as Wally put it, "to get into your very bones and make them lazy."

At length Jim rolled over.

"Well, I'm off for a bathe," he said. "Coming, Cecil?"

"Oh, yes," Cecil answered, a little doubtfully; while Wally jumped up as a matter of course.

"Ugh!" groaned Norah. "Pigs! Why was I born a girl?"

"So's we could lay ourselves at your feet!" said Wally solemnly, suiting the action to the word, and placing his forehead forcefully in the dust before her.

"M'f!" Norah wrinkled her nose. "It's very nice of you, but I don't

54

quite see what use it would be. Anyhow, I'd far rather go bathing." She huddled on the ground, and looked tragic. "Go—leave me!"

"Sorry, old girl," grinned Jim. "We won't be long."

"Be as long as you like," said the victim of circumstances, cheerfully. "I'm going to sleep."

The three boys disappeared along the bank, finding, apparently, some difficulty in discovering a suitable bathing place, for it was some time before shouts and laughter from a good way off told Norah that they were in the water. She sighed, looking ruefully at the river flowing beneath her, and half decided to go in herself; but her father did not care for her bathing in the open alone, and she gave up the idea and shut her eyes so that she would not see temptation rippling down below. Presently she fell asleep.

She did not know how long it was before she woke. Then she jumped up with a start, thinking, for a moment, that it was dark. The sun had disappeared behind a huge bank of deep-purple cloud that had crept up, blotting out everything. It was breathlessly hot and quite still—not a leaf stirred on a tree, and the birds were quiet.

"Whew!" said Norah. "We're going to have a storm—and a big one!"

She listened. From far up faint calls and laughter still met her ears. It was evident that the boys were finding the water very much to their taste.

"Duffers!" Norah ejaculated. "We'll have the loveliest soaking—and Dad'll be anxious."

She coo-ee'd several times, but no response came. Finally she rose, with a little wrinkle in her brow.

"I guess I'd better saddle up," she said.

The horses were tied up in a clump of trees not far off, the saddles out of reach of their restless feet. Norah saddled Bobs first, and then the two stock horses—which was easy. To get Monarch ready, however, was not such a simple matter: the youngster was uneasy and sweating, and would not keep still for a moment; to get the saddle on and adjust breastplate and rings was a fairly stiff task with a sixteen-hands horse and a groom of fourteen years, hampered by a divided riding skirt. At length the last buckle went home, and Norah gave a relieved sigh.

"Bother you, Monarch!" she said. "You've taken me an awful time. Come on, Bobs."

Leaving the other horses tied up, she mounted and cantered down the bank, calling again and again. An answer came sooner than she had expected, and the three boys, somewhat hastily arrayed, came running through the trees.

"Jimmy, have you seen the weather?" asked his sister, indicating the blackened sky.

"Only a few minutes ago," Jim said, visibly annoyed with himself. "We were diving in a hole with the trees meeting overhead, and the scrub thick all around us—hadn't an idea it was working up for this. Why didn't you call us, you old duffer?"

"I did—but I couldn't make you hear," said Norah, somewhat injured. "Hurry—I've saddled up."

"You have? You didn't saddle Monarch?" asked Jim quickly.

"Yes, he's all ready, and the valises are on. We're in for a ducking, anyway, don't you think, Jim?"

"I think you hadn't any business to saddle Monarch," Jim said, soberly. "I wish you wouldn't do those things, Norah."

"Oh, it was all right." She smiled down at him. "He was only a bit fidgety; I believe he's frightened of the weather, Jim." She looked across at Cecil, seeing that young gentleman, wonderful to relate, with his stock folded awry, and his hair in wild confusion. "Do you mind thunderstorms, Cecil?"

"I—don't care for them much," Cecil panted. Running evidently did not agree with him, and he was finding his tweed riding suit very unfitted for the heat of the day. Jim, jogging easily, clad in white silk shirt, cord breeches and leggings, looked at him pityingly.

"Carry your coat, Cecil?" he sang out.

"No, thank you. I'd rather wear it," said Cecil, who disapproved of being coatless at any time, and had looked with marked disfavour at Jim and Wally as they set off in the morning.

"Stupid donkey!" Jim muttered, under his breath. "Ah, there are the horses!"

He made for Betty at once, and tossed the breathless Cecil into her saddle, advising him to ride on quickly.

Wally was up in a twinkling; but to mount Monarch was no such easy matter, for the black horse was dancing with restlessness, and a low growl of thunder far to the west evidently terrified him. Finally, with a quick movement, Jim was in the saddle, whereat Monarch promptly reared. He came down, and tried to get his head between his legs, but the boy was too quick for him, and presently steadied him sufficiently to move away in the wake of the others.

"Go on!" Jim shouted. "Don't lose a minute!"

They went down the river bank at a hand gallop, chafing now and then at the necessity of striking away from the track to find gates or slip-rails, as one paddock followed another. At first Monarch gave Jim all he knew to hold him, and at the gates Wally and Norah had to do all the work, for the black thoroughbred was too impatient to stand an instant, and threatened to buck a score of times. Jim

56

watched the sky anxiously, very disgusted with himself. He knew they had no chance of getting home dry, but at least they must be out of the timber before the storm broke. It was coming very near now—the thunder was more frequent, and jagged lightning tore rents in the inky curtain that covered the sky. He took Monarch by the head, and sent him tearing along the track, passing the boys—Wally riding hard on Nan, and Cecil sitting back on Betty with a pale face. Before him Bobs was galloping freely, Norah riding with her hands well down, and on her face a smile that was like a child's laugh of sheer happiness. Norah loved thunderstorms; they seemed to call to something in her nature that never failed to respond. She glanced up at Jim merrily as he passed her.

"Grand, isn't it?" she said. Then her face changed. "He isn't getting away with you, Jim?"

"Not he!" said her brother, grinning. "But we've got to get out of this jolly soon—hurry your old crock, Norah!" Norah's indignant heel smote Bobs, and they raced neck and neck for a moment.

They swung out of the trees just in time, the plain clear for home before them. Almost simultaneously, the storm broke. There was a mad flash of lightning across the gloom, and then a rattling peal of thunder that rang round the sky and finished with a tremendous crack overhead. The black horse stopped suddenly, wild with terror. Then his head went down, and he bucked.

Norah and Wally pulled up, regardless of the rain beginning to fall in torrents. Monarch was swaying to and fro in mad paroxysms, trying to get his head between his knees, his back humped in an arch, all his being centred in the effort to get rid of the weight on his back, and the iron in his mouth, and the control that kept him near that terrible convulsion of nature going on overhead. Jim was motionless, each hand like iron on the rein—yet with gentleness, for he knew the great black brute was only a baby after all, and a badly frightened baby at that. Cecil, coming by on Betty, his face white, looked aghast at the struggle between horse and rider, and fled on homewards. The thunder pealed, and the lightning lit the sky in forked darts.

Possibly the rain steadied Monarch, or sense came back to him through Jim's voice. He stopped suddenly, planting all four feet wide apart on the ground. Jim patted his neck, and spoke to him, and the tension went out of the big horse. He stood trembling a little.

"Slip along," nodded Jim to Norah.

Bobs and Nan went off together. Behind them, Monarch broke into a canter, obedient once more.

Five minutes later they were at the stables, Billy out in the wet to take the horses. The storm was raging still, but there were coolness and refreshment in the air. Billy grinned at the three soaked riders as they slipped to the ground, and then at Brown Betty, trotting down the hill in the rain. There was no sign of Cecil, who had fled indoors.

"Him plenty 'fraid," said the black retainer, his grin widening. "Him run like emu!" His eagle gaze dwelt on Monarch, who was still trembling and excited.

"Been buck?" he asked, his eyes round.

"Plenty!" Jim laughed. "All right, Billy, I'll let him go myself."

CHAPTER IX

THE BILLABONG DANCE

The slope beyond is green and still,
And in my dreams I dream,
The hill is like an Irish hill
Beside an Irish stream.

Kendall.

"Don't dress to-night, if you don't mind, Cecil," said Jim, putting his head into his cousin's room.

"Not dress?" Evening clothes were part of Cecil's training, and he kept to them rigidly, putting on each night for dinner what Murty O'Toole, having seen in wonder, referred to as "a quare little cobbed-shwaller-tail jacket." He regarded with fine scorn the cheerful carelessness of the boys where clothes were concerned. To Jim and Wally who were generally immensely occupied until dinner-time, and more often than not had further plans for the time following, putting on regulation evening dress seemed a proceeding little short of lunatic; but since Cecil "liked that sort of thing," they let him alone. To-night, however, was different, and when Cecil repeated his query half impatiently, Jim nodded.

"No. Didn't we tell you? It's the dance in the loft."

"Oh—don't you people ever dress for dances then?"

"Not for these dances," Jim answered. "It's the men's spree—all the hands and their friends; and you can be jolly well certain they won't run to dress clothes. So we make a point of not putting 'em on. Father did one year, and felt very sorry he had."

"I don't know that I'm keen on going, anyway," said Cecil.

"Oh, I think you'd better. Dad likes us to go, and it's really rather fun," Jim responded, patiently. "Norah's quite excited about it."

"Norah's young and enthusiastic," said Cecil.

"Oh, well, you're hardly hoary-headed yourself yet!" Jim grinned. "Might as well be cheerful while you're alive, Cecil, 'cause you'll be a long time dead!" He withdrew his head, shut the door with an unconcerned bang, and his whistle died away up the corridor.

"Hang it!" said Cecil, disgustedly, looking at his forbidden garments. "Who wants to go to a beastly servants' ball, anyhow?" He donned a dark suit reluctantly, a little consoled in that its very

59

recent cut would certainly be an eye-opener to Billabong, and went down to dinner, meeting on the way Norah, in a muslin frock, with her hair flying and her eyes sparkling.

"Oh! I'm so glad you haven't dressed up!" said she. "It's such fun, Cecil!—we've been helping to decorate the loft, and really you'd hardly know it was a loft, it looks so decent. And it's so funny to see the men; they pretend they don't care a bit, but I do believe they're quite excited. Murty came in with a trememdous lot of ferns, and he's been nailing them all on the wall in streaks, and he and Mick Shanahan nearly had a fight 'cause Mick leaned against one of them and the erection came down, and the nail tore Mick's coat. Still, it was Murty who seemed most aggrieved! And the musicians have come out from Cunjee, and they've been practising—they can play, too!" She paused for lack of breath.

"What sort of music does Cunjee supply?"

"Violin and flute and a funny little piano," said Norah. "They had quite an exciting time getting the piano up into the loft with the block and pulley. But the music sounds very well up there. The only trouble is old Andy Ferguson, the fencer—he's always been accustomed to fiddle for them, and he's very crushed because we've got out these men. Dad says he'd never have got them if he'd dreamed how disappointed old Andy would be."

Cecil had seen Andy, who struck him as a peculiarly uninteresting old man. That such consideration should be shown to his wishes and feelings was a thing beyond him, and he merely stared.

"However, he's going to play the supper dances and some others," said Norah, not noticing his silence, "so he's a bit consoled." They entered the drawing-room at the moment, finding Jim and Wally in armchairs, tweed clad and unusually tidy, and chafing miserably against the tyranny of white shirts after days of soft variety. "And a big buggy load of girls has come out from Cunjee already; and Brownie says there's a tremendous demand for hot water for shaving from the men's quarters, and Dave Boone came in for some mutton fat for his hair, but she wouldn't give it to him. Now she's half sorry she didn't, 'cause she believes he'll use the black fat they keep in the harness room; he's so dark no one would be able to tell—from the look! Who are you going to dance with, Cecil?"

"You, if I may," drawled Cecil.

"Why, of course, if you want to," Norah said, laughing. "But we always dance with every one on these occasions. It's one of the sights of one's life to see Wally leading Brownie out!"

Cecil gasped.

"And am I expected to dance with Mrs. Brown?"

"Very possibly she won't have a dance to spare you," said Wally serenely. "Brownie's no end popular, you see. Thank goodness. I've booked mine with her already!"

Cecil's stare spoke volumes.

"And who are your partners, Norah?"

"Any one who asks me," said that maiden promptly.

"And your father allows it?"

"Certainly he does," said Jim. "Don't get tragic, Cecil. The men on the place are an awfully decent lot, and most of them have been here ever so long—besides, it's their one night in the year, and they never overstep their limits. Dad always plans this spree himself specially. Of course, if you don't like—"

Jim stopped short, and bit his tongue. It had suddenly occurred to him that he was host—and he had nearly said something rude. So he whistled vaguely, and asked Wally if he were going to dance with Lee Wing, who was the Chinese gardener.

"Wish I could get the chance," said Wally, his eyes twinkling. "Think of piloting fat old Lee Wing through a polka—he'd get so beautifully puffed, and his pigtail would wave in the breeze, and he'd be such an armful!"

"Do you mean to say that Chow comes, too?" queried Cecil.

"No; he's shy," Wally answered. "We've tried to get him, but in vain; he prefers to go to bed and dream of China. And Billy hangs about like a black ghost, but he won't come in. So we lose a lot of international enjoyment; but, even so, what's left is pretty good, itsn't it, Norah?"

"I love it," said Norah.

"And you don't get any of your own friends to come? It seems to me the queerest arrangement," said Cecil.

"It's the men's dance, don't you see? There wouldn't be much fun for them if the place were filled up with our friends."

"Well, I should think a few of your own sort would be better. Aren't there any girls or boys within reach that you know? I suppose you've a juvenile sweetheart or two in the district?"

Norah looked at him blankly. Wally gave an expressive wriggle in his chair, and Jim sat up suddenly, with a flush on his brown face.

"We never talk that sort of rot here," he said angrily. "Norah's not a town girl, and her head isn't full of idiotic, silly bosh. I'll thank you—"

Mr. Linton came in at the moment, and the point on which Jim intended to express his gratitude remained unuttered. Cecil had reddened wrathfully, and the general atmosphere was electric. Mr.

Linton took, apparently, no notice. He pulled Norah's hair gently as he passed her.

"You're all remarkably spruce," he commented. "Can any one tell me why almost every maid I have met in my house this day turns and flees as though I were the plague? Sarah is the only one who doesn't shun me, and her mind appears to be taken up with affairs of State, for I asked her twice if she had seen my tobacco pouch, and she brought me in response a jug of shaving water, for which I have had no use for some time!" He laughed, stroking his iron-grey beard. "Can you explain the mystery, Norah?"

"It's easy," said his daughter. "Sarah's hair has a natural friz, so she's the only girl in the house without curling pins concealed—more or less—in her front hair. Brownie gave permission for the pins to-day; I guess she thinks it would give Sarah an unfair start if she didn't!"

"But the shaving water?"

"Ah, well, I expect Fred Anderson wanted that. She's engaged to him, you know," said Norah, simply.

"Well, I hardly see why she should give me his shaving water, either from Anderson's point of view or mine; but I suppose it's all right," said Mr. Linton. "The whole place is upset. I really wanted some work done, but the men who should have been sinking a well were tacking up ferns, and those whose mission in life is—or ought to be—hoeing out ragwort were putting French chalk on the floor of my loft! Judging from my brief inspection, it seemed to me that the latter occupation was far more strenuous than the ragwort job; but they seemed much happier than usual, and were working overtime without a struggle!"

"To hear you talk so patiently," quoth Norah, "no one would imagine that you'd bought the French chalk yourself!" She perched on the arm of his chair, and looked at him severely, while the boys laughed.

"The men are like a lot of kids to-day," Jim said. "Did you hear about old Lee Wing, Dad? He was standing under the block and pulley after they'd hoisted up the piano, and I expect the sight of the hook on the end of the dangling rope was too much for the men, for they slipped it through Wing's leather belt and hauled him up too! You should have seen him, with his pigtail dangling, kicking at the end of the rope like the spider in 'Little Miss Muffet!' They landed him in the loft, and Fred Anderson insisted on waltzing with him, while one of the musicians hammered out The Merry Widow on the piano. Poor old Wing was very wild at first, but they got him laughing finally."

"Why that long-suffering Chinaman stays here is always a

mystery to me," said his father, laughing. "He's the butt of the whole place; but he fattens on it."

"There's the dinner gong!" said Norah, jumping up. "Come on, gentlemen, we've to hurry to-night, so that the girls can get free early."

The loft over the stables, which had been built with a view to such occasions, was quite transformed when the house party entered it a couple of hours later. The electric light—Billabong had its own plant for lighting—had been extended to the loft, and gleamed down on a perfect bower of green—bracken and coral ferns, the tender foliage of young sapling tops, Christmas bush, clematis and tall reeds from the lagoon—the latter gathered by Jim and Wally during their morning bathe. Rough steps had been improvised to lead from outside up to the main door of the loft, over which still dangled from the block and pulley the rope that had suspended the irate Lee Wing earlier in the day. It was also possible to enter by the usual method—a trapdoor in the floor over a ladder leading from the floor below; but this was considered by the men scarcely suitable for their partners. All traces of its usual contents had, of course, been removed from the big room, and the floor gleamed in the light, mute evidence of the ardour with which Mr. Linton's French chalk had been applied. At one end, near the railing guarding the trapdoor, the Cunjee musicians were stationed, and close to them a queer old figure hovered—old Andy Ferguson, gnarled and knotted and withered; Irish, for all his Scotch name, and with his old blue eyes full of Irish fire at the thought of "a spree." He held his old fiddle tenderly as he might hold a child; it, too, was the worse for wear, and showed in more than one place traces of repair; but when Andy wielded the bow its tones were just as mellow to him as the finest instrument on earth. He kept a jealous eye on the Cunjee men; they might oust him for most of the night, but at least his was to be the old privilege of opening the ball. "The Boss" had said so.

The homestead men had lined up near the door to receive their guests—to-night they were hosts to Mr. Linton and his children, as to every one else. They were a fine lot of fellows—Murty O'Toole, and Mick Shanahan, the horse breaker, and Willis and Blake and Burton—all long and lean and hard, with deep-set, keen eyes and brown, thin faces; Evans, who was supposed to be over-seer, and important enough to arrive late; younger fellows, like Fred Anderson and David Boone (the latter's hair suspiciously smooth and shiny); Hogg, the dour old man who ruled the flower garden and every one but Norah; and a sprinkling of odd rouseabouts and boys, very sleek and well brushed, in garments of varying make, low collars, and the tie the bushman loves "for best"—pale blue satin, with what Wally termed "jiggly patterns" on it. Of the same type were the guests—men from other stations, cocky farmers and a very small sprinkling of township men.

The ladies kept rigidly on arrival to the other side of the loft. There was Mrs. Brown, resplendent in a puce silk dress that Norah remembered from her earliest childhood, with a lace cap of monumental structure topped by a coquettish bow of pale pink ribbon. Her kind old face beamed on every one. Close to her, very meek under her sheltering wing, were Sarah and Mary, the housemaids—very gay in papery silks, pink and green , with much adornment of wide yellow lace. Norah had helped to dress them both, and she smiled delightedly at them as she came in. There was Mrs. Willis, who ruled over the men's hut, and was reckoned, as a cook, only inferior to Mrs. Brown; and Joe Burton's pretty wife, in a simple white muslin—with no doubt in big Joe's heart, as he looked at her, as to who was the belle of the ball. Then, girls and women from that vague region the bush calls "about," in mixed attire—from flannel blouses and serge skirts, to a lady who hurt the eye it looked at, and made the lights seem pale, in her gorgeous gown of mustard-coloured velveteen, trimmed with knots of cherry-coloured ribbon. They came early, with every intention of staying late, and cheerfully certain of a good time. The Billabong ball was an event for which an invitation was much coveted.

Norah kept close to her father's wing, as they entered, shaking hands gravely with the men by the door, and with Mrs. Brown—which latter proceeding she privately considered a joke. The boys followed; Jim quiet and pleasant; Wally favouring Murty O'Toole with a solemn wink, and Cecil plainly bored by the little ceremony. He let his fingers lie in each man's hand languidly—and would probably have been injured had he seen Murty wipe his hand carefully on the side of his trousers after he had passed on. The men had no love for the city boy.

"S'lect y'r partners!" It was Dave Boone, most noted "M.C."—in demand at every ball in the district. Dave knew what he was about, and saw that other people understood the fact; no shirking when he was in command, no infringement of rules, no slip-shod dancing. Even as he kept his eagle eye on the throng, he "selected" one of the prettiest girls himself, and bore her to the head of the room. There was never any doubt of Dave's generalship.

Cecil turned to Norah.

"May I have this?"

"Sorry," Norah said, "I always dance with Jim first."

"P'f!" said Cecil, lightly. "That old brother-and-sister idea is exploded."

64

"Not with Jimmy and me," Norah answered. "Why don't you ask Mary? She can dance awfully well."

"No, thank you," said Cecil, with elevated nose. "I'll watch."

Wally had approached Mrs. Brown, and bowed low.

"Ours, I think?"

"Now, Master Wally, me dancin' days are over," said Brownie. "Go an' get one of the girls, now, dearie, do!"

"A girl!—when I can get you?" Wally ejaculated. "Not much I" He tucked her hand into his arm and led her off in triumph.

"Promen-ayde y'r partners!"

Dave turned and nodded to Andy Ferguson, who, with fiddle tucked lovingly under his chin, was waiting for his signal. He broke into a march—the time a little shaky, the tune a little old, for the hand that held the bow was old and shaky, too; but still a march, with a swing to it that set the feet going at once. The dancers promenaded round the room in a long procession, led proudly by Wally and Mrs. Brown. At one end a few men, disappointed in obtaining partners, clustered by the wall; near them stood Mr. Linton, watching in his grave, pleasant way that was so like Jim's, with Cecil at his elbow, his delicate face dull and expressionless. Round and round marched the couples.

"Circular waltz, please!"

The music swung into a waltz without a break, and simultaneously the march broke into the dance as every man seized his partner by the waist and began to revolve solemnly and silently. Cecil gaped.

"What on earth is a circular waltz?"

"Blest if I know for certain," replied his uncle, laughing. "Much like any other waltz—but you mustn't use the middle of the floor. Watch young Boone."

Dave was keeping an eagle eye on the dancers. For the most part they were content to gyrate near the wall; but should any more daring couple approach the unoccupied space in the middle of the room, they were instantly detected and commanded to return. As Cecil looked, Wally, who was dancing with a broad grin of sheer happiness on his face, swung his ponderous partner right across the centre—and was greeted by the vigilant M.C. with the stern injunction—"Keep circle!" Quite oblivious that this outbreak had anything to do with him, while Mrs. Brown, feeling the most miserable of sinners, was far too breathless to explain, Wally presently repeated his offence, whereupon Boone pulled him up gravely, and pointed out his enormity to him. The culprit grinned the more widely, promised amendment, nodded vigorously, and danced off, Mrs. Brown remaining speechless throughout. Mr. Linton smothered a laugh in his beard.

Presently the music came to an end. Old Andy put his fiddle down and looked along the loft with a happy little smile. The dancers stopped, and Mr. Boone's voice rose sonorously.

"Seats, please!"

At this, each man rushed with his partner to the side of the loft previously tenanted by the ladies, and deposited her on the long forms ranged there. Then the men retreated hastily to the other side.

There was no conversation, nor had there been any through the dance. It seemed that the poetry of motion must suffice for enjoyment.

Norah and Jim, who had been dancing vigorously, pulled up near the others.

"Did you see me get hauled over the coals?" asked Wally gleefully. He had placed Mrs. Brown on a seat, and followed the example of his sex in retreating.

"Rather—we were in fits, behind you!" said Jim. "Was Dave cross?"

"Oh, quite mild; took my assurance that I didn't know I was sinning, and forgave me like a man and a brother. And why shouldn't a fellow cross that floor?"

"Goodness knows; but it's a rule. They dance very strictly, and in many ways more correctly than we do."

"There are two lovely couples," said Wally, gleefully. "They hold each other firmly round the neck, and they revolve on the space of a threepenny bit. It's beautiful. May I try that way with you, Norah?"

"No, you mayn't," laughed Norah; "at least, not here. They might think we were imitating them."

"Curious penetration on their parts!" rejoined Wally. "Well, can you tell me why lots of men hold one arm behind their backs?"

"In my young days that was quite ordinary," Mr. Linton put in. "I always danced that way—and I was remarkably run after," he added, modestly. Whereat Wally meekly assured him that he thought the practice a highly desirable one, and had serious thoughts of adopting it himself.

"I've been looking at the programme nailed up for the musicians," said Cecil. "There are some dances I never saw— Varsoviana, Circassian Circle, and Caledonians."

"In the Varsoviana," said Mr. Linton, retrospectively, "I used to shine."

"Well, they beat us," said his son. "We can't dance 'em; but we

66

look on. The first two are round dances, and the Caledonians is a square. I suppose they'd be all right, only they're not taught now."

"And there are no two-steps," said Cecil, in a tone of personal injury.

Jim laughed outright.

"It'd be so much simpler for you if you'd remember you're at what's commonly known as 'a bush hop'," he said. "You can't expect the last adornments of a city spree. Anyway, they get more honest fun out of this than most people do at a Melbourne or Sydney ball."

Cecil looked patient.

"May I have the next dance, Norah?"

"I'm sorry, truly, Cecil, but I've promised it to Murty."

"Oh!" said Cecil. "The next?"

"That's Mick Shanahan's," said Norah, laughing. "But you may have the one after that if you like."

"I must be thankful for small mercies, I suppose," said he, unthankfully.

"Won't you dance with any one else?"

'No, thanks, I don't care to." The tone was final.

"Well, I'm going to collar Sarah or die!" said Wally, manfully. "I'll probably die, anyway, 'cause Fred has his eye on her. Still, here goes!"

The musicians gave a preliminary blast, on which followed a shout from the M.C.

"Select y'r partners for the lancers!"

At the word there was a general stampede. Youths who had been timid before, grown bolder now, dashed towards the long row of girls. Where more than one arrived simultaneously, there was no argument; the man who failed to speak first shot off to find another damsel. In a moment every available fair one had been secured firmly, and the dancers awaited further commands.

Wally had not waited for permission from Mr. Boone. At the first sound of the music he had darted towards Sarah, arriving beside the lady with "the natural friz" a yard in front of Fred Anderson.

It was not etiquette to refuse to dance, and the fact that he was "the Boss's" guest, if only a boy, carried weight. Sarah rose, with a rueful glance at her disappointed swain. The two disconsolate faces moved Wally to compassion.

"I say—I'm awfully sorry," he said. "'Fraid I got ahead of you unfairly, Fred—perhaps you'll excuse me this time, Sarah? You don't mind? Well, you'll give me the next, won't you? Thanks, awfully." He relinquished her to the beaming Fred, and returned, partnerless, to Mr. Linton and Cecil.

Then it was a marvellous sight to behold young Dave Boone!

With Mrs. Brown on his arm, he "took the floor" at the head of the room, seeing that the dancers were correctly sorted out in sets; and thence proceeded to dance and instruct the room simultaneously, in a manner truly amazing. With what agility did he "set to partner" and "swing corner," with his eagle eye all the time scanning the sets to make sure no one mixed up the commands!—how ably bear his part in "First lady and second gent.," not even put out of step by the necessity of telling the further end of the room that it was going wrong!—how splendidly issue the edict to "chassee-crossee" and "gent. solo," finding time, even in the press of his double occupation, to propel his panting partner in the way she should go! His voice rang out over the room, indicating each figure as it came— there was no excuse for making any mistake in a square dance when Mr. Boone was in command. And all the while he danced with a wholehearted energy and a face of absolute gravity. No one, watching him, could have possibly imagined that this was a pastime.

"I've seen Boone looking infinitely more cheerful when fighting a bush fire!" said Mr. Linton.

"Talk about a conjurer!" was Cecil's astonished comment. "I never saw one man do so many things at once!"

The music ceased at last, and the "Seats, please!" marked the temporary termination of the labours of the M.C. Murty brought Norah back to her father, thanked her gravely, and made off.

"What happened to you, Wally?" queried Jim, restoring a blushing damsel in blue to her form and rejoining his relations. "Did Sarah turn you down?"

"I resigned gracefully in favour of Fred," Wally said. "He looked murderous, and Sarah looked woe-begone, so it seemed the best plan. But she's mine for the next—and ill befall the caitiff that disputes my claim!"

"No one'd dare!" said Jim, hastily. "I'm after Brownie, myself."

"Ah, Jim, be steady with her," said Norah. "It's a polka!"

"I'll be steady as old Time," Jim told her, smiling. True to his promise, when the music began he danced mildly and moderately, and Brownie emerged from the ordeal in far better order than might have been expected.

After that the evening flew. Dance after dance went by in rapid succession—for the guests were out to dance, and where no time is wasted in talking much may be done with a few hours. Cecil steadfastly declined any partner but Norah, and as that maiden had no mind to spare him more than two, his evening was dull, since his sense of humour was not equal to finding any fun in the entertainment. He was the object of considerable curiosity among the visitors, and was generally voted "stuck-up," and "too big for his

68

boots." As for Jim and Wally, they flung themselves cheerfully into the business of the night, and even succeeded in making most of their partners talk, albeit this was a daring proceeding, and not looked upon with favour by the M.C. They were too popular, however, to come in for any real criticism, and being regarded by the majority of the men as "just kids," were allowed to do very much as they liked.

Supper was a majestic meal, spread on long tables in a big tent. Mr. Linton led the way to it with Mrs. Brown, followed by Mick Shanahan, who conveyed Norah much in the way he danced with her—as if she were a piece of eggshell china, and apt to crack with careless handling. There was no "head of the table"; every one sat in the place that seemed good, and tongues flew as fast as the knives and forks. At the end Mr. Linton made a little speech.

"My friends," he said, "it's a great pleasure to Billabong to see you all here. I hope you'll keep it up till morning, and come again next year; you're always welcome. However, it is time my daughter went to bed." (Dissent, and cries of "Not her!") "Before she goes, though, I would like to see one more dance. I move that our old friend Andy Ferguson play the 'Royal Irish.'"

There was frantic applause, and supper adjourned hastily, while every one hurried back to the loft; in the midst old Andy, his quavering voice a little raised in excitement, his fiddle held firmly in one hand. "Too old to work," some called him, wondering why David Linton kept the old fencer, when younger men were always wanting work on Billabong; and now, as he faced the long room with his faded blue eyes a little misty, Andy looked an old man indeed. But the pride of work was in him, and his master knew it— knew how the gnarled hands ceased to tremble when they grasped the adze and mattock, just as there was now no quiver in them as he raised the brown fiddle and cuddled it under his chin. Age would seize on Andy only when he could work and play no more. The light came back into his eyes as he saw the boys and girls waiting for the music—his music.

He drew the bow lovingly across the strings, and swung into the Irish dance the old, common tune with the little gay lilt to it that grips the heart and makes the feet beat time, and has the power to wake old memories across the years. There were no memories to wake in the happy young hearts in the loft at Billabong that night. But Andy looked over the heads of the dancers at his master, meeting his eyes as man to man, and each knew that the mind of the other had gone back to days long dead.

The long floor echoed under the dancers' feet—up and down, swing in the centre, hands across; the pace was always a good one

69

when Andy Ferguson played the "Royal Irish." One foot tapped out the time, and his grey head nodded in sympathy with it. They called to him now and again, "Bravo, Andy! Good man, Andy! Keep it going!" and he smiled at the friendly voices, watching them with the keenness of the Irishman for a light foot in a dance.

Just before him, Mrs. Brown, dancing with Jim, was footing it in and out of the figures like a girl, holding her skirts quaintly on either side as she advanced and retired, and came back to sweep a curtsey that shamed the quick bow of the younger generation, while the tall lad she had nursed waited for her with a grave gentleness that sat prettily on his broad shoulders. Near, too, the old man's eyes dwelt lovingly on Norah, whose eyes were dancing in time with her feet as Wally pranced her madly up and down, his own brown face glowing.... just for a moment Andy saw "the little mistress" who had known her baby for so brief a time fourteen years before; her face looked at him through her child's grey eyes. He looked across at his master again, a little wistfully.

The tune broke into "St. Patrick's Day," and Murty O'Toole gave a sudden involuntary shout, his hand above his head, Mick Shanahan echoed it; the Irish music was in their blood, and the old man with the brown fiddle had power to make them boys again. He, too, had gone back on the lilt of the tune; back to his own green country, where the man with the fiddle has his kingdom always, and the lads and lasses are his subjects. There was a girl with blue Irish eyes, coming to meet him on St. Patrick's morning... the tune wavered ever so little then, as his heart cried out to her. Then the dream passed, and he knew that he was a boy no more, but old Andy Ferguson, playing for the boys and girls in the loft at Billabong. The bow moved faster and faster yet—only a good pair could see him right through the "Royal Irish." They were panting when he dropped his hand at last and stood looking at them a little vaguely. Then they crowded round him, thanking him. Even the Cunjee musicians were saying that he could beat them all, and Miss Norah had put her hand into his, and was patting his arm. There was a mist before him—he could not see them all, though he knew his triumph.

"'Tis wid the kindness of all of y'," he murmured. "So good to me y' all are!"

David Linton's hand was on his shoulder.

"Come on, old friend," he said, gently; "we're getting old and we're tired, you and I." He led him away, Norah still holding his hand. Behind them the music broke out again, cheerily, and the flying feet made the loft echo until the dawn.

CHAPTER X

CHRISTMAS

O mellow air! O sunny light!
O Hope and Youth that pass away,
Print thou in letters of delight
Upon each heart one glorious day!

G. Essex Evans.

Norah woke up early.

Close outside her open windows a magpie in the magnolia tree was carolling as though he knew it was a special morning, and that he had a special message to deliver. The linen blinds were rolled tight up, and she could see him near one of the great creamy blossoms, each big enough for his bath; his black and white coat very spruce and smart, his head thrown back in utter enjoyment of his own song. Norah smiled at him sleepily from her pillow.

"Nice old chap!" she said; and then she remembered.

"Oh!–Christmas." She gave a little happy laugh, for to-day was going to be such a very good day. There was something that had taxed all her patience; it was so hard to keep the secret until Christmas. Norah was not a very patient person by nature, and she was glad that the need for it was almost over.

She turned over lazily, and then burst out laughing as something caught her eye at the foot of the bed–a huge football stocking, assuming extraordinary shapes by reason of strange packages within it, while from the top a monkey on a stick grinned at her. Norah jumped up and brought the stocking back to bed for examination, weak with laughter when she had finished. A big box of chocolates; a scarlet Christmas cracker; a very flowery mug of thickest china, with "Love the Giver" on it, and tied to the handle a label with "For a Good Little Girl" in the best handwriting of Wally, who evidently considered it not sufficiently adorned by nature; a live frog in a glass-covered box; a huge bundle, which took her many minutes to unwrap, and was finally found to contain a tiny pig of Connemara marble; a Christmas pudding the size of a golf ball; and finally, in the very toe, a minute bottle labelled "Castor Oil; Seasonable at Any Time."

"Oh, you nice donkeys!" said the recipient of these varied gifts, lying back and investigating the chocolates. A sound at the window made her look up, and Jim's laughing face peeped round the curtain.

"Like 'em?"

"They're lovely," said Norah, fervently. "Come in, Jimmy, you old duffer. Merry Christmas!"

Jim came in, immensely tall and lean in his pyjamas, and sat down on the bed.

"Merry Christmas, old kid!" he said, and kissed her. "Taken your oil?"

"Pudding first—and chocolates," said Norah, solemnly, indicating the box. "Take lots, Jim, they're beauties. How did you get that thing into my room?"

"Waited until I could hear your cheerful snores, and then sneaked in by the window," said her brother, dodging a chocolate. "My best stocking; I think I was jolly good to lend it to you—you'll kindly notice that the frog's box tore a hole in it, and take steps accordingly! It's a ripping morning—but it's going to be hot. Do you know what time it is?"

"I don't," said Norah.

"Five o'clock," said Jim; "isn't it ridiculous!—and you wide awake and playing with pigs and frogs! I'm off to bed again for a bit—besides, young Wally's bursting to know how you liked your sock. Go to sleep again, old chap."

"I'll try," said Norah, obediently, snuggling down, "Take some chocolates to Wally—and the castor oil!"

At the moment Norah was quite convinced that sleep was the last thing possible for her, and merely laid down to please Jim, just as she would cheerfully have endeavoured to jump over the moon had he expressed any wish in that direction. Thus she was considerably surprised on waking up two hours later to hear the dressing gong pealing through the house. Further off came the cheerful voices of Jim and Wally on their way to the lagoon. Cecil preferred the bath in the house, saying that he considered it cleaner, which remark had incensed Norah at the time. But they were learning not to worry about Cecil's remarks, but to regard him with a kind of mild toleration, as one who "could not help it."

Norah tore in haste to the bath, and returning made a speedy toilet; breakfast was to be half an hour later than usual, but still there was much to do. Her gifts to the men's quarters had gone over the night before, in charge of Mrs. Willis; still there were parcels for the girls in the house, together with the envelopes containing cheques for them, which Mr. Linton always gave into Norah's care, and of course Brownie's gifts, besides the nearer and dearer excitement of the breakfast table. To the latter she attended first, scattering parcels at each plate before any one else arrived on the scene. Then she raced off, just escaping in the hall Jim, who immediately put his hands behind him and began to whistle with great carelessness. Jim was a man of tact.

Mrs. Brown, narrowly watching some fried potatoes, heard flying footsteps, and turned to receive Norah bodily.

"Merry Christmas, Brownie, dear!" said the breathless one. She hung over the stout shoulders a tiny shawl of softest white wool.

"It's only a shawl-let," Norah explained, "just for when you feel the summer evenings get cool, you know."

"An' you made it, my precious!"

"Why, of course," said Norah, lifting her brows; "do you think I'd buy it, when you taught me to knit? Ah, Brownie, I'm having such a good time!"

"Look at me!" said Mrs. Brown, sitting down in rapture, and forgetting her frying pan entirely. "This lovely shawl–an' your Pa's cheque–and here's even Master Wally brung me down a cap, an' Master Jim–don't 'e always think!–a frame with the photer 'e took of you an' your Pa, an' it's sollud silver, no less, if you'll believe me, an' then it's none too good for the photer, but the dear lamb knew wot I'd like more than anything on earth! Of all the loving–kindest children–" At this point Brownie's feelings overcame her, and she sniffed and, inhaling a threat of burnt potato, rushed to conceal her emotions over the stove.

Sarah and Mary felt delighted with the pretty collars Mrs. Stephenson had chosen for Norah in Melbourne; the daughter of the house encountered Jim returning from the back regions, with a broad smile on his brown face. Jim's invariable gift to Lee Wing was a felt hat, and as the Celestial still wore the one first given, eight Christmases before, it was popularly supposed that the intermediate half-dozen went to support his starving relatives in China! Lee Wing had never mentioned the existence of any starving relatives, but Wally said it was well known that all Chinese gardeners had them– speaking, as Norah remarked, as though it was a new complaint, like measles or mumps!

"You didn't give Wing another hat, Jim?" queried his sister.

"I did, though," returned Jim, firmly. "Asked him at midwinter what he'd have, and he grinned and said, 'Allee same hat!' So he got it–a lovely green one!"

"Jim!–not green! For Lee Wing!"

"There weren't any other colours left," said Jim; "next year it would have had to be pale blue! He took it with a heavenly smile, and looked at it all over inside and out; then he looked down at his feet, and I beheld his toe sticking out of his boot. He didn't say 'Thank you' at all. What he did say was 'Nex'-Clis'mas-socks,' all in one word, and you couldn't have widened his smile without shifting his ears further back!"

"Merry Christmas, Norah, asthore!" said a cheerful voice, and Norah turned to greet Wally. So Wally had to hear the story of Lee Wing all over again, and they were laughing over it when Mr. Linton came out on the verandah, pausing in the doorway a moment to look at the slender figure in the blue frock, with white collar and tie, and the tall lads in white flannels beside her.

Three greetings flashed at him simultaneously as he came into view.

"Merry Christmas, every one!" he said, one hand on his small daughter's shoulder. "Going to be a hot Christmas, too, I believe. Where's Cecil?"

"Coming," said that gentleman, exchanging good wishes with a languid air. "Sorry to be late, but I couldn't open the bathroom door."

Wally started.

"Good gracious, was it you in there?" he asked anxiously. "I thought it was Norah—and we wanted her out of the way at the moment, so I barricaded the door! Then I saw her afterwards, so I reckoned she'd got out all right, and I never bothered to take down the barricade. I'm awfully sorry!"

Every one laughed but Cecil, who saw nothing humorous in having been obliged to climb through the bathroom window, and said so with point.

"I'm a fearful ass, truly," said Wally, with contrition. "Norah, you've no need to laugh like a hyena—you ought to have been there, if you weren't!"

"That's why I laugh," Norah explained kindly. "Never mind, it's Christmas—and there's breakfast!"

It was the gong, but not breakfast. Mrs. Brown knew better than to send in the porridge with the gong on Christmas morning. Instead, the table was heaped with parcels, a goodly pile by every plate.

"What an abominable litter!" said Mr. Linton, affecting displeasure. "Norah, kindly oblige me by getting those things out of your way. How are you going to eat breakfast?"

"You're as bad as I am, Daddy!"

"Dear me!" said her father. "I seem to be. Well, yours is decidedly the most untidy, so you had better begin."

They watched the eager face as Norah turned to her bundles. Books from Cecil and his mother; warm slippers made by Brownie;

a halter exquisitely plaited from finest strips of hide by Murty O'Toole, the sight of which brought the whole gathering to Norah's side; from Wally a quaint little bronze inkstand, and from Jim the daintiest horse rug that Melbourne could produce, made to fit Bobs, with a big scarlet B in one corner, and Norah's monogram in the other. "Not that he needs it just now," Jim explained, as Norah hugged him–"but a store's no sore, as Brownie'd say!" Last, a tiny velvet case, which concealed a brooch–a thin bar of gold with one beautiful pearl. Norah did not need the slip of paper under it to know it came from Dad.

Then things became merry, and even Cecil warmed at the gifts on his plate, while the boys were exclaiming in delight over Norah's knitting, and Wally was shaking hands with Mr. Linton and looking half-shamefacedly at the plain gold sleeve links from him and the silver watch chain from Jim; and Mr. Linton's face was alight with pleasure at the waistcoat Norah had made for him, and the little oak bookshelf for his bedside that was the work of Jim's spare hours. Finally all the bundles were unwrapped, and there was a lull, though Norah's eyes were still dancing, and she exchanged glances with her father.

Jim spoke.

"There's a string under my plate," said he, faintly puzzled. "At least, there's one end."

"Strings always have two ends," said Wally, wisely. "Where's the other?"

"I'm blessed if I know," said Jim. "It goes down to the floor."

Wally came round, investigating.

"Seems to me it goes out of the window," he said. "Guess you'd better follow it, Jimmy."

Jim looked round, a little doubtful. Then he saw Norah's face, and knew that there was something he did not understand. He laughed a little.

"Some one pulling my leg?" he asked, good-humouredly. "Oh, well, I'll chase it."

The string went somewhere–that was evident. Outside it was at the height of Jim's hand, and ran along the wall, so that it was easy to follow. They trooped after him as he went along, Norah completely unable to walk steadily, but progressing principally on one foot, while David Linton's eyes were twinkling. The chase was not a long one; the string suddenly cut across to the door in the high fence dividing the front and back gardens, and there disappeared.

"What next?" said Jim.

"If it was me," said Wally, with a fine disregard of grammar, "I should open the door."

"Good for you, Wally," grinned Jim. "Here goes!" He flung the door open, and then stood as if rooted to the spot.

The string went on. It ended, however, just through the door, where its end was spliced to a halter, held by black Billy, whose smile disclosed every tooth in his head. Fidgeting in the halter was a big bay horse, showing all Monarch's quality, and all his good looks; a show ring horse, picked by a keen judge, and built for speed as well as strength. He looked at Jim with a kind eye, set well in his beautiful head. There was no flaw in him; from his heels to his fine, straight forelock he was perfection.

Jim had no words. He did not need to be told anything—Norah's face had been enough; but he could not speak. He took refuge with the big bay, moving forward and putting out a hand, to which the horse responded instantly, rubbing his head against him in friendly fashion. Then, across the arched neck, Jim's eyes met his father's, and the colour flooded into his brown face.

"Well, old son—will he do?"

"Do!" said Jim, weakly. "Dad!—by Jove, I–I–" He stopped helplessly; then his hand went out and took his father's in a grip that made David Linton realize that this big son of his was nearly a man.

"Oh, Jimmy, I'm so glad—and isn't he lovely?"

"Why, he's perfect," Jim said, stepping back and running his eye over his Christmas box. "My word, Dad, he'll jump!"

"Yes, he'll jump all right," said David Linton. "Gallop, too, I should say."

"Plenty!" said Billy, with unexpected emphasis, whereat every one laughed.

"Billy and Norah have had this little joke plotted for some time," Mr. Linton said—"and the experiences they have undergone in keeping strings and steed out of your way this morning have, I believe, whitened the hair of both!"

Jim looked gratefully round.

"You're all bricks," he said. "Has he got a name, Dad?"

"'A tearin' foine wan,' Murty says," responded his father; "since it's Irish: Garryowen, unless you'd like to change it."

"Not me!" said Jim. "I like it." He looked round as the sound of the gong came across the garden. "I say, don't mind me," he said—"go into breakfast. I don't want any this morning." His eye went back to the bay.

"Rubbish!" said his father—"he'll be alive after breakfast! Come along," and reluctantly Jim saw Billy lead his horse away to the stable. He discovered, however, on reaching the breakfast room,

76

that he was remarkably hungry, and distinguished himself greatly with his knife and fork.

Afterwards it was necessary to try the bay's paces without delay, and they all watched Jim take him round the home paddock. Garryowen moved beautifully; and when Jim finally put him at the highest part of the old log fence, and brought him back again, he flew it with a foot to spare. The boy's face was aglow as he rode up.

"Well, he's perfect!" he said. "I never was on such a horse." He came close to his father. "Dad," he said in a low tone—"are you sure you wouldn't like him instead of Monarch? He's far more finished."

"Not for anything, thanks, old chap—I prefer my pupil," said his father, his look answering more than his words. "You see he never bucks with me, Jim!"

Jim laughed, dismounting. "Like to try him, Cecil?"

"Thanks," said Cecil, scrambling up and setting off down the paddock, while Jim watched him and writhed to think of possible damage to his horse's back and mouth. Billy, who was near, said reflectively, "Plenty bump!" and Murty O'Toole roundly rebuked Jim for "puttin' up an insult like that on a good horse!" They breathed more freely when Cecil came back, albeit the way in which he sawed at the bay's mouth was calculated to strike woe to the heart of any owner. Then Wally tried Garryowen, and finally Norah, having flown to the house for a riding skirt, had a ride also, and sailed over the log fence in a manner fully equal to Jim's. She came back charged with high compliment.

"He's nearly as good as Bobs, Jim!"

"Bobs!" said Jim, loftily. "We don't compare ponies with horses, my child!"

"Then he's not to be compared with Bobs!" Norah retorted sturdily, and, the laugh being on her side, retired quickly to dress for dinner.

Dinner was typical of Billabong, and an Australian Christmas—one with the thermometer striving to reach the hundred mark. Everything was cold, from the mammoth turkey, with which Mr. Linton wrestled, to the iced peaches that topped off what the boys declared "a corking feed." There was plum pudding, certainly, but it was cold, too. Wally found in his piece no fewer than four buttons; and, deeply aggrieved, went afterwards to remonstrate with Mrs. Brown, who was amazed, declaring she had put in but one, which to her certain knowledge had fallen to the unhappy lot of Sarah. Further inquiries revealed the fact that Jim had come to the table well supplied with buttons, with which he had contrived to enrich Wally's portion as it travelled past him—which led to a battle on the lawn, until both combatants, too well fed and weak with mirth to fight, collapsed, and slept peacefully under a pine tree.

Later on the horses were saddled, and every one rode out to the river, where Brownie and the maids had already been driven by Fred Anderson, and where they picnicked for tea. Afterwards they lay on the soft grass, with the water murmuring past them, and Mr. Linton told them stories—for Christmas was ever, and will ever be, the time for stories. Simple, straightforward tales, like the man himself: old Christmases overseas, and others in many parts of Australia—some that brought a sadder note into the speaker's voice, and made Norah draw herself along the grass until she came within touch of his hand. Words were never really needed between them— being mates.

So they stayed until the golden western sky had grown rose colour, and the rose glow faded into night, that brought with it a little cool breeze. Then the horses were saddled, and they rode home by the longest possible way, singing every imaginable chorus, from Good Old Jeff to the latest medley of pantomime ditties, and ending with a wild scurry across the paddock home. They all trooped into the house, waking its quietness to youth and laughter.

But David Linton called to Norah.

"Come on," he said, "we'll finish up with the real Christmas songs."

So they all gathered round the piano while Norah played, and joined in the old Christmas hymns and carols—none the less hearty in that they sang of frost and snow with all around them the yellowing plain, dried up by the scorching sun, and, beyond that, the unbroken line of the little trodden Bush. The young voices rang out cheerily, David Linton listening in his armchair, his hand over his eyes.

Norah was in bed when her father looked in, in passing, to say good-night. She put up her face to him sleepily.

"It's been a beautiful Christmas, Daddy dear!" she said.

CHAPTER XI

"LO, THE POOR INDIAN!"

I mind the time when first I came
A stranger to the land.

Henry Lawson.

The house was unusually quiet. It was New Year's Day, and every man on the place, and most of the maids, had gone off to a bush race meeting, ten miles away. Even Mrs. Brown had allowed herself to be persuaded to go and, arrayed in her best silk gown, had climbed laboriously into the high double buggy, driven by Dave Boone, and departed, waving to Norah a stout reticule that looked, Wally said, as though it contained sausages! Only Mary, the housemaid, remained. Mary was a prim soul, and did not care for race meetings. She had remarked that she would stay at home and "crocher"!

Mr. Linton and the boys had ridden away after lunch. A valuable bull had slipped down the side of a steep gully and injured himself, and bush surgery was required. David Linton was rather notable in this direction, and he had seen to it that Jim had had a thorough course of veterinary training in Melbourne. Together they made, the squatter remarked, a very respectable firm of practitioners! Cecil and Wally were ready to perform unskilled labour as required, and it was quite possible that their help might be needed, since no men were available. So the picnic planned for the afternoon had had to be abandoned, and Norah was left somewhat desolate, since she could not take part in the "relief expedition."

"Hard on you, old girl," Jim had said; "but it can't be helped."

"No, of course it can't," Norah replied. She was well trained in the emergencies of the country, and would probably have been perfectly cheerful had this particular one only been something that would not have excluded her. As it was, however, it was certainly disappointing, and she felt somewhat "at a loose end" as she watched the four ride off. There seemed nothing for her to do. It was beyond doubt that being a girl had its drawbacks.

Within, the silence of the house was depressing, and the rooms seemed much too large. Norah saw to one or two odd jobs, fed some chickens, talked for a while to Fudge, the parrot, who was a companionable bird, with a great flow of eloquence on occasions, wrote a couple of letters—always a laborious proceeding for the maid of the bush—and finally arrived at the decision that there was nothing to do. In the kitchen Mary sat and "crochered" placidly at a fearful and wonderful set of table mats. Norah watched her for a while, with a great scorn for the gentle art that could produce such monstrosities. Then she practised for half an hour, and at length, taking a book, sauntered off to read by the creek.

Meanwhile Mary worked on contentedly, unconscious of outer things, dreaming, perhaps, such dreams as may come to any one who makes crocheted table mats of green and yellow. Now and then she rose to replenish the fire, returning to her needle in the far-away corner of the great kitchen, where Mrs. Brown's cane armchair always stood. She glanced up in surprise after a while, when a shadow fell across the doorway. Then, for Mary was a girl with "nerves," she jumped up with a little scream.

An Indian hawker stood there—a big, black-bearded fellow, in dusty clothes that had once been white, and on his head a turban of faded pink. His heavy pack hung from his shoulder, but as the girl looked, he slipped it to the ground, and stood erect, with a grunt of relief. Then he grinned faintly at Mary, who had promptly put the table between them, and asked the hawker's universal question:

"Anything to-day, Meesis?"

The Hindu hawker is still a figure to be met frequently in the Bush—where he is, indeed, something of an institution. "Remote from towns he runs" a race that no poetical licence can stretch to complete the quotation by calling "godly." He carries a queer mixture of goods—a kind of condensed bazaar-stall from his native land, with silks and cottons, soaps, scents, boot laces and cheap jewellery, all packed into a marvellously small space; and so he tramps his way through Australia. No life can be lonelier. His stock of English is generally barely enough to enable him to complete his deals; the free and independent Australian regards him as "a nigger," and despises him accordingly; while the Hindu, in his turn, has in his inmost soul a scorn far deeper for his scorners—the pride of tradition and of caste. It is the caste that keeps him rigidly to himself, since, as a rule, he can touch no food that others have handled. He sits apart, over his own tiny fire, baking his unappetising little cakes; and in many cases even the shadow of a passer-by falling across his cookery is held to defile it beyond possibility of his eating it. As a rule he has but one idea in life—to make enough money to carry him back to end his days in comfort by the waters of the Ganges.

There are certain well recognized hawkers in many districts—men who have kept for a long time to a particular beat, and may be regarded as fairly regular, and likely to turn up at each place at their route three or four times a year. Such men have generally arrived at the dignity of a pack-horse—no unmixed benefit in the eyes of people driving, since most of the country horses are reduced to frenzy by the sight of the lean screw with his immense white pack—the hawker is merciless to his horse—led by the "black" man in flapping clothes and gay turban. Still the regular hawkers are a more respectable class of men, and their visits are often eagerly welcomed by the housewife in the lonely country, many miles from a township, who finds herself confronted with such problems as the necessity for lacing Johnny's Sunday boots with strips of green hide, or the more serious one of a dearth of trouser-buttons for his garments.

It is the casual hawker who is looked on with disfavour, and strikes terror to the heart of many women. He has very frequently no money and less principle; and being without reputation to sustain in the district, is careless of his doings along a route that he probably does not intend to visit again. He knows perfectly well that women and children are afraid of him, and as a rule is very willing to work upon that fear—though the sight of a man, or of a dog with character, is sufficient to make him the most servile of his race. But where he meets a lonely woman he is a very apparition of terror.

There was one hawker who came regularly to Billabong; a cheery old fellow, well known and respected, whose caste was not strict enough to prevent his refusing the station hospitality, and whose appearance was always welcome. He had been coming so long that he knew them all well, and took an almost affectionate interest in Jim and Norah, always bringing some little gift for the latter. The men liked him, for he had been known to "turn to" and work at a bush fire "as hearty as if he weren't a fat little image av a haythen," said Murty O'Toole; Norah was always delighted when old Ram Das came up the track, his unwieldy body on two amazingly lean legs. Even Mary would not have been scared at his appearance.

But this was not Ram Das—this Indian who stood looking at her with that queer little half-smile, so different from the old man's wide and cheerful grin. It was a strange man, and a terrible one in Mary's sight. She gaped at him feebly across the table, and he watched her with keen, calculating eyes. Presently he spoke again, this time a little impatiently.

"You ask-a meesis annything to-day?"

"Nothin' to-day," said Mary, quickly and nervously.

"You ask-a meesis."

"She don't want anything," the girl quavered.

81

"You ask-a."

"I tell you she don't want anything—there ain't any missis," Mary said. He looked at her unbelievingly, and broke into a speech of broken English that was quite unintelligible to the frightened girl behind the table. Then, as she did not answer him, he came a few steps nearer.

It was more than enough for Mary. She gave a terrified shriek and ran for the nearest cover—the half-open door of the back kitchen behind her. She banged it violently as she dashed through. There was no lock on the door, so she could not stay there—but the window stood open, and Mary went through it with all the nimbleness of fear. She came out into the yard where the way lay clear to the house; and across the space went Mary, cometwise, a vision of terror and flying cap strings, each moment expecting to hear pursuing feet. Puck, the Irish terrier, sleeping peacefully on the front verandah, leapt to his feet at the sudden bang of the back door, and came dashing through the house in search of the cause. Mary, half sobbing, welcomed him with fervour.

"Good dog, Puck!" she said. She reconnoitred through the nearest window.

The Indian had come out of the kitchen, and now stood on the back verandah, his dark face working. He looked uncertainly about him. Then the back door opened a few inches—just so far that an enthusiastic Irish terrier could squeeze through—and Mary's voice came.

"Good dog, Puck!—sool 'im!"

The door banged again, and the heavy lock shot home. Mary flew back to the window, shutting and locking it frantically. She watched.

Puck wasted no time. He dashed at the hawker, with every fighting instinct aroused, and the Hindu leaped back quickly, seizing with one hand a broom that leaned against the wall. He met the terrier's onslaught with a savage blow that sent the little dog head over heels yards away. Puck picked himself up and came again like a whirlwind. Then Mary screamed again, for the Hindu dropped the broom, and something flashed in the sunlight—a long knife that came swiftly from some hiding place in his voluminous draperies. He crouched to meet the dog, his eyes gleaming, his lips drawn back from his teeth.

Puck was no fool. He arrested himself almost in midair, and planted himself just out of the hawker's reach, his whole enraged little body a vision of defiance, and barked madly. The Indian moved backwards, uttering a flood of furious speech, while for each step that he moved the terrier advanced another. Then Mary's heart gave a sudden leap; for the hand that held the knife suddenly went behind him as he reached for his pack and swung it to his shoulder. Puck was nearly upon him in the moment that the knife no longer menaced, but the Hindu was quick; and again the little dog drew back, rending the air with his barking. Slowly the man backed off the verandah and along the path to the yard gate, Puck following every step, loathing with all his fury that unfair advantage of gleaming steel that kept him from his enemy. The Hindu backed through the gate, and slammed it in the terrier's face, spitting a volley of angry words as he went. Mary flung the window open and called her protector anxiously, lest he should find some means of exit and leave her alone; and Puck came back a few steps, turning again to bark at his retreating foe. The tall form in the dusty clothes went slowly down the track. Mary watched him out of sight. Then she fled to her own room, locked herself in securely, and went, very properly, into hysterics.

Meanwhile, at the creek, Norah was nodding sleepily over her book. It was hot, and naturally a lazy day; everything seemed sleepy, from the cows lying about under the willows on the banks to the bees droning overhead. Tait, near her, was snoring gently. Even the water below seemed to be rippling more lazily than usual; the splash of a leaping fish made an unusual stir in the stillness. Moreover, her book was not calculated to keep her awake. It was poetry, and Norah's soul did not incline naturally to poetry, unless it were one of Gordon's stirring rhymes, or something equally Australian in character. This was quite different, but it had been Cecil's Christmas gift, and it had seemed to Norah that politeness required her to study it.

"It's the rummiest stuff!" said the Bush damsel, hopelessly. She turned to the cover, a dainty thing of pale blue and gold. "William Morris? Didn't we have a stockman once called Bill Morris? But I'm pretty certain he never wrote this. The name's the same, though!" thought Norah, uncertainly. She turned back, and read anew, painstakingly:

> No meat did ever pass my lips
> Those days. (Alas! the sunlight slips
> From off the gilded parclose dips,
> And night comes on apace.)

"Then I'm positive it wasn't our Bill Morris, 'cause I never saw a stockman who was a vegetarian. But what's a parclose? I'll have to ask Cecil; but then he'll think me such a duffer not to know, and he'll be so awfully patronizing. But what on earth does it all mean?"

She closed the book in despair, let her eyelids droop, and nodded a little, while the book in its blue and gold cover slipped from her knee to the grass. It was much easier to go to sleep than to read William Morris. What a long time Dad and the boys were, doctoring Derrimut! It was certainly dull.

A quick bark from Tait startled her. The collie had jumped up, and was bristling with wrath at an unusual spectacle coming through the trees towards her—a tall man, with a face of dusky bronze, surmounted by a pink turban. His face was working angrily, and he muttered as he walked, slowly, as if the pack on his shoulder were heavy. When Tait barked he started for a moment, but then came on steadily—a collie is rarely as formidable as an Irish terrier.

Norah paled a little. She was not timid, but no Australian girl takes naturally to an encounter with a Hindu and there was no doubt that this man was in a very bad temper. The place was lonely, too, and out of sight of the house, even if she had not been painfully conscious that there was not a man on the place should she need help. Still, there was nothing to be gained by running. She backed against the tree, keeping one hand on Tait's collar as the man came up.

"What do you want?"

He stopped, and the pack slipped to the grass. Then he broke into a flood of rapid speech in his own tongue, gesticulating violently; occasionally indicating the house with a sweep of his hand in that direction. As he talked he worked himself up to further wrath—his voice rose almost to a shout sometimes, and his face was not pleasant to see. Once or twice he held his left hand out, and Norah saw that it was bandaged.

For a minute or two she was badly frightened. Then, watching him, she suddenly came to the conclusion that she had nothing to fear—that he was telling her something he wanted her to know. She listened, trying hard to catch some word in the flood of fluent foreign speech, and twice she thought she made out the name of Ram Das. Then he finished abruptly with almost the one word of Hindustani she knew, since it was one the old hawker had taught her. "Sumja," ("Do you understand?" he hurled at her.

Norah shook her head.

"No, I don't 'sumja,'" she said: but her tone was friendly, and some of the anger melted from the Indian's face, and was succeeded by a quick relief. "Can't you speak English? You know Ram Das— Ram Das?" she repeated, hoping that the name might convey something to him. To her immense relief, the effect was instantaneous.

"Know Ram Das," said the man, struggling for words. "Him— him." He swept the horizon vaguely with his hand.

"I know Ram Das," Norah put in. "Him good man."

The Hindu nodded violently. His face was natural again, and suddenly he smiled at her. "You a meesis?" he asked. "Ram Das say l'il meesis."

"I'm little meesis," Norah said promptly. It was the old man's title for her. "Did Ram Das send you?"

"Him send me," said the man, with evident pleasure in finding the word. He struggled again for English, but finally gave it up, and held out his left hand to her silently.

"Why, you're hurt!" Norah said. "Is that why Ram Das sent you?"

He nodded again, and began to unroll the long strip of cotton stuff round his hand and wrist. It took a long time, and at last he had to go down to the water and bathe the stiffened rag before it would come away. Then he came back to Norah and held it out again—a long, hideous gash right up the wrist, torn and swollen and inflamed.

"Oh!" said Norah, drawing back a pace, instinctively. "You poor fellow! How did you do it?"

"Barb wire," said the Indian, simply. "Three days. Him bad. Ram Das, him say you help." With this stupendous effort of eloquence he became speechless again, still holding the torn wrist out to her.

"I should think so!" said Norah, forgetting everything in the sight of that cruel wound. "Come on up to the house quickly!" She turned to lead the way, but the man shook his head.

"Woman there," he stammered.

"It's all right," Norah told him. "Come along."

"Small dog," said the Hindu, unhappily. "Them afraid of me." He pointed towards the house. "Been there."

"Oh-h!" said Norah, suddenly comprehending. She knew Mary. Then she laughed. "You come with me; it's all right." She led the way, and the hawker followed her. A few yards further on, Norah bethought herself of something, and turned back.

"You must have that covered up," she told him. "No, not with that awful rag again," with a faint shudder. She took out her handkerchief and wrapped it lightly round the man's wrist. "That'll do for the present—come on."

Puck, still in a state of profound indignation in the back yard, was thrown into a paroxysm of fury at the sight of his enemy returning. Norah had to chain him up before the Hindu would come inside the gate. Then she led the way to the kitchen and called Mary.

No Mary answered, so Norah went about her preparations alone—a big basin of hot water, boracic acid—standby of the Bush—soft rags, and ointment from the "hospital drawer" Mrs. Brown kept always ready. She shuddered a little as she began to bathe the

85

wound, while the Indian watched her with inscrutable face, never flinching, though the pain was no small thing. It was done at last—cleansed, anointed, and carefully bandaged. Then he smiled at her gratefully.

"Ram Das him say you good," he said. "Him truth!"

Norah laughed, somewhat embarrassed.

"Hungry?" she asked. "You take my food?"

It was always a delicate question, since the Hindu is easily offended over a matter of caste. This man, however, was evidently as independent as Ram Das, for he nodded, and when Norah brought him food, fell to work upon it hungrily.

Thus it was that Mary, brought from the hysterical sanctuary of her room by the pressing sense of the necessity of looking after the kitchen fire, and coming back to her duties like a vestal of old, found her dreaded enemy cheerfully eating in the kitchen, while Norah sat near and carried on a one-sided conversation with every appearance of friendliness, with Tait sleepily lying beside her—at which astonishing spectacle Mary promptly shrieked anew. The Hindu rose, smiling nervously.

"Come here, you duffer, Mary!" said Norah, who by this time had arrived at something of an understanding of the previous happenings. "He's as tame as tame. Why, old Ram Das sent him!"

"Miss Norah, he's got a knife on him!" said Mary, in a sepulchral whisper. "I saw it with me own eyes. He nearly killed Puck with it!"

"Well, Puck was trying to kill him," said Norah, "and I guess if you had a wrist like his, you'd defend yourself any way you could, if Puck was at you! He's terribly sorry he frightened you—you didn't understand him, that was all. Ram Das sent him to have his wrist fixed up, and his name's Lal Chunder, and he's quite a nice man!"

"H'm!" said Mary doubtfully, relaxing so far as to enter the kitchen, but keeping a respectful distance from the hawker, who took no further notice of her, going on with his meal. "I don't 'old with them black creechers in any shape or form, Miss Norah, an' it's my belief he'd kill us all in our beds as soon as wink! Scarin' the wits out of one, with his pink top-knot arrangement—such a thing for a man to wear! Gimme white Orstralia!"

"Look out, he'll hear you!" said Norah, laughing. "He—"

"What talk is this?" said a cheerful voice; and Ram Das, very plump, very hot and very beaming, came in at the kitchen door, and stood looking at them. "I sent this young man to the li'l meesis, for that he was hurt and in pain, and I know the fat woman is kind, and has the brassic-acid." He glanced at Lal Chunder's bandaged wrist, and shot a quick question at him in their own tongue, to which the

86

other responded. The old man turned back to Norah, not without dignity.

"We thank the l'il meesis," he said. "Lal Chunder is as my son: he cannot speak, but he will not forget."

"Oh, that's all right," said Norah, turning a lively red. "It wasn't anything, really, Ram Das–and his wrist was terribly sore. You'll both camp here to-night, won't you? And have some tea–I'm sure you want it, it's so hot."

"It will be good," said Ram Das, gratefully, sitting down. Then voices and the sound of hoofs and the chink of bits came from outside; and presently Mr. Linton and the boys came in, hot and thirsty.

Cecil's eyebrows went up as he beheld his cousin carrying a cup to the stout old Hindu.

"It's the most extraordinary place I was ever at," he told himself later, dressing for dinner, in the seclusion of his own room. From the garden below came shouts and laughter, as Jim engaged Norah and Wally in a strenuous set on the tennis court. "Absolutely no class limits whatever, and no restrictions–why, she kept me waiting for my second cup while she looked after that fat old black in the dirty white turban! As for the boys–childish young hoodlums. Well, thank goodness I'm not condemned to Billabong all my days!" With which serene reflection Mr. Cecil Linton adjusted his tie nicely, smoothed a refractory strand of hair in his forelock, and went down to dinner.

CHAPTER XII

OF POULTRY

A man would soon wonder how it's done,
The stock so soon decreases!

A. B. Paterson

"Where are you off to, Norah?"

"To feed the chickens."

"May I come with you, my pretty maid?"

"Delighted!" said Norah. "Here's a load for you."

"Even to stagger under thy kerosene tin were ever a joy!" responded Wally, seizing the can of feed as he spoke—the kerosene tin of the bush, that serves so many purposes, from bucket to cooking stove, and may end its days as a flower pot, or, flattened out, as roofing iron. "Anyhow, you oughtn't to carry this thing, Norah; it's too heavy. Why will you be such a goat?"

Under this direct query, put plaintively, Norah had the grace to look abashed.

"Well, I don't, as a rule," she said. "It's really Billy's job to carry it for me, but Jim has been coming with me since he came home, so of course young Billy's got out of hand. And Jim's gone across with Dad to see old Derrimut, so I had no one. I looked for you and couldn't find you. And I asked Cecil politely to accompany me, but he put his eyebrows up, and said fowls didn't interest him. Oh, Wally, don't you think it's terribly hard to find subjects that do interest Cecil?"

"Hard!" said Wally expressively. "Well, it beats me, anyhow. But then Cecil regards me with scorn and contumely, and, to tell you the truth, Nor., when I see him coming I quiver like—like a blancmange! He's so awfully superior!"

"You know, I'm sure he's not enjoying himself," Norah went on; "and it really worries us, 'cause we hate to think of anyone being here and not having a good time. But he does keep his nose so in the air, doesn't he?"

"Beats me how you're so nice to him," Wally averred. "My word, it would do that lad good to have a year or two at our school! I guess it would take some of the nonsense out of him. Was he ever young?"

"I shouldn't think so," Norah said, laughing—"he has such a lofty

88

contempt for anything at all juvenile now. Well, at least he's looking better than when he came, so Billabong is doing him good in one way at any rate, and that is a comfort. But I'm sure he's counting the days until he goes away."

"Well, so am I," said Wally, cheerfully. "So at least there are two of us, and I should think there were several more. It's pleasant to find even one subject on which one can be a twin-soul with Cecil. Norah"–solemnly–"I have counted eleven different pairs of socks on that Johnny since I came, and each was more brilliant than the last!"

"I don't doubt it," Norah laughed. "They're the admiration of the laundry here, and even the men stopped and looked at them as they were hanging on the line last week. Dave Boone was much interested in that green pair with the gold stripes, and asked Sarah what football club they belonged to!"

"Great Scott!" said Wally explosively. "Can you imagine Cecil playing football?"

"I can't–I wish I could," Norah answered. "Well, never mind Cecil–he's a tiring subject. Tell me what you think of my chicks."

Norah's special fowl yard was a grassy run divided into two parts, with small houses and wire-netted enclosures in each. At present one was devoted to a couple of mothers with clutches of ten and twelve chickens–all white Orpingtons. The mothers were stately, comfortable dames, and the chicks, round little creamy balls, very tame and fascinating. They came quite close to Norah as she stooped to feed them, and one chick, bolder than his brethren, even stood on the back of her hand. Wally admired without stint, and proceeded to discharge the practical duty of rinsing out the water tins and filling them afresh.

In the other yard a number of older chickens grew and prospered; these also were all white, of the Leghorn breed, and Norah was immensely proud of them. She sat down on the end of a box and pointed out their varied beauties.

"I should have more–lots more," she said, dolefully. "But I've had horrible trouble with pigs. Why anybody keeps pigs at all I can't imagine!"

"They're handy when preserved," Wally remarked. "But what did they do to you?"

"I had a lot of hens sitting this year," said the owner of the yard– "sitting on lovely eggs, too, Wally! Some I got from Cunjee, and some from Westwood, and two special sittings from Melbourne. I was going to be awfully rich! You couldn't imagine all I'd planned with the immense sums I was going to make."

"There's a proverb," said Wally, sententiously, "about counting your chickens."

"You're quite the twelfth person who's mentioned that," Norah said, with some asperity. "Anyhow, I never counted them; I only became rich in a vague way, and it was very comforting. I'm glad I had that comfort, for it was all I had."

"Norah, you thrill my very soul with awful fears," Wally gasped. "Tell me the worst!"

"Donkey!" said Norah, unsympathetically. "Well, they were set. I fixed up the boxes myself, and lined them so beautifully that when they were ready, and the eggs in, it was all I could do to prevent myself sitting on them!"

"I know," Wally nodded. "And then the hens wouldn't sit, would they? They never do, when you make the nests especially tempting. I had an old Cochin once who used to sit quite happily for six months at a time on a clod and a bit of stone, expecting to hatch out a half-acre allotment and a town hall; but if you put her on twelve beautiful eggs she simply wouldn't look at them! Makes you vow you'll give up keeping hens at all."

"It would," Norah said. "Only mine didn't do that."

"Oh!" said Wally, a little blankly. "What did they do, then?"

"Sat—"

"And ate the eggs—I know," Wally burst in. "My old brute used to eat one a day if you got her to sit. I remember once it was a race between her and the eggs, and I used to haunt the nest, wondering would she get 'em all eaten before they hatched. They beat her by one—one poor chick came out. The shock was too much for the old hen, and she deserted it, and I poddied it in a box for a week, and called it Moses, and it would eat out of my hand, and then it died!" He gasped for breath, and Norah gazed with undisguised admiration at the orator.

"So I know how you'd feel," Wally finished.

"I might—but my hens weren't cannibals. They didn't eat any."

"You had luck," said the unabashed Wally. "Well, what happened?"

"They sat quite nicely—"

"And the eggs were addled, weren't they? It's always the way with half these swagger sittings you buy from dealers. They—"

"Oh, Wally, I wish you wouldn't be so intelligent!" said Norah, with not unnatural heat. "How am I ever going to tell you?"

"Why, I thought you were telling me as hard as ever you could!" Wally responded, visibly indignant "Well, fire away; I won't speak another word!"

"I don't think you could help it," Norah laughed. "However, I'd eight hens sitting, and I really do believe that they understood their responsibilities, for they set as if they were glued, except when they came off for necessary exercise and refreshment. Even then, they never gave me any of the usual bother about refusing to go back into the right box, or scratching the eggs out. They behaved like perfect ladies–I might have known it was too bright to last!" She heaved a sigh.

"I know you're working up to some horrible tragedy, and I'm sure I won't be able to bear it!" said her hearer, much agitated. "Tell me the worst!"

"So they sat–"

"You said that before!"

"Well, they sat before–and after," said Norah, unmoved. "Two of them brought their eggs out, beautiful clutches, twelve in one and thirteen in the other. Such luck! I used to be like the old woman who pinched herself and asked, 'Be this I?' They all lived in a fox-proof yard–fence eight feet high with wire-netting on top. I wasn't leaving anything to chance about those chicks."

"Was it cholera? Or pip?"

"Neither," said Norah. "They were the very healthiest, all of them. The chickens grew and flourished, and when they were about a week old, the other six hens were all about to bring out theirs within two days. Oh, Wally, I was so excited! I used to go down to the yard about a dozen times a day, just to gloat!"

"Never gloat too soon," said Wally. "It's a hideous risk!"

"I'm never going to gloat again at all, I think," said Norah, mournfully. The recital of her woes was painful. "So I went down one morning, and found them all happy and peaceful; the six old ladies sitting in their boxes, and the two proud mammas with their chicks, scratching round the yard and chasing grasshoppers. It was," said Norah, in the approved manner of story-tellers," a fair and joyous scene!"

"'Specially for the grasshoppers!" commented her hearer. "And then–?"

"Then I went out for a ride with Dad, and I didn't get back until late in the afternoon. I let Bobs go, and ran down to the fowl yard without waiting to change my habit." Norah paused. "I really don't know that I can bring myself to tell you any more!"

"If you don't," said Wally, indignantly, "there'll certainly be bloodshed. Go on at once–

"Am I a man on human plan

Designed, or am I not, Matilda?"

"H'm," said Norah. "Well, I'm not Matilda, anyway! However, I

91

opened the gate of the yard. And then I stood there and just gaped at what I saw."

"Dogs?"

"Our dogs are decently trained," Norah said, much offended. "No, it wasn't dogs—it was pigs!"

"Whew-w!" whistled Wally.

"Pigs. They had burrowed in right under the fence; there was a great big hole there. And they'd eaten every chicken, and every egg in the yard. My lovely boxes were all knocked over, and the nests torn to bits, and there wasn't so much as an eggshell left. The poor old hens were just demented—they were going round and round the yard, clucking and calling, and altogether like mad things. And in the middle of it all, fat and happy and snoring—three pigs!"

"What did you do?" Wally felt that this case was beyond the reach of ordinary words of sympathy.

"Couldn't do anything. I chased the beasts out of the yard, and threw everything I could find at them—but you can't hurt a pig. And Dad was horrid—advised me to have them killed, so that at least we could have eggs and bacon!" Norah laughed, in spite of her woebegone tone.

"And he calls himself a father!" said Wally, solemnly.

"Oh, he wasn't really horrid," Norah answered. "He wrote off to town and bought me a very swagger pair of Plymouth Rocks—just beauties. They cost three guineas!"

"Three guineas!" said the awestruck youth. "What awful waste! Where are they, Norah? Show me them at once!"

"Can't," Norah responded, sadly.

"You don't mean—?"

"Oh, I've had a terrible year with fowls," said the dejected poultry keeper. "Those Plymouth Rocks came just before the Cunjee show, and Dad entered them for me, 'cause the dealer had told him they would beat anything there. And I think they would have—only just after he sold Dad mine, a Cunjee man bought a pair for five guineas. He showed his, too!" Norah sighed.

"Oh!" said Wally.

"So I got second. However, they were very lovely, and so tame. I was truly fond of Peter."

"Why Peter?"

"Oh, Peter means a Rock," said Norah. "I heard it in a sermon. He was a beautiful bird. I think he was too beautiful to live, 'cause he became ill—I don't know what it was, but he pined away. I used to nurse him ever so; for the last two days of his poor young life I fed him every hour with brandy and strong soup out of the spout of the

92

invalid feeder. Brownie was quite annoyed when she found I'd used it for him," said Norah, reflectively.

"But he was an invalid, wasn't he?" asked Wally.

"Of course he was—and it's an invalid feeder. I don't see what it's for, if not for the sick. But it didn't do him any good. I went out about ten o'clock one night and wrapped him in hot flannel, and he was rattling inside his poor chest; and in the morning I went out at five and he was dead!"

"Poor old Nor.!"

"So I tied a bit of black stuff on the gate and went back to bed," said Norah, pensively.

Wally grinned. "And what became of Mrs. Peter?"

"Oh, Mrs. Peter was a lovely hen," Norah said, "and very healthy. She never seemed to feel any of Peter's delicacy. He was a very refined bird. There was another show coming on at Mulgoa, and I found among the other fowls another Mr. Peter, and it struck me I would have a try for the prize. Mrs. Peter was so good that I felt I'd get it unless the five-guinea Plymouth Rock man came up. So I fed up the new Peter and had them looking very well the day before the show. And then—"

"Yes?" said Wally, as she paused.

"Then a new dog of Burton's killed Mrs. Peter," said Norah, "so I gave up showing poultry!"

"I should think you did," said the sympathetic auditor. "What did your father say?"

"He was very nice; and very angry with the dog; but he didn't buy me any more valuable fowls—and I expect that was just as well," said Norah, laughing. "I don't seem to have luck when it comes to keeping poultry. Jim says it's management, but then Jim never kept any himself. And it does make a difference to your views if you keep them yourself."

"It does," Wally agreed. "I used to lose ever so many in Queensland, but then things are really rough on fowls up there—climate and snakes and lots of odd things, including crocodiles! When I came down to school I left a lot of hens, and twelve eggs under one old lady hen, who should have hatched 'em out a few days after I left. And the whole lot went wandering and found some poison my brother had put out for a cat!" Wally wiped his eyes elaborately.

"And died?"

"It was suicide, I think," said Wally, nodding. "But I always had comfort about that lot, because I still have hopes that those twelve eggs hadn't hatched."

"I don't see what that has to do with it," Norah said, plainly puzzled.

"Why, don't you understand? If they hatched I must have lost them along with the others; but if they didn't hatch, I didn't lose so many, for, not having them to lose, I couldn't very well lose them, could I? Q.E.D.!" finished Wally, triumphantly. "That's Philosophy!"

"You're a credit to your teachers, old man," said a new voice; and Jim made his appearance behind the fence, over which he proceeded to climb laboriously.

"Yes, I'm a nice boy," said modest Mr. Meadows. "Sometimes I think you don't appreciate me—"

"Perish the thought!" said Jim, solemnly.

"But I always feel that honest worth will tell in the end," finished Wally. "Jim, you great, uncivilized rogue, unhand me!" There was a strenuous interlude, during which the Leghorn chicks fled shrieking to the farthest corner of their domain. Finally Jim stepped unwittingly, in the joy of battle, into the kerosene tin, which was fortunately empty, and a truce was made while he scraped from a once immaculate brown leather legging the remains of the Leghorns' breakfast.

"Serve you right," said Wally, adjusting his tie, which had mysteriously appeared under his right ear. "Norah and I were talking beautifully, and you hadn't any business to come poke your nose in, if you couldn't behave, had he Nor.?" Whereat Norah and Jim grinned cheerfully at each other, and Wally collapsed, remarking with indignation that you couldn't hope to get justice for either of the Linton twins when it came to dealing with the other.

"We're not twins!" said Norah.

'No," said her guest, "I think you're worse!" Withdrawing, he sat in melancholy isolation on a hen coop, and gave himself up, very appropriately, to brooding.

"Well, I'm sorry if I broke up the party," Jim said, relinquishing the task of polishing his leggings with marshmallow leaves and looking at its streaked surface disconsolately. Jim might—and did—scorn coats and waistcoats in the summer, and revel in soft shirts and felt hats; but his riding equipment was a different matter, and from Garryowen's bit and irons to his own boots, all had to be in apple pie order. "Norah, may I have your hanky to rub this up? No? You haven't one! Well, I'm surprised at you!" He rubbed it, quite ineffectually, with the crown of his hat, and still looked pained. "Never mind, I'll get hold of some tan stuff when I go in. What I came to say when you attacked me, young Wally—"

"When I attacked you! I like that!" spluttered the justly indignant Wally.

"Didn't you? I thought you did," grinned Jim. "My mistake, I suppose. Well, anyhow, when you attacked Norah–quiet, Wally, bother you; how can a fellow get a word out?–what I came to mention was that Dad wants us."

"Oh!" said Norah, gathering herself up. "Why didn't you say so before?"

"Too busy, and you and Wal. do prattle so. Anyhow, he's not in a tearing hurry, 'cause he said he was going to have an hour at his income-tax–and you know what that means."

"Solitude is always best for Dad when he's income-taxing," said Norah. "It has the most horrible effect on his usual serenity. My dear old Hermit used to help him, of course; but now–well, no wonder he's starting early! How's Derrimut, Jimmy?"

"Going on splendidly; Dad and I are quite proud of ourselves as vets.," said her brother. "We made quite a good job of the old chap; I believe he'll hardly have a blemish. By George, you should have seen Cecil at that operation! He had one rope to hold and he was scared to death."

"So was I," said Wally, grinning. "I was always as timid as a rabbit."

"You!" said Jim, laughing. "Well, you held three ropes, anyway, and I didn't notice that you looked pale."

"My face won't let me," said his chum. "But I felt pale!"

"Well Cecil looked and felt it," Jim said. "Of course, you don't exactly blame a town chap for not taking to that sort of thing like a duck to water. Still, there's a limit–and I'll swear Norah would have made a fuss. As far as that goes, Dad says he's known our grandmother, in the early days, have to help at a much worse job for a beast than fixing up old Derry's leg. Lots of women had to. They wouldn't like it, of course, but they certainly wouldn't have made it harder for the man they were helping by putting on frills!"

"Well, you'd hate to have to get a woman to do a job like that."

"Of course you would. You'd never do it unless it came to a question of saving a beast or easing its pain. But if it did come to the point, a decent woman with backbone would lend a hand, just as she's help if it was the man himself that was hurt. At least, most Australian women would, or most of those in the country, at any rate. I'd disown Norah if she didn't."

"I should hope so!" said Norah, quietly.

"At the same time, I've not the remotest intention of employing you as a vet., old woman," said Jim, untying her hair ribbons in a brotherly fashion. "Quite enough for you to act in that capacity for that rum beggar, Lal Chunder–who's departed, by the way, leaving

95

you his blessing and a jolly little brass tray. The blessing was rather unintelligible, but there's no doubt about the tray."

"Bother!" said Norah, vexedly. "Silly man! I don't want him to give me presents—and that wound of his ought certainly to have been looked after for a few days."

"He said he was going to travel with Ram Das—and old Ram'll see that he ties it up, I expect," said Jim, with unconcern. "I wouldn't bother, old first-aid; it looked tip-top when you dressed it before breakfast."

"I'd have given him rag for it, anyway," said Norah, still troubled.

"He can always tear half a yard or so off that turban of his," Jim said. "Don't go out of your way to meet worry, my girl—it'll always come quickly enough to meet you. Which is philosophy quite equal to Wally's!" He sighed. "Here's trouble coming to meet us now, that's certain!"

CHAPTER XIII

STATION DOINGS

I see as I stand at the slip-rails, dreaming,
Merry riders that mount and meet;
Sun on the saddles, gleaming, gleaming,
Red dust wrapping the horses' feet.

W. H. Ogilvie

They had turned the corner of the house leading to the verandah off which Mr. Linton's office opened, and where that gentleman was presumably to be found, wrestling with the intricacies of his income-tax schedule–the squatter's yearly bugbear. Along this verandah came, slowly, Cecil, beautiful to behold in a loose brown suit, with buff coloured shirt and flowing orange tie. Wally cast a swift glance at his ankles, and chuckled.

"He's got new socks on!" he said, in a sepulchral whisper.

"Shut up, you duffer–he'll hear you!" Jim said. He raised his voice. "Looking for us, Cecil?"

"Yes," Cecil drawled. "Uncle David asked me to find you. Fed the–ah–poultry, Norah?"

"Yes, thank you," said that damsel.

"Awfully uninteresting things, fowls," said Cecil, turning and walking back with them. "Noisy and dirty–I can't imagine you bothering your head over them."

"They're not dirty when they're kept properly," Norah said, a little warmly. "And I don't think any animal's uninteresting if you look after it yourself. Of course, if you do nothing more than eat them–"

"I assure you that's all I care to do!" said Cecil. At this point, they arrived at the door of the office, which was perhaps as well, and found Mr. Linton half submerged in a sea of stock returns, books, and bill-files.

"Oh, here you are," he said, smoothing the furrows out of his brow to smile at Norah. "I had an idea I sent you for the others some time ago, Jim."

Jim looked somewhat sheepish.

"Yes." He admitted, laughing. "Fact is, I–I got into a kerosene tin!" He glanced at his left leg expressively.

97

"I see," said his father, with a smile. "Well, I don't know that it matters—only a note has just come out from Anderson, and his chauffeur is waiting for an answer. It seems Cunjee is playing Mulgoa in a great cricket match on Thursday, and they're short of men. They want to know if they can recruit from Billabong. "

"Good business!" said Jim, joyfully, while Wally hurrahed below his breath. "But will they let us play, Dad—Wal. and me?"

"Oh, they've fixed that up with the Mulgoa fellows," said his father. "It's all right. They're kind enough to ask me to play, but it's out of the question—even if I weren't approaching senile decay"—he smiled—"I wouldn't be able to go. Mr. Darrell has a buyer coming to look at his young stock on Friday, and he writes me that if I want any of them—he knows I did want some—I can have the first pick if I am over at Killybeg on Thursday. So that means I'll be away from Wednesday morning—and I think this match will be as efficacious as anything else in keeping you out of mischief during my absence!"

"I'm glad we'll have something!" Jim said, his grin belying his meek voice. "Well, we'll have to see who can play."

"You two boys, of course," said his father. "And Cecil—do you play?"

"Not for worlds, thank you," said Cecil, hastily. "It's not in my line."

"Oh," said his uncle. "Then you can be Norah's escort—if she wants to go, that is!"

"Want to go! Well, Daddy!" said Norah in expostulation—whereat everybody laughed.

"Murty can slog, I believe, and of course, Boone is a cricketer," the squatter said. "They only want four, so if those two fellows are willing—of which I'm not very doubtful!—that will be just right. You might go out and see if they're anywhere about, Jim."

Jim and Wally dashed off, to return presently with the tidings that Murty would play "wid all the pleasure in loife." Boone was away at work, but his acquiescence could be taken for granted.

"Then I'll send a line to the doctor," Mr. Linton said. "He and Mrs. Anderson want you all to go there for lunch on the day of the match—a very good arrangement, seeing that you'll have Norah with you. You'd better get away from here quite early; it's pretty certain to be hot, and the day will be a fairly long one, in any case. It will be far better to get the ride over before the sun is very formidable. And if you'll take my advice, boys, you'll make those fellows have some practice before Thursday. You two should be in good form, but they scarcely ever touch a bat."

Jim and Wally approved of his advice, and each evening before the day of the match saw the Billabong contingent of the Cunjee eleven hard at work on a level stretch of ground close to the homestead; while Norah was generally to be found making herself useful in the outfield. Her sex did not hinder the daughter of the house from being able to return balls with force and directness, and when, as a reward for her aid, she was given a few minutes with the bat, to carefully regulated bowling from Wally, Norah's cup of joy was full. She was even heard to say that school might be bearable if they let you play cricket most of the time!—which was a great admission for Norah, who had kept her word rigidly about not mentioning the dreaded prospect before her. That she thought of it continually, Jim knew well and he and his chum were wont, by all means in their power, to paint school life for girls in attractive colours without appearing to be directly "preaching" to Norah; which kindly thought she saw through very well, and was silently grateful, though it was doubtful if her sentence lost any of its terrors.

It was always more or less before her. Her own circle had been too limited to give Norah much experience of the outer world, and she shrank instinctively from anything that lay beyond Billabong and its surroundings. No one, meeting her in her home, would have dreamed that she might be shy; but the truth was that a very passion of shyness came over her when she thought of confronting a number of girls, all up to date and smart, and at ease in their environment, and all, if Cecil were to be believed, ready to look down upon the recruit from the Bush.

For Cecil lost no opportunity to point out to Norah her drawbacks, and to hint at her inferiority to ordinary girls of her own age; "properly trained girls" was his phrase. When he talked to her—which was prudently when no one else was about—Norah felt a complete rustic, and was well assured that the girls at Melbourne would very soon put her in her place, even if they did not openly resent the presence among them of a girl reared in the country, and in so unusual a fashion. She even wondered miserably sometimes if Dad and Jim were rather ashamed of her, and did not like to say so; it was quite possible, since the city boy evidently held her in such low esteem. But then would come a summons from her father, or Jim would appear and bear her off imperiously on some expedition with him, and she would forget her fears—until the next time Cecil persevered in his plan of educating her to a knowledge of her own deficiencies. It is not hard for a boy, on the verge of manhood, to instil ideas into an unsuspecting child; and Cecil's tuition gave poor Norah many a dark hour of which her father and the other boys never dreamed. It would have gone hard with Cecil had they done so.

Between cricket-practice, occasional rides and exploring expeditions, boating on the lagoon, and fishing in the river, to say nothing of much cheerful intercourse, the days passed quickly—at least to most of the inhabitants of the homestead, and when Wednesday came Norah rode across the run with her father to see him on his way to Killybeg. The Darrells' station was some thirty-five miles away by the usual roads; but a short cut over the ranges reduced the journey by fifteen miles, although it was a rough trip, and an impossible one for vehicles. Mounted on Monarch, however, Mr. Linton thought nothing of it; and Norah laughed at his self-accusation of old age as she rode beside him, the lean, erect figure in the saddle giving easily to the black horse's irresponsible bounds—for Monarch had been "spelled" for the trip, and was full of spirits and suppressed energy.

"Take care of him, Daddy, won't you?" she said, a little anxiously, as Monarch executed a more than ordinarily uproarious caper. "He's awfully fresh."

"He'll steady down presently," said her father, smiling at the upturned face. "There's some steep country ahead of him."

"Yes, but he's such a mad-headed animal—and those paths on the sides of the gullies are very steep."

"You sound like the nervous young woman in 'Excelsior,'" David Linton said, with a laugh. "Cheer up, my girl—there's no need to worry about Monarch and me. He's only playful; hasn't an atom of vice, and I know him very well by now. I never put my leg over a better horse."

"Oh, of course," said Norah, cheered, but not altogether convinced. "Every one knows he's a beauty—but just look out that he doesn't try to be too playful on the sidings, Daddy. It would be so easy to slip down."

"Not for anything with four good legs and a fair allowance of sense," said her father. "Do you think you could make Bobs slip down?"

Norah laughed.

"Oh, Bobs is like a mountain goat when it comes to sure-footedness," she said. "You've said yourself, Daddy that it would hardly be possible to throw him down! But then, Bobs is Bobs, and he's seven years old, and ever so sensible—not like that big four-year-old baby. So promise me you'll be careful, Daddy."

"I will, little daughter." They were at the boundary fence now, and it was time for Norah to turn back. "Hurry home—I don't quite like you being so far afield by yourself."

"Oh, Bobs will look after me." Norah hugged her father so far as Monarch would permit—Mr. Linton had got off to wrestle with a stiff padlock on the seldom-used gate, and the black horse was pulling away, impatient of the delay.

"I expect he will," said the father. "That pony is almost as great a comfort to me as he is to you, I believe! Make haste home, all the same." He stood still a moment to watch the little white-coated figure and the handsome pony swinging across the plain at Bobs' long canter; his face tender as few people ever saw it. Then he mounted the eager Monarch, and rode off into the rough country that led to the ranges.

It was comparatively early, but already very hot. Norah was not sorry when she left the long stretch they called the "Far Plain" behind her, and came into the welcome shade of a belt of timber. She walked Bobs through it slowly. Then came the clear stretch to the homestead, and they cantered steadily across it.

Near the stockyard a cloud of dust hovered, through which might be seen dimly the forms of Jim, Wally and O'Toole–all engaged in the engrossing pursuit of inducing three poddy calves to enter the yard. They had but one dog, which, being young and "whip shy," had vanished into the distant landscape at the sound of Murty's stockwhip, leaving them but their own energies to persuade the calves; and when a poddy calf becomes obstinate there are few animals less easy to persuade. Each was possessed of a very respectable turn of speed and a rooted determination to remain in the paddock. When, as frequently happened, they made separate rushes away in the direction of freedom it was all but impossible for those on foot to head them off and keep them in the corner by the yards. They raced hither and thither like mad things, cutting wild capers as they fled; backed and twisted and dodged, and occasionally bellowed as they bolted, much as a naughty child might bellow. To an onlooker there was something distinctly funny in the spectacle.

Murty and the boys, however, might be excused for failing to see the finer points of the joke. They were hot beyond expression; they were also extremely dirty, and were verging on becoming extremely cross. To and fro they darted wildly, striving to head off the cheerful culprits: lifted up their voices in fruitless shouting, and wasted much necessary breath in uttering wild threats of what might be expected to happen when–if ever–they succeeded in yarding the enemy. Not one had a hat; they had long ago been used as missiles in checking a rush, and now lay in the dust, trampled under the racing feet of the poddies. Moreover, it was distressingly evident that they were becoming tired, whilst the calves remained fresh and in most excellent spirits. The chances, as Norah arrived, were distinctly in favour of the calves.

101

From a comfortable seat on a rail Cecil watch the battle, for once ceasing to look bored. In his opinion it was funnier than a circus. Once or twice he shouted words of encouragement to the combatants, and frequently he laughed outright. As an entertainment this quite outshone anything that had been offered him on Billabong—and Cecil was not the man to withhold applause where he thought it due. Finally his attitude attracted the notice of the perspiring Mr. O'Toole.

"Yerra, come down out o' that an' len' a hand!" he shouted, panting. "It is laughin' ye'd be, wid these loonattic images gittin' away on us—!" Further eloquence on Murty's part was checked by a determined rush on the part of a red and white calf, which would certainly have ended in freedom but for a well-aimed clod, which, hurled by the Irishman, took the poddy squarely between the eyes and induced him to pull up and meditate. Unfortunately Murty tripped in the act of delivery, and went headlong, picking himself up just in time to stop a second rush by the calf, which, on seeing his enemy on the ground, promptly ceased to meditate. Cecil rocked with laughter.

"Oh, get off that fence and try and block these brutes, Cecil!" sang out Jim, angrily. "Another hand would make all the difference, if you'd exert yourself!"

Cecil's laughter came to a sudden stop. He looked indignantly at his grey suit, and with pain at his patent leather shoes; then, apparently coming to the conclusion that there was no help for it, descended gingerly, and came into the line of defenders. A sturdy little Shorthorn singled him out for attention, and charged in his direction.

"Block him! Block him, I say!"

Jim's voice rang out. Cecil uttered a feeble yelp as the calf came racing past, waved his arms, and executed a few mild steps towards him—attentions which but served to accelerate the Shorthorn's flight. He went by the city lad like a meteor, rendering useless a wild run by Wally, who was just too late to head him. Murty O'Toole uttered a shout of wrath.

"Howly Ann! He's lost him! The blitherin'—yerra, glory be, there's Miss Norah!"

The change from indignation to relief was comical. Norah and Bobs came like a bolt from the blue upon the vision of the astonished Shorthorn, which made one last gallant effort for freedom, dodging and twisting, while gallant effort for freedom, dodging and twisting, while Bobs made every movement, propping and swinging to cut him off in a manner that would have disturbed any rider not used to the intricate ways of a stock horse. Finally the calf gave it up abruptly, and raced back towards the yard, the pony at his heels. He bolted in at the open gate, promptly followed by his companions, and Murty cut off their exit with a grunt of relief.

"Wisha, it's hot!" he said, mopping his brow. "Sure, Miss Norah, y' kem in the nick av time—"twas run clane off our legs, we was."

"They can run, can't they?" said Norah, who was laughing. "Did you hurt yourself, Murty?"

"Only me timper," said the Irishman, grinning. "But 'twas enough to make a man angry to see that little omadhaun dancin' an' flapping his arrums f'r all the world loike a monkey on a stick—an' pardon to ye, Miss Norah, but I do be forgettin' he's y'r cousin."

"Oh, he's not used to stock; you mustn't be hard on him, Murty," Norah laughed. "Are you very hot, you poor boys?"—as Wally and Jim came up, panting. Cecil had withdrawn towards the house, in offended dignity.

"Hot!" said Wally, casting himself on the ground—

"'Far better in the sod to lie,
    With pasturing pig above,
Than broil beneath a copper sky,
    In sight of all I love!'
That's me!"

"Don't know how you've energy to spout Dr. Watts at that rate," said Jim, following his example.

"I don't think it is Dr. Watts; I fancy it's Kendall," said Wally, uncertainly. "Not that it matters, anyhow; I'm not likely to meet either of them! Did you ever see anything like the way those little beggars ran?"

"Hope I never will again—with the thermometer at this height," Jim answered. "Norah, no words can say how glad I was to see you return, my dear!"

"I can imagine how much of your gladness concerned me, and how much was due to that Shorthorn calf!" said Norah, laughing.

"Well, he'd have been fleeing yet into the offing if it hadn't been for you," said Wally. "Will any one take my hand and lead me for a drink?"

"We'll go up to the house—it's cool there," Jim said. "I want a lemon squash three feet long. There'll be one for you, Murty, if you come up."

"I will that same," said Mr. O'Toole, promptly. "There's no vegetable loike the limon on a day loike this!" So they let Bobs go, and all trooped inside, where Cecil was found, well brushed, and wearing a martyred expression—which, however, was not proof against refreshments. He even went so far as to express mild regret for his slowness to render assistance, remarking that it was against

103

his doctor's advice for him to run; which remarks were received with fitting demeanour by his hearers, though, as Wally remarked later, it was difficult to see how any one who knew Cecil at all could ever have contemplated the possibility of his running!

"Well, I must go back and help Murty brand those youngsters," Jim said, at length, bringing his long form in stages off the sofa. "Coming, Wal.? And, Norah, just you take things quietly. It's uncommon hot, and you'll have a long day to-morrow."

Norah assented with surprising meekness, and the day passed calmly, enlivened by an enthusiastic cricket practice in the evening; after which she was called into requisition at the piano, and played to an audience stretched on basket chairs and lounges on the verandah outside. Finally the performer protested, coming out through one of the long windows for a breath of cooler air.

"Well, then, it's bed," said Jim, yawning prodigiously. "Norah, the men are going to drive in, with our playing togs, to-morrow; would you rather go in the buggy?"

"I'd rather drive, thanks, Jim."

"Thought so. Then hurry off to bed, for we're going to make an early start." Jim paused, looking up at the star-filled sky. "And I give you all warning, it's going to be a caution for heat!"

104

CHAPTER XIV

CUNJEE v. MULGOA

I remember
What it was to be young, and glad, and strong,
By a creek that rippled the whole day long.

M. Forrest.

There was no doubt whatever that the heat was, as Jim had prophesied, "a caution." Pretty little Mrs. Anderson, walking down to the cricket ground at Cunjee, between Jim and Cecil, inwardly wondered what had made her come out of her cool, shaded house to encounter so scorching a sun—with nothing ahead but a bush cricket match. However, Cunjee was no more lively than other townships of its class, and even a match was something. Besides, her husband was playing, and the Billabong contingent, who did not seem to mind the heat at all, had arrived full of most infectious high spirits, filling her house with a cheerful atmosphere of youth and jollity. Norah had at once succumbed to the charms of the baby, and as the baby seemed similarly impressed with Norah, it had been hard to remove him from her arms even for purposes of nourishment for either. She had quite seriously proposed to take him to the match, and had been a little grieved when his mother hastily vetoed the proposition. As mother of three babies, Mrs. Anderson knew precisely their worth at an entertainment—particularly on a hot day.

Even Cecil was more than usually inclined to be—if not happy, at least less bored; although he had begun the day badly, and considered himself scarcely on speaking terms with Jim. This attitude was somewhat difficult to sustain, because Jim himself ignored it cheerfully, and addressed to his cousin whatever remarks came into his head—which Cecil privately considered a demeanour showing the worst of taste.

Bobs had been the "unhappy cause of all this discord." The bay pony was always an object of envy to Cecil, and in his heart he was determined to ride him before leaving Billabong. Particularly he coveted him for the ride into Cunjee. It was bad enough, he considered, to be condemned to Brown Betty in the paddocks, but she was certainly not stylish enough to please him when it came to a

105

township expedition. So he had sauntered out when the horses were being saddled, and delicately hinted to Jim that he might ride Bobs.

Jim, wrestling with Garryowen's girth, had found it the easiest way out of the difficulty to avoid hearing the hint—which he considered "like Cecil's cheek," and as nothing short of Norah's own command would have induced him to accede to it, silence seemed the better plan. Cecil had waited a moment until his head came up from under the saddle flap, and repeated his remark.

"Afraid not," said Jim, driven to bay, and speaking shortly to cover his annoyance. "Norah's going to ride him herself." He led Garryowen off to tie him under the shade of the pepper trees, and did not return to saddle Bobs until Cecil had retreated to the house, looking very black.

This little incident—which Jim had not thought is necessary to report to Norah—had slightly marred the harmony of the early morning. But Jim's unfailing good humour make it hard to keep up a grievance, and if Betty were not exactly stylish, her paces were good enough to make her rider enjoy the trip into Cunjee, especially as Wally and Norah were in the best of spirits and kept things going with a will. Then had come lunch at the Andersons', an occasion which called all Cecil's reserve powers into play. Mrs. Anderson was pretty and smart, and he assumed his best society manner in talking to her, monopolized most of the conversation and flattered himself on making a distinct impression on his country hostess. Possibly he would have been pained had he heard Mrs. Anderson's remark to her husband while putting on her hat after lunch.

"Did you ever see such a contrast, Jack?" she asked—"that conceited boy, and those nice Grammar School youngsters—they're so jolly and unaffected!" To which the doctor had responded that if he had his way he'd boil Cecil, and it was time she had that veil fixed—and had led her forth, protesting that "half the pins weren't in!"

Cecil, however, knew nothing of these comments, and was very well satisfied with himself as they walked slowly along the lane leading to the cricket ground. Jim, on the other side of Mrs. Anderson, tall and handsome in his flannels, with his white hat pulled over his eyes, discoursed cheerfully of school matches, and promised them something worth seeing if young Wally got going with the bat—conversation which did not interest Cecil, who turned it as speedily as might be to matters more to his taste, whereat Jim grew silent, listening with a smile hovering on his well-cut mouth to society doing in the city, told with a view to impressing his hearers with a sense of the narrator's own important share therein. Once Mrs. Anderson met Jim's eye in a brief glance, and reflected the smile momentarily. Behind them, Norah, Wally, and the little doctor kept up a flow of chatter which Wally described as "quite idiotic and awfully comfortable!" The party arrived at the cricket ground on very good terms with itself.

The ground boasted no pavilion save a shed used for the preparation of afternoon tea—a building of which the extreme heat made it almost possible to boil the kettle without lighting a fire! Naturally, no one used it for purposes of watching the play, but there was a row of wattle trees along one side of the ground, and seats placed in their shade made an excellent natural grand stand. Here the non-players betook themselves, while the doctor and the two boys went off to the spot where already most of the other players were gathered—a lean-to under a huge gum-tree, used as a dressing-room by most of the combatants, a number of whom arrived on horseback from long distances. The Billabong boys had changed at the hotel, after putting up their horses, and before repairing to the Andersons', so that they had no dressing to do— which was more than fortunate for them, since the lean-to was so thick with men, boys, valises, discarded garments, leggings and boots, that it resembled a hive in a strong state of disorganization.

Finally, the men were ready; a somewhat motley crowd—not more than seven or eight in flannels, while the remainder were in ordinary dress, with occasionally riding breeches and leggings to be seen, and not a few football jerseys. The Mulgoa men, on being mustered, were found to be a man short, while Cunjee had one to the good. So Murty O'Toole, to his intense disgust, was solemnly handed over to Mulgoa. Then Dr. Anderson, who captained Cunjee, won the toss, and Murty took the field along with his new allies, amid heartless jeers from Mr. Boone, smoking comfortably under a tree, who desired to know should he fetch Mr. O'Toole an umbrella?

The story in detail of a cricket match is generally of particular interest to those who have been there; and as, unfortunately, the number of spectators of the famous battle between Cunjee and Mulgoa was limited, little would be served by an exhaustive description of each over bowled on that day of relentless heat. Cunjee shaped badly from the start. Their two most noted batsmen, a young blacksmith and the post-master, fell victims, without getting into double figures, to the crafty bowling of the Mulgoa captain, Dan Billings—who drove a coach in his spare moments, and had as nice an understanding of how to make a ball break on a fast wicket as of flicking the off leader on the ear with the cracker of his four-in-hand whip. Dr. Anderson scored a couple of fours, and then went out "leg before." He remarked, returning to the "pavilion" sorrowfully, that when one was as round and fat as he, it was difficult to keep out of the way of three little sticks! Then Dave Boone and Wally made a stand that roused the perspiring spectators to something like enthusiasm, for Mr. Boone was a mighty "slogger," and Wally had a neat and graceful style that sent the Cunjee supporters into the seventh heaven. Between them the score mounted rapidly, and the men of Mulgoa breathed a sigh of relief when at length Dave skied a ball from Billings, which descended into the ample hands of Murty O'Toole, who was quite undecided whether to treat his catch as a triumph or a calamity. There was no doubt, however, on the part of his colleagues for the day, who thumped him wildly on the back and yelled again with joy. Mr. Boone retired with a score of forty-five and a wide grin.

Then Jim joined Wally, and kept his end up while his chum put on the runs. Nothing came amiss to Wally that day—slow balls, fast balls, "yorkers," "googlies"—the science of Mulgoa went to earth before the thin brown schoolboy with the merry face. Jim, however, was never at ease, though he managed to remain in a good while; and eventually Dickenson, a wiry little Mulgoa man, found his middle stump with a swift ball—to the intense dismay of Norah, to whom it seemed that the sky had fallen. Cecil smiled serenely

"I had an idea Jim fancied himself as a bat!" said he.

"Jim never fancies himself at anything!" said Jim's sister, indignantly. "Anyway, he's a bowler far more than a bat."

"Ah, it's possibly not his 'day out.' What a pity!" Cecil murmured.

"Well, we can't always be on our best form, I suppose, " said Mrs. Anderson, pacifically. "And, at any rate, Norah, your friend is doing splendidly. Wasn't that a lovely stroke?"

Alas! it soon was apparent that Cunjee was not going to support its ally. One after another the wickets went down, and the batsmen returned from the field "with mournful steps and slow." Wally, seeing his chances diminishing, took liberties with the bowling, and hit wildly, with amazing luck in having catches missed. At last, however, he snicked a ball into cover-point's hands, and retired, amid great applause, having made forty-three. The remaining Cunjee wickets went as chaff before the wind, and the innings closed for 119.

Then there was a rush for the refreshment shed, and monumental quantities of tea were consumed by the teams and their supporters, administered by the admiring maidens of Cunjee. Wally and Jim, prone on the grass in the shade, were cheerful, but by no means enthusiastic regarding their chances. Norah had half expected to find Jim cast down over his batting failure, and was much relieved that he exhibited all his usual serenity. Jim's training had been against showing feeling over games.

"Absolutely fiery out there," said he, accepting a cup gratefully. "Thanks, awfully, Mrs. Anderson; you people are no end good. Didn't we make a beautiful exhibition of ourselves?—all except Dave and this kid, that is."

"Kid yourself," said Wally, who was sucking a lemon slowly and luxuriously. "No tea, thanks, Norah. I'm boiling already, and if I took tea I don't know what might happen, but certainly heat apoplexy would be part of it. Have half my lemon?"

"I don't think so, thanks," said Norah, unmoved by this magnificent offer. "You seem to be getting used to that one, and I'd hate to deprive you of it. Do you boys think we've any chance?"

"It's highly doubtful," Jim answered. "The general opinion is that Mulgoa's good for 150 at the very least—they've got a few rather superior men, I believe, and of course that Billings chap is a terror. And the wicket, such as it is, is all in favour for the bat—which doesn't say much for us And one of our men has gone down with the heat and can't field—fellow from the hotel with red hair, who made five—remember him, Wal.? He's out of training, like most hotel chaps, and as soft as possible, So we're playing a man short."

"I wish they'd give you Murty back!" said Norah, with feminine ignorance.

"Much hope!" returned her brother. "Anyway, Murty's not over good in the field; he's too much in the saddle to be a quick man on his feet. I wouldn't mind you as substitute, Nor."—which remark, though futile, pleased Norah exceedingly.

She was rather more hopeful when the Cunjee team at length took the field, with Boone and the blacksmith bowling against Billings and another noted Mulgoa warrior. But her hopes were rapidly put to flight, and the spirits of the Cunjee "barrackers" went down to zero as it became distressingly apparent that Mr. Billings and his partner were there to stay. Alike they treated the bowling with indifference, hitting the Billabong stockman with especial success—which soon demoralized Dave, who appealed to be taken off, and devoted his energies to short slip fielding. Here he had his revenge presently, for the second Mulgoa man hit a ball almost into his hands, and Dave clung to it as a drowning man to a straw—one wicket for thirty-five.

Then the score mounted with alarming steadiness, and the wickets fell all too slowly for the home team. Dan Billings appeared as comfortable at the wickets as though on the box of his couch, and smote the bowling all round the ground with impartiality. The heat became more and more oppressive, and several of the Cunjee men were tiring, including plump little Dr. Anderson, who stuck to his work as wicket-keeper pluckily—to the unconcealed anxiety of his wife. His reward came when a hot return from the field by Wally gave him a chance of stumping one of the Mulgoa cracks. But the enthusiasm was only momentary; the game was considered, even by the most sanguine small boy of Cunjee, to be "all over bar shouting."

Jim had been bowling for some time from one end with fair results. The batsmen certainly took fewer liberties with him, and he managed to account for three of them for a comparatively low average. He had allowed himself to become anxious, which is a bad thing for a bowler when the score is creeping up and the batsmen are well set. Wally watched his chum with some anxiety—there was none of the fire in his bowling that had so often brought down the ground in a School match.

"Wish he's wake up," said Wally to himself. "I'd like a chance to talk to him."

The chance came when the field crossed over, disposed anew to harry a left-handed batsman. Jim came over with his long, swinging walk, his head a little bent. He started a little at his friend's voice.

"You'll snore soon!" said Wally, incisively. "What on earth's the matter with you? Play up, School!"

Jim stopped short a moment—and burst out laughing, Wally's indignant face glanced back over his shoulder as he ran off. There was a new spring in the bowler's walk as he went to his crease, and the smile still lingered.

The left-handed man faced him confidently—not many local bowlers could trouble him much, and being a large and well-whiskered gentleman, the tall schoolboy opposite to him sent no thrill of fear through his soul. But Jim had learned a thing or two at school about left-handed bats. He took a short run.

On returning to the pavilion the whiskered one admitted that he knew really nothing about the ball. It seemed to come from nowhere, and curl about his bat as he lifted it to strike. How the bails came off was a mystery to him, though it was unfortunately beyond question that they had not remained on. The left-hander removed his pads, ruminating.

Cunjee, meanwhile, had cheered frantically, and Wally sent a School yell ringing down the field. Jim's eye lit up anew as he heard it.

"I do believe I've been asleep," he muttered.

The new man was waiting for him, and he treated his first two balls with respect. Then he grew bolder; hit him for a single, and snicked him to the fence for four. There was a perceptible droop in the Cunjee spirits at the boundary hit. Then Jim bowled the last ball of the over, and there was a composite yell from Cunjee as the Mulgoa man pushed the ball gently into the air just over Dr.

110

Anderson's head. The little doctor was pitifully hot, but he did not fail. The Mulgoa batsman returned to his friends.

Dan Billings was a little worried. Much, he felt, depended on him, and he had never been more comfortably set; but his men— would they be as reliable? He decided to hit out, and Mulgoa roared as the hundred went up for a beautiful boundary hit. Six wickets were down, and Mulgoa was 107 at the end of the over. It seemed safe enough.

Jim took the ball again, his fingers pressing the red surface almost lovingly. He had quite waked up; his head was buzzing with "theories," and his old power seemed to have come back to his fingers. The first ball came with a beautiful leg-break, and the Mulgoan bat swiped at it wildly, and vainly. Seven for 107.

Cunjee was getting excited as the eighth man came in—a wiry and long youth with a stolid face. He contented himself with blocking Jim's bowling, snatching a single presently so that Billings would have the responsibility—to which that gentleman promptly responded by smiting Jim for three. That brought the stolid youth back to power—an honour he did not wish. He hit the next ball softly back to the bowler. Eight for 111; and Cunjee howling steadily, with all its youth, and some of its beauty, battering with sticks on tins. A dog ran across the ground, and was greeted with a yell that made it scurry away in terror, its tail concealed between its legs. Just then Cunjee had no time for dogs.

But it was Mr. Billings' turn, and Mr. Billings was busy. He made good use of the over—the score mounted, and the Cunjee hopes swung lower. It was still eight—for 115—when a single brought his companion to face little Harry Blake, the other Cunjee bowler, who was plainly feeling the weight of his position. He sent the ball down nervously—it slipped as it left his hand, and the Mulgoan stepped out to meet it, while Harry gasped with horror. Up, up, it soared—a boundary surely! Then there was a roar as Wally Meadows gathered himself together, raced, and sprang for the red disc, spinning over his head just at the fence. It seemed to hover above him—then his hands closed, and, unable to stop himself, Wally somersaulted, rolling over and over in the long grass of the outfield. He sat up, his brown face lit by a wide smile, the ball still clutched, held above his head. Nine for 115!

The tension was on bowlers and batsmen alike now—all save Dan Billings, whose calmness was unimpaired. He greeted the tenth man cheerfully—and the tenth man was Murty O'Toole, very hot and nervous, and certainly the most miserable man on the ground as he faced "Masther Jim's" bowling, and knew that the alien hopes of Mulgoa depended on him. Out in the open a Mulgoa man shrugged

111

his shoulders, remarking, "He won't try!" and was promptly attacked furiously by three small boys of Cunjee, who pelted him with clods and abuse from a safe distance. Murty looked at Jim with a little half-apologetic gesture, and Jim grinned.

"Play up, Murty, old chap!" he said.

It was not in vain that he had schooled the stockman in the paddock at Billabong. He sent down a treacherous ball, and Murty met it and played it boldly for two, amid Mulgoan shrieks. Two to tie and three to win—no, one fewer now, for the Irishman had turned a swift ball to leg, and only quick fielding had prevented a boundary. A hundred and seventeen! Murty heaved a sigh of relief as he leaned on his bat at the bowler's end and glanced across at Jim.

"Praises be, 'twill be Billings to hit it, an' not O'Toole!" he muttered. "I have put me fut in it sufficient f'r wance!"

The ball left Jim's hand with a whizz, and Billings stepped out to meet it. Just what happened no one saw clearly for a moment, it all came to pass so quickly. Then an Irish yell from Murty O'Toole woke the echoes, even as the bowler's hand flashed up above his head—and the big stockman flung up his bat in an ecstasy of delight. Billings bit off a sharp word and left his crease; and Cunjee woke to the fact that the Mulgoan captain was caught and bowled. The match was theirs—by one run!

When Cunjee woke it became very thoroughly awake. They rushed the ground, cheering, shouting and hurling hats and caps into the air, irrespective of their owners' wishes. There was a demonstration to carry Jim in, which that hero promptly quenched by taking to his heels and leaving his too affectionate friends far in the rear. Behind him Cunjee and Mulgoa seethed together, and the air was rent with cheers. Free fights were in active progress in at least five places on the ground. It was clearly Cunjee's day out.

Jim met Wally with a grin that was distinctly sheepish.

"Knew you could!" said the Mentor, patting him happily on the back. "Good old School! But what an ass you were, Jimmy!"

"I was," said Jim, meekly.

CHAPTER XV

THE RIDE HOME

In the gathering of night-gloom o'erhead in
The still, silent change.

Gordon.

"Well, old girl?"

Norah laughed up at the big fellow delightedly.

"Oh, wasn't it lovely, Jimmy?" she said. "I was so excited—and you were grand! And wasn't Wally's catch a beauty? It's been a lovely match, hasn't it, Jim?"

"H'm—in spots," said Jim, a little doubtfully, but laughing back at her. "Rather like the fellow who said his egg was 'excellent—in parts,' don't you think? Anyhow, we won, and that's the main thing—and I never did see a catch to beat that of Wal's."

"We're all immensely proud of you, Jim," Mrs. Anderson said. "And didn't my old man do well?"

"He did, indeed," Jim agreed heartily. "But I'm not a bit proud of myself—I think I was asleep most of the time, till old Wal., here, woke me up with a few well-chosen words. However, it's over now—and Norah, I want you to get along home."

"Aren't you coming?" Norah asked, a little blankly.

"We'll have to catch you up. I don't quite like the look of the weather; we're in for a storm, that's certain, and you may possibly escape it if you get away now. I can't start just yet; the Mulgoa fellows are insisting on 'shouting' for all hands, and we can't very well refuse; besides"—he dropped his voice—"you know what Boone is—I must see that he and Murty leave Cunjee. Cecil will look after you, won't you, Cecil?"

That gentleman assented without any pleasure. He did not feel impressed with the prospect of acting as escort to a small girl when he might have remained in Cunjee. Norah was quick to notice his manner.

"I needn't bother Cecil, Jim," she said, "I can quite easily ride on by myself."

"Indeed you won't," her brother responded. "Why, it'll be dark before long—let alone the state of the weather. You don't mind, Cecil, do you?"

113

Thus directly questioned, Cecil could do nothing but express his entire willingness.

"That's all right, then," Jim said. "Hurry on down to the hotel and get the saddles on, there's a good chap. Goodness knows whether you'll find any one there, but I fancy that pretty well the whole township is up at the match. You'll only escape that storm if you're lucky--don't lose a minute." He made his farewells to Mrs. Anderson, and turned to Norah again. "Better look after your own girth," he told her--"run after Cecil and lend him a hand if he wants it."

Cecil had already started; his slim, correctly attired figure was hastening along the dusty lane. He hated rain, and the hint of the coming storm had made him hurry when no other consideration would have done so. There was no one visible about the hotel yard, as he entered, and he called in vain; then, seeing no help for it, he entered the stables, where the Billabong horses occupied the stalls at one end. Bobs whinnied sharply as the door opened, and Cecil looked at the inquiring head; and then, sourly, towards Brown Betty, standing peacefully, half asleep, in her stall.

"Wonder if she'd mind?" Cecil muttered, pondering. "Let her, anyhow!" With which cryptic remarks he moved towards the saddles.

Norah arrived on the scene a few minutes later, coming straight to the stables. For a moment she could not see Cecil, then, peering into Betty's stall, she made him out, busily girthing up. Bobs was already saddled, and Norah went up to him.

"Why, you have been quick, Cecil," she said, cheerfully. "I thought I was going to help you, but there doesn't seem anything for me to do. Thanks very much for saddling Bobs." She led the pony out, and then stopped. "Oh, what a pity," she said. "You've got the wrong saddles on, Cecil."

Cecil came out, leading the brown mare, and a little flushed.

"I did it on--ah--purpose," he said. "You don't mind, I suppose if I ride Bobs home?"

Norah looked at him a moment, and then flushed in her turn. To let her cousin ride Bobs seventeen miles was unthinkable. She had the profoundest regard for her pony's back; and she knew that even Brown Betty's seasoned hide was giving way under the unskilled horsemanship of the city boy. It was very doubtful, moreover, that it would be safe to mount him on Bobs, who was already excited with the coming storm and the prospect of home. She knew every turn, and thought of the high-spirited pony--he went quietly for her, but with a new-chum it might be a different matter.

Moreover, Norah was distinctly annoyed. She was a sweet-

114

tempered maiden, but she did not like being treated lightly; and in assuming that he might coolly appropriate her special property, it seemed to her that Cecil was treating her very lightly indeed. She had a moment's swift wish that Jim were there to take her part. It was not quite easy to oppose any one nearly grown up like Cecil—who in addition was a guest, and had a special claim on courtesy. She flushed deeply as she answered him in a low voice.

"I can't let you ride Bobs, I'm afraid, Cecil."

"Oh, can't you?" said Cecil, staring. "Why not?"

"Well, no one rides him but me," said Norah unhappily. "And he's a queer pony, Cecil. I'm not a bit sure that he'd go nicely with you. You see, I understand him."

"You evidently think no one can ride but yourself," Cecil said disagreeably. "I really think I can manage the famous Bobs."

"If you knew him it might be all right," Norah answered. "But I'd really rather not, Cecil. He's eager and impatient, and quite unaccustomed to strangers. Dad would be awfully annoyed if you had any trouble with him."

"I don't fancy Uncle David would be given any need for annoyance," Cecil replied. "I'm a bit sick of this old mare, and I don't think it would hurt you to lend me Bobs. It's uncommonly selfish of you to want to keep him always."

Norah's flush deepened.

"I'm awfully sorry you think that," she said. "And I'll speak to Dad about your riding him, if you like—another time."

"Another time? Then what's the matter with my riding him now? I suppose," said Cecil with a sneer, "you want to show off in Cunjee."

Norah stared at him blankly for a moment. Rudeness had been always so far from her that she did not for a moment comprehend that this boy was being deliberately rude. Then she walked round Bobs without replying, and unbuckled the girth.

"Please let me have my saddle," she said. Her voice was quite final.

Cecil was pale with anger. He flung round without a word, tugging at the buckle until Betty, who was patient but girth-galled, pulled away in protest. As it yielded Norah laid his saddle on the mare's withers, and slipped her own away. Their eyes met for a moment as she did so—the child's steady and a little scornful, the young man's shifty. Then Norah lifted her saddle across to Bobs, and girthed him up in silence.

The pony was restless and excited, and objected to the second saddling out in the space of the yard, when he was keen to get away. It seemed unreasonable to Bobs, and he ran round and generally behaved in a frivolous manner, while Norah struggled with the girth. When it was done, she took her head, somewhat dishevelled, from under the saddle flap. She laughed a little.

Cecil, every line of his back showing offended dignity, was riding out of the yard. As he came to the gate he dug his heel into Betty, who broke into a canter at once. Norah's escort disappeared round a turn in the street without looking back.

"Well, if he isn't a donkey!" was her comment. "He's awfully unpleasant—I wish he wouldn't make things so uncomfortable." She mounted Bobs, and subdued that excitable steed's impatience while she settled her habit. "Jim will be so angry if he finds out. I must get away before he comes."

She rode into the street. Some distance away a crowd was moving slowly in her direction. Cheers and snatches of triumphant choruses were wafted to her. In the midst she could see some figures in white flannels. Norah rounded the corner of the street, seeing ahead of her a fast-receding speck—Brown Betty and her rider. It was evident that she was not to have the benefit of Cecil's presence on the ride home; and Norah could not help laughing again, although she was annoyed at the whole occurrence. For all his airs, he was such a baby, this cousin of hers.

"I'll tell Dad all about it," she reflected. "The he can say whether he thinks Cecil can ride Bobs. Only I won't tell him he cleared out and left me, 'cause there would be a row straight away." Thus pondering in the Australian manner, she took the road home.

Jim's storm was coming up slowly, and though the sun had not yet set, already it was growing dusk; and still it was very hot. She let Bobs canter slowly, not wishing to appear to be hurrying after Cecil. Norah never bore malice, but she had her pride! Often she glanced back over her shoulder, hoping to see the boys. She knew they would not let the grass grow under their horses' hoofs, once they were able to take the road home. But the track lay bare behind her, and ahead Cecil had quite disappeared. By the time she was five miles out of Cunjee she seemed the only person in the whole landscape, and the only sound that met her ear was the steady beat of the cantering hoofs, mingled with the creak of the saddle leather.

The metalled road ended, and she struck into the bush track. It was very lonely now; trees overhung the path, and the eerie light of the coming storm threw strange shadows, at which Bobs shied constantly. Once or twice there was a distant roll of thunder. There was just light enough left to see the way. The road wound in and out among the trees. By day it was Norah's favourite part of the journey; but now she could not help wishing that it were possible to look further ahead, or to watch the road over which she had passed, to catch the first glimpse of Jim and Wally. There was a pleasant security in feeling that they were coming. Norah was not a nervous girl; but she had rarely been allowed to ride any but short distances alone. If Dad and Jim were not available, it was an understood thing that Billy must act as her escort. Certainly she had never been in the dark alone, and so far from home. She was not afraid—she would have laughed at the very notion. Still, it was a little queer. She knew she would be glad when she was out of the timber.

There came a bend in the track, and Bobs swung round it sharply. Then a dark figure loomed up suddenly in the gloom, and the pony shied violently, and propped. Norah struck her heel into him, her heart giving a great bound. He struggled and plunged. A hand was on his bridle, and a rough voice threatened him savagely. In the gloom Norah could just make out a brutal-looking man, young, but with something in his face that made her shudder. Her heart stood still for a moment, after that first wild leap. Then she realized that he was asking her for money, and she commanded her voice to answer.

"I haven't any."

It was true. When she rode with her father or brother it never occurred to Norah to carry money, and she wore nothing of value at all to tempt any thief. Her hunting-crop was silver mounted; she remembered it suddenly, glad that it was dark and that the man would not be likely to notice the gift that had been Jim's.

"I don't believe y'," he said.

"Well, you can, then," Norah answered. She was beginning to recover herself, a little ashamed of that first moment of unreasoning terror. If she had no money he would surely let her go. She scarcely knew the meaning of fear—how should she, in the free, simple life that had always been guarded, yet had left her only a little child in mind? "I haven't so much as a penny," she went on. "Let go my bridle."

"What are y' doin' here alone?" The slow voice was crafty; something in it brought back that stupid first fear. She pulled herself together.

"My people are coming—you'd better let go. If my brother gets hold of you—"

"Oh, your brother's comin', is he?"

"Yes; let go my bridle."

"Shut up about your bridle!" said the man, and Norah shrank back as if she had been stung. He began to lead Bobs off the track.

"What are you doing?" she asked angrily. She kicked Bobs again, and the pony tried to rear, caught between the sudden blow and that compelling hand on his rein. The man pulled him down savagely, jerking at his bit and flinging threats at him and at Norah.

117

"Y' might as well stop playin' the fool," he told her. "I want that pony, an' I'm goin' to have it."

To have Bobs! She tried to speak, but the words died before she could utter them. Bobs! In her bewildered terror she scarcely realized for a moment what he meant; then she raised her whip and cut with all her strength at the hand that held the rein. He gave a sharp yell of pain as the stinging whalebone caught him, but he did not relinquish his grasp, and Norah struck at him again and again, half blindly in the darkness, but always with the strength of desperation. It could not last long—the struggle was too pitifully unequal. It was only a minute before he had wrested the whip from her and held her wrists in one vice-like hand. His voice was thick with rage.

"I'll teach y'," he said, "y' little spitfire! Get off that pony."

He began to drag her off. She clung to the saddle wildly, knowing how hopeless it was, but somehow feeling that she must not leave that one poor haven of safety. Then she felt herself going, and in that sickening moment screamed for help—a child's piteous cry:

"Jim! Jim! Jim!"

There was no Jim to aid her—she knew it, even as she cried. The rough grasp tightened; she could feel his breath as he dragged her from the saddle.

Then from the darkness came a tall, stealthy shadow, and suddenly her wrists were free, as her assailant staggered back in the grip of the newcomer. She made a violent effort and found herself back in the saddle; and Bobs was plunging wildly, his bridle free. The necessity of steadying him in the timber helped her to calm herself. Before her the men were swaying backwards and forwards, blocking the way to the track; her enemy's savage voice mingling with a lower one that was somehow familiar, though she could not tell what he said. Then she saw that the struggle was ending—the tall man had the other pinned against a tree, and turned to her. His dark face was close, and she cried out to him, knowing him for a friend.

"Oh, Lal Chunder, it's you!"

"Him beat," said Lal Chunder, breathlessly. "L'il meesis orright?"

"I'm all right," she said, struggling with—for Norah—an unaccountable desire to cry. "Oh, don't let him go!"

"No," said the Hindu, decidedly. "Him hurt you? Me kill him."

The last remark was uttered conversationally, and the man against the tree cried out in fear. Lal Chunder flung at him a flood of rapid Hindustani, and he collapsed into shivering silence. Probably it was rather awe-inspiring—the great black-bearded Indian, with

118

his keen, enraged face and the voice that seemed to cut. But to Norah he was a very haven of refuge.

"Oh, you mustn't kill him," she said. "The boys will be here—men coming—quick! Can you hold him?"

"Hold him—yes—tight," said Lal Chunder, tightening his grip as he spoke, to the manifest discomfort of the man against the tree. Then came distant voices, and a snatch of a School song, mingled with quick hoofs; and Norah caught her breath in the sharpness of the relief. She rode out on the track , calling to Jim.

The boys pulled up, the horses plunging.

"Norah! What on earth—"

Norah explained rapidly, and Jim flung himself off, tossing Garryowen's rein to Wally, and ran to her.

"Kiddie—you're all right? He didn't hurt you?" The boy's voice was shaking.

"Only my wrists," said Norah, and then began to shudder as the memory of the struggle in the trees came back to her. Jim put his arm about her.

"Thank heaven for that blessed Indian!" said he. "Steady, old girl—you're all right," and Norah recovered herself.

"Yes, I'm all right, Jimmy," she said, a little shakily. "What about Lal Chunder?"

"Here's the buggy," said Wally, and in a moment Murty and Boone were on the scene, when it was the work of a few minutes to tie the prisoner with halters and hoist him into the buggy, where he lay very uncomfortable, with his head close to the splashboard. There was much explanation, and it would probably have gone hard with the prisoner but for Jim, as Murty and Boone wanted to deal out instant justice.

"Not good enough," Jim said. He was rather white, in the glow of the buggy lamps. "He'll be better safe in gaol." He turned to Lal Chunder, who had drawn close to Norah, and was contemplating his right hand, which had been nearly shaken off by the four from Billabong. The Hindu's English was not equal to his sense of friendship, and conversation with him lacked fluency. It was some time before Jim could make him understand that they wanted him to return to the station—and indeed, it was Norah who made it clear at last.

"Me want you," she said, taking the dusky hand in hers. "Come back to my home." She pointed towards the direction of Billabong. Lal Chunder capitulated immediately.

"It is an order," he said, gravely; and forthwith climbed into the buggy, a weird figure between the two stockmen, their faces still flushed with anger as they looked at the man lying between their feet.

"We'll put him away in the lock-up, an' be out agin in no time, Masther Jim," said Murty. "Take care of her me boy." And the stockman, who had known Norah since her babyhood, choked suddenly as he looked at her pale face. Norah was herself again, however, and she smiled at him cheerily.

"I'm right as rain, Murty!" she said, in the Bush idiom. "Don't you worry about me."

"'Tis pluck y' have," said the Irishman. He turned the buggy with some difficulty, for the track was narrow, and they spun off on the return journey to Cunjee, while Norah, between the two boys, was once more on the way to Billabong.

"You're sure you're all right, Nor.?" Jim said, looking at her keenly.

"Yes—truly, Jim." Norah had made up her mind not to say too much. There was nothing to be gained by harrowing them with unnecessary details—and, child-like, the memory of her terror was already fading, now that care and safety had again wrapped her about. "I was a bit scared, but that's all over."

"Then," said Jim, "can you tell me where is Cecil?" His voice was dangerously calm.

"Oh, he—he went on," Norah said. "We had a dispute, and he was a bit put out."

"A dispute? What about?"

"He wanted to ride Bobs."

"Did he? " Jim said. "And because you wouldn't let him, he cleared out and left you?"

"Well, he was offended," Norah replied slowly, "and I dare say he thought I would catch him up—instead of which I hung back, hoping you boys would catch me up. So it wasn't really his fault."

"He must have known you would be coming through that timber by yourself in the dark."

"Oh, most likely he reckoned I'd have you with me by that time. He doesn't understand very well, does he? He didn't mean any harm, Jim."

"I don't know what he meant," Jim said, angrily. "But I know what he did—and what he'd have been responsible for if Lal Chunder hadn't happened along in the nick of time. Great overgrown calf! Upon my word, when I see him—"

"Oh, don't have a row, Jim," Norah pleaded. "He's a guest."

"Guest be hanged! Do you mean to say that's excuse for behaving like a cad?"

120

"Ah, he wouldn't mean to. Don't tell him about—about Lal Chunder—and the man."

"Not tell him?" Jim exclaimed.

"Well, not to-night, anyhow. Promise me you won't have a row to-night—and if you tackle him when you get home there will be a row. Wait until Dad comes home." finished Norah, a little wearily.

Behind her, Wally leaned across to his chum. They pulled back a little.

"I say—don't worry her, old man," Wally said. "I guess she's had a bit of a shock—let's try and keep her mind off it. Do what she asks." And Jim nodded.

"All right, old woman," he said, coming alongside again. "I won't slay him to-night—don't bother your little head. We'll let Dad fix him."

Norah's grateful look rewarded him.

"Thanks, Jimmy," she said. "I—I'm feeling like having a little peace. And he'd never understand, no matter what you said."

"I suppose he wouldn't," Jim agreed. "But he's a worm! However—the storm's coming, and if we don't want wet jackets we'd better travel." They tore homewards through the hot night. Presently Wally started a chorus, and both boys were relieved when Norah joined in. They nodded at each other cheerfully behind her back. So, singing very lustily, if not in the most artistic fashion, they reached the Billagong stables just as the first heavy drops were falling.

Within, Cecil met them, a little nervously.

"I thought you were lost," he said.

"H'm," said Jim, passing him, and struggling with his promise. "Sorry you and Norah had any difference of opinion."

Cecil flushed.

"Possibly I was—ah—hasty," he said. "I did not consider I asked Norah much of a favour."

"That's a matter of opinion. At any rate, Cecil, I may as well tell you straight out that I don't consider it would be at all wise for you to ride Bobs."

"I'm not likely to hurt him."

"He might very likely hurt you. He's not an easy pony to ride."

Cecil's little laugh was irritating.

"What?" he said. "I don't profess to be a jockey, but—a child's pony?"

Jim very nearly lost his temper.

"You won't be convinced," he said, "and I've no desire to convince you with Bobs. But take my advice and let Norah alone about her pony. You've a very good mare to ride."

"That old crock!" said Cecil, scornfully.

Jim stared.

"Crock!" he said. "Well, you won't find many hacks to beat old Betty, even if in your mighty judgment she is a crock. And, anyhow, Bobs is Norah's, and no one else has any say about him. There's the bell; ready, chaps?"

The meal was scarcely lively. Cecil maintained an offended silence, and Jim was too angry to talk, while Norah was silent and a little pale. However, Cecil retired to his room immediately he had finished; and the boys set themselves to the task of diverting Norah, fearful lest the evening's adventure should have any bad effect on her. They succeeded so well that by bedtime Norah had forgotten all her troubles, and was weak with laughter. When Wally set out "to blither," as he said, he did not do things by halves.

Jim came into Norah's room and switched on her light.

"Sure you're all right, kiddie?"

"Rather!" said Norah. "I've laughed too much to be anything else."

"Then go to sleep laughing," said Jim, practically. "I'm quite close if you want anything."

"Oh, I won't want anything, thanks," Norah answered. "Good-night, Jimmy."

"Good-night, little chap."

Norah tumbled hastily into bed and slept dreamlessly. She did not know that Jim dragged a sofa and some rugs along the corridor, and slept close to her door.

"Kid might dream and wake up scared," he said to Wally, a little apologetically, before mounting guard. It was Jim's way.

CHAPTER XVI

A CHILD'S PONY

With the spirit of fire and of dew
To show the road home to them all.

Kendall.

It was quite early next morning when Cecil awoke. One of his
grievances against the country was the way in which the birds acted
as alarum clocks every day, rousing him from his well-earned
slumbers fully an hour before even the earliest milk cart rattling
along the suburban street fulfilled a similar purpose at home.
Generally, he managed to turn over and go to sleep again. This
morning, however, he was unusually wakeful.

He lay turning in his mind his anger against his cousins. Little
causes for annoyance, simple enough in themselves, had been
brooded over until they made up a very substantial total; and now,
last night's happenings capped everything. In his own heart of
hearts he knew that he had small justification for his childish
outbursts of anger; only it was not Cecil's nature to admit any such
thing, and if justification were not evident, his mind was quite equal
to manufacturing it. At the end of half an hour's gloomy pondering
he had worked himself up into a fine state of ill usage, and into the
firm belief that Norah and the boys had no intention but to insult
and humiliate him.

To some natures there is a certain comfort in nursing a
grievance, and reasoning themselves into a plaintive state of
martyrdom. When Cecil finally rolled angrily out of bed, he was
almost cheerful in the contemplation of his own unhappiness. They
were determined to sneer at him and lessen his pride, were they?
Well, they should see.

Just what they were likely to see, Cecil did not know himself, but
the reflection was soothing. Meanwhile, the birds were maddeningly
active, and an unusual restlessness was upon him. He dressed
slowly, putting on flannels, for the day promised heat, and went
downstairs.

Sarah and Mary were busy in the hall, and lifted astonished
eyebrows at seeing the boy down before the others; as a rule Cecil
strolled into the dining-room barely in time for breakfast, or was

late altogether. He took no notice of them, but wandered out to the back, where Brownie was found instructing a new kitchen assistant in the gentle art of cleaning a stove. She, too, showed amazement at the apparition, but recovered sufficiently to offer him tea and scones, to which Cecil did justice.

"Be you all going out early?" Brownie asked.

"Not that I know of." Cecil's tone did not encourage conversation.

"Seein' you so unusual early, I thought there was some plan on," said Brownie. "Master Jim's great on makin' plans, ain't he? (Meriar, elbow grease is one of the necessariest things in gettin' a shine on a stove–don't let me catch you merely strokin' it again!) An' Miss Norah's always ready to back him up–wunnerfull mates them two has alwuz been, an' Master Jim has ever and alwuz looked after her, from the d'rekly-minute he could walk!"

"Ah?" said Cecil.

"Well may you say so," said Brownie, inspired by her subject. "As loving-kind a pair as could be, have them two been; and as proud of each other–! Well, any one who reads may run! An', Master Jim never mindin' her being on'y a girl; not that that has 'ampered Miss Norah much, I will say, seein' how she rides an' all. I'm sure it's a picture to see her on that there Bobs, an' the dumb beast knows every single word she says to him. They'll fret for each other cruel, Bobs an' her, when she goes to school."

Brownie's enthusiasm was ill-timed, as far as Cecil was concerned; indeed, she could scarcely have hit upon a subject less palatable to him. Still, it was useless to interfere with the old woman; so he gulped down his tea hastily, listening with ill-concealed impatience to her talk of Norah and Bobs, and then escaped abruptly.

"H'm!" said Brownie, looking after him. "Not a word out of me noble–not even a thank you! Too much of a fine gentleman for Billabong, like his ma before him!"

"Young gent don't seem to cotton to Miss Norah," remarked the astute, if new, Maria, who had been listening with all her ears.

"When you're asked for your opinion about your betters, Meriar, it may be time to shove in your oar; but until then let me advise you to keep it in your own head," said Brownie severely. "At present your work is rubbin' that stove, and if it ain't done in remarkable quick time it'll have to be blackleaded all over again, bein' as how it'll have got too dry!" Appalled by which awful possibility, Maria fell to work with wonderful vigour, dismissing all lesser matters from her mind.

Meanwhile, Cecil strolled across the yard, and thence towards the stockyards, where a trampling of feet and a light cloud of dust showed that the men had got in the horses for the day. He selected a clean place on the top rail carefully, and cast his eye over the little mob standing in groups about the enclosure–a dozen stock horses; the big pair of greys that were used in the covered buggy or the express wagon; the brown ponies that Norah drove; his own mount Betty, and Wally's mare Nan; and then the aristocrats, Garryowen and, last of all, Bobs. Norah's pony was standing near an old black horse for which he had a great affection. They were nearly always to be found together in the yards or paddocks. Even unbrushed as he was, the sunlight rippled on his bay coat when he moved, showing the hard masses of muscle in his arched neck.

"Beauty, ain't he?" It was Mick Shanahan, on his way to another paddock to bring in some colts. He pulled up beside Cecil, the youngster he was riding sidling impatiently.

"Yes, he's a nice pony," said Cecil, without enthusiasm.

"Well, I've seen a few, but he beats 'em all," said the horsebreaker. "A ringer from the time he was a foal–and he's only improved since I first handled him, four year ago. Worth a pot of money that pony is!" He laughed. "Not as his particular owner'd sell him, I reckon. Miss Norah acts more by that chap than by anything else she's got!"

"I suppose so," Cecil said, seeing that he waited for a reply.

"Yes, my word! Take 'em all round, they'd be hard to beat as a pair," said Mick, lighting his pipe in apparent ignorance that his horse was indulging in caracoles that appeared likely to end in a bucking demonstration. He threw the match away after carefully extinguishing it, and puffed out a cloud of smoke. "Quiet, y' image, can't y'? Who's hurtin' y'? Well, I must be goin'–so long." Cecil nodded casually, and the impatient pupil went off in a series of bounds that struck the city boy as alarming, although Mick did not appear to notice that his mount was not walking demurely.

Several other men came to the stockyard, selected each a horse, and saddled it, and disappeared in various directions. The old black horse, Bob's mate, was taken by Joe Burton, who harnessed him into a dray that stood near, loaded up a number of fence rails, and drove off over the paddock, evidently to a job of repairing some boundary. Cecil watched them crawl across the plain, until they were only a speck on the grass. Then he turned his sullen eyes on Bobs, who, left alone, had come nearer to the fence where he sat, and was sleepily flicking with his tail at an intrusive fly, which insisted on walking round his hip. Cecil stared at him for some minutes before his idea came to him.

Then he flushed a little, his hand clenching on the post beside him. At first the idea was fascinating, but preposterous; he tried to

125

put it from him, but it came back persistently, and his mind held it with a kind of half-fearful excitement. They had said he could not ride him—a child's pony! Would he show them?

Once he entertained the idea at all he could not let it go. It would be such an easy way of "coming out on top"—of showing them that in one thing at least their opinion was worthless. That Jim's words were true, and that he could not master Bobs, he ridiculed loftily. It was impossible for him to believe that what a child of fourteen did so easily he might not be able to do. He had never seen Bobs other than quiet; and though big and well bred and spirited, he was still only a pony—a child's pony. Visions floated before him of increased respect paid him by the men, and even by his uncle, when he should have demonstrated his ability to manage something better than old Brown Betty, flicking at the flies in her corner of the yard, with down-drooped head, and then—he wanted to ride Bobs; and all his life Cecil Linton had done what he wanted.

He slipped down from the fence and went across to the stables for a saddle and bridle, entering the harness room a little nervously, but relieved on finding no men about. Returning, he caught Bobs—who stood like the gentleman he was—and brought him outside, where his unaccustomed fingers bungled a little with the saddle. The one he had chosen in his haste had a breastplate, but this he could not manage at all; and at last he managed to get the bewildering array of straps off, and hang it over the fence. He buckled on a pair of spurs he had found in the harness room. Then he gathered up the reins and clambered into the saddle. Possibly, had he let Bobs feel the spur, his ride would have ended there and then, and there would have been no further developments in Cecil's excursion; and it is certain that he would have spurred him cheerfully, had not the pony moved off at once. As it was he sat back and felt exceedingly independent and pleased with himself. He turned him down the home paddock.

"Phwat are y' doin' on that pony?"

Murty O'Toole had come out of the men's quarters, and was gazing open-mouthed at the unfamiliar figure on Bobs—"the city feller," for once not apparelled in exaggerated riding clothes, but in loose flannels; already the legs of the trousers had worked up from his low shoes, disclosing a vision of brilliant sock. Cecil took no notice.

"Hallo, there! Shtop a minnit! Who put y' on Bobs?"

"Mind your own business," said Cecil, between his teeth, looking round.

"My business, is it? Sure, 'tis my business, if 'tis anny man's on Billabong! Did Miss Norah say y' could ride her pony?"

126

"What's that to you?"

"Be gob!" said Murty, "'tis more to me than it is to you, seein' 'tis meself knows Miss Norah's feelin's an' disposition about Bobs! Did she give y' leave? Tell me, or I'll pull y' off, if y' was the Boss' nevvy ten times over!"

"Will you?" Cecil spat the words at him bitterly. He shook the reins, and Bobs, impatient enough already, broke into a canter that carried him away from the good friend who had intervened on his behalf. They shot across the paddock.

Murty, left helpless, said a few strong things as he looked after the retreating pair.

"It's a guinea to a gooseberry he's taken Frinch lave wid him," he said, "bitther tongued little whipper-snapper that he is! Sure if Bobs gets rid av him it'll serve him sorry, so 'twill. But phwat'll I do about it, at all?" He scratched his head reflectively. "If I go over 'twill only worry Miss Norah to hear–an' it's most likely he'll have enough av it pretty soon, an' the pony'll come home–an I do not care if he comes home widout him! I'll lave it be f'r awhile." He went slowly over to the stockyards.

Cecil, cantering over the grass with Bobs' perfect stride beneath him, was, for the moment, completely satisfied with himself. He had routed the enemy in the first engagement, and, if he had not left him speechless, at least he had had the last word. Murty and he had been at daggers drawn from the very first day, when the grinning Irishman had pulled him out of the wild raspberry clump in the cutting-out paddock; and the cheerful friendliness with which Jim and Norah treated the stockman had always irritated him. He was exceedingly pleased that on this occasion he had scored at his expense.

Where should he go? There were three gates leading out of the home paddock–one to the Cunjee road; another to a similar well-cleared plain to that on which the house stood; and a third into a smaller paddock, which in its turn led into part of the rougher and steeper part of the run. Cecil wanted to get out of sight quickly. In his mind there was a half-formed idea that Murty might saddle a horse and come out in pursuit; and a hand-to-hand encounter with the justly indignant Irishman was just at that moment the last thing that the boy wanted. So he decided upon the bush paddock, and headed in that direction.

Now, a horse that is always ridden by one person is apt to develop ideas of his own–possibly through acquiring habits insensibly from his usual rider. Also, he becomes accustomed to that one rider, and is quite likely to be annoyed by a change–not alone in weight and in style of riding, but in the absence of the sympathy that always exists between a horse so managed and the one who cares for him and understands him. The alien hand on his mouth had irritated Bobs from the first; it was heavy, and jerky, where Norah's touch was as a feather; and the light, firm seat in the saddle was changed for a weight that bumped and shifted continuously. Further, it was not very usual for Norah to ride in this direction—he had headed naturally for the second gate before his tender mouth was suddenly wrenched aside towards the third. Bobs arrived at the gate in something considerably removed from his usual contented state of mind.

The gate was awkward, and Cecil clumsy at shutting it; he hauled the pony's mouth roughly in his efforts to bring him into position where he could send home the catch. The same performance was repeated at the next gate—the one leading into the bush paddock; and when at length they turned from it Bobs' mouth was feeling the bit in a manner that was quite new to him, and as unpleasant as new. He sidled off in a rough, jerky walk, betraying irritation in every movement, had Cecil been wise enough to know it.

Cecil, however, was still perfectly content. He was out of sight of the house, which was comforting in itself; while as for the idea that he was not completely master of his mount, he would have been highly amused at it. It was pleasant to be out, in the morning freshness; and there was no need to hurry home, since the scones and tea in the kitchen had made him independent of breakfast. The paddock he was in looked interesting, too; the plain ended in a line of rough, scrub-grown hills which it occurred to him would be a good place to explore. He headed towards them.

Bobs walked on, inwardly seething; jerking his head impatiently at the unceasing pressure on his bit, and now and then giving a little half kick that at length attracted Cecil's attention, making him wonder vaguely what was wrong. Possibly something in the saddle; it had occurred to him when cantering that his girth was loose. So he dismounted and tightened it, bringing it up with a jerk that pinched the pony suddenly, and made him back away. This time Cecil did not find it so easy to mount. He was a little nervous as he rode on—and there is nothing that more quickly communicates itself to a horse than nervousness in the rider. Bobs began to dance as be went, and Cecil, hauling at his mouth, broke out into a mild perspiration. He decided that he was not altogether an easy pony to ride.

A hare jumped up abruptly in the grass just ahead. Bobs shied and plunged—and missing the hand that always understood and steadied such mistaken energy, gave a couple of rough "pig-jumps." It was more than enough for Cecil; mild as they were, he shot on to

128

the pony's neck, only regaining the saddle by a great effort. The reins flopped, and the indignant Bobs plunged forward, while his rider clawed for support, his feet and hands alike flying. As he dropped back into the saddle, the spurs went home; and Bobs bolted.

He had never in his life felt the spur; light and free in every pace, Norah's boot heel was the utmost correction that ever came to him. This sudden cruel stab on either side was more than painful—it was a sudden shock of amazement that was sharper than pain. Coming on top of all his grievances, it was too much for Bobs. Possibly, a mad race would rid him of this creature on his back, who was so unlike his mistress. His heels went up with a little squeal as he bounded forward before settling into his stride.

Cecil gave himself up for lost from the first. He tugged frantically at the rein, realizing soon that the pony was in full command, and that his soft muscles might as well pull at the side of a house as try to stop him. He lost one stirrup, and clung desperately to the pommel while he felt for it, and by great good luck managed to get his foot in again—a piece of good fortune which his own efforts would never have secured. The pommel was too comforting to be released; he still clung to it while he tried to steady himself and to see where he was going.

The plain ended abruptly just before him, and the rough hills sloped away to the south. Perhaps, if he put Bobs at the steepest it might calm him a little, and he might be able to pull him up. So he wrenched the pony's mouth round, and presently they were racing up the face of the hill, which apparently made no difference whatever to Bobs. Cecil had not the slightest idea that his heels were spurring the pony at every stride. He wondered angrily in his fear why he seemed to become momentarily more maddened, and sawed at the bleeding mouth in vain. They were at the top of the hill now. The crest was sharp and immediately over it a sharp drop went down to a gully at the bottom. It was steep, rough-going, boulder-strewn and undermined with wombat holes. Perhaps in his calmer moments Bobs might have hesitated, but just now he knew nothing but a frantic desire to escape from that cruel agony in his sides. He flung down the side of the hill blindly, making great bounds over the sparse bracken fern that hid the ground. Cecil was nearly on his shoulder now—a moment more would set him free.

Then he put his foot on a loose boulder that gave with him and went down the slope in a flurry of shifting stones. He made a gallant effort to recover himself, stumbling to his knees as Cecil left the saddle and landed in the ferns—but just as he struck out for firmer footing his forefoot sank into a wombat hole, and he turned a complete somersault, rolling over and over. He brought up against a big boulder, struggled to rise and then lay still.

* * * * *

Presently Cecil came limping to him, white and angry.

"Get up, you brute!" he said, kicking him. When there was no response, he took the bridle, jerking it. Bobs' head gave a little at every jerk, but that was all.

Between rage and fear, Cecil lost his head. He kicked the pony savagely; and finding that useless, sought a stick and thrashed him as he lay. Once Bobs struggled, but only his head and shoulders came up, and presently they fell back again. Cecil gave it up at last, and left him alone, limping down to the gully and out of sight. He sat down on a log for a long while, until the sun grew hot. Then he pulled his hat over his eyes and set off towards home.

Bobs did not know he had gone. He lay quite still.

CHAPTER XVII

ON THE HILLSIDE

Never again, when the soft winds blow,
We shall ride by the river.

G. Essex Evans.

Wally came into breakfast with a rush and a scramble, bearing traces of a hasty toilet. At the table Norah and Jim were eating solemnly, with expressions of deep disapproval. They did not raise their eyes as Wally entered.

"Awfully sorry!" said he. "You've no idea of the difficulties I've had to overcome, Norah, and all along of him!" indicating Jim with a jerk of his head. "Oh, Norah, do be sympathetic, and forget that he's your brother. I assure you I'd be a far better brother to you than ever he could, and you can have me cheap! Look up at me, Norah, and smile—one perfect grin is all I ask! He took my towel and dressed Tait in it, and for all he cared I would be swimming in that beastly lagoon yet, and dying of cramp, and nervous prostration, and housemaid's knee. And she goes on gnawing a chop!"

He sat down, and buried his face in his hands tragically, and began to sob, whereat Norah and Jim laughed, and the victim of circumstances recovered with promptitude.

"Cream, please," he said, attacking his porridge. "Oh, he's a beast, Norah. I'm blessed if I know why you keep him in the family—it can't be for either his manners or his looks! I have a hectic cough coming on rapidly. My uncle by marriage three times removed died of consumption, and it's a thing I've always been nervous about. When I occupy the family urn with my ashes you'll be sorry!"

"I should be more than sorry if it were this urn," Jim put in, grinning. "It might be an honour, of course; but we've other homely uses for the urn. How long did you swim, Wal.?"

"Never you mind," returned Wally wrathfully. "I don't see why I should satisfy any part of your fiendish curiosity—only when Brownie finds Tait wearing one of the best bath towels as a toga, and makes remarks about it, I shall certainly refer her to you!"

"I never saw a dog look so miserable as he did," Norah said, laughing. "He came straight up to me, with a truly hang-dog air, and folds of towel ever so far behind him in the grass, and didn't get back his self-respect until I took it off. Poor old Tait! You really ought to be ashamed of yourself, Jimmy."

"I am," said Jim cheerfully. "Toast, please."

"When I saw Tait last he was disappearing into the landscape with all his blushing honours thick upon him!" Wally said. "I don't see why you waste all your sympathy on the brute, and give me none. It's the greatest wonder I'm here at all!"

"Where's Cecil, anyhow?" asked Jim, suddenly.

"Haven't an idea—how should I? He wasn't in the lagoon, which is the only place I could give an expert opinion on this morning."

"Oh, he's late as usual," Norah said. "I suppose he's still cross about last night. Really, Jim, I'm sorry we've managed to rub him up the wrong way."

"Why, the difficulty would be to find the right way," Jim retorted. "He's such a cross-grained beggar—you never know when you're going to offend him; and of course he's perfectly idiotic about the horses. Wonder if he thinks we like horses with sore backs and mouths! He'll have to give poor old Betty a spell, anyhow, for she's a patch on her back the size of half a crown, thanks to him."

"Oh, dear!" said Norah, with a little shiver. "That's awfully bad news—'cause I'd about made up my mind to offer him Bobs!"

"Offer—him—Bobs!" said Jim slowly. Wally gasped.

"Just for a ride, Jimmy. He's a guest, you know, and I don't like him to feel ill-used. And you let him on Garryowen.

"Only for a moment—and then with my heart in my boots!" said Jim. "Norah, I think you're utterly mad if you lend him Bobs—after last night, too! Why, you know jolly well I've never asked you for your pony!"

"Well, you could have had him," Norah answered, "you know that, Jimmy. I don't want to lend him to Cecil—I simply hate it; but I don't like the idea of his thinking we treated him at all badly."

"He's the sort of chap that would find a grievance if you gave everything you had in the world," Jim said. "It's all rot—and I tell you straight, Nor., I don't think it's safe, either. Bobs is all right with you, of course, but he's a fiery little beggar, and there's no knowing what he'd do with a sack of flour like that on his back. I wish you wouldn't."

"What do you think, Wally?"

"Me? Oh, I'm with Jim," Wally answered. "Personally, I think a velocipede is about Cecil's form, and it's absolute insult to a pony like Bobs to ask him to carry him! And you'd hate it so, Nor.'!"

"Oh, I know I would," Norah said. "He's such a dear—"

"What! Cecil?"

"No, you donkey–Bobs," Norah continued, laughing. "I'd feel like begging his pardon all the time. But–"

"Murty wants to see you, Master Jim," said Mary, entering. "Says he'd be glad if you could spare him a minute."

"All right, Mary–thank you," said Jim, getting up lazily and strolling out. "Back in a minute, you two."

"What happens to-day, Norah? Marmalade, please," said Wally, in a breath.

"The marmalade happens on the spot," laughed Norah, handing it to him. "Otherwise–oh, I don't know, unless we ride out somewhere and fish. We haven't been out to Angler's Bend this time, have we?"

"No, but that's fifteen miles. You'd never let Cecil ride Bobs that distance?"

"Oh, I couldn't!" said Norah, hastily. "I don't think I possibly could ride anything except Bobs out there. Cecil might have him another day, if Jim doesn't think me quite mad. Perhaps I won't be sorry if he does, 'cause I'd hate to go against Jim! And Bobs is–"

"Bobs," said Wally gravely; and Norah smiled at him. "Hallo, Jamesy–what passion hangs these weights upon thy brow?"

Jim had entered quickly.

"It's that beauty Cecil," he said, angrily. "My word, Norah, I'll let that young man know what I think about him! He's taken Bobs!"

"What!"

"Gone out on Bobs before breakfast. Must have got him in the yard, and saddled him himself. Murty saw him just as he was riding off, and tried to stop him. Here's Murty–he'll tell you."

"Sure, I towld him to stop, Miss Norah," said the stock-man. "Axed him, I did, if he'd y'r lave, and he gev me back-answers as free as y' please. I was perfickly calm, an never losht me timper, an' towld him I'd pull him off av the little harse if he'd not the lave to take him; an' he put the comether on me by cantherin' off. So I waited, thinkin' not to worry y', an' that he'd be comin' back; or more be token Bobs widout him, an' small loss. But he's elsewhere yit, so I kem in f'r Masther Jim."

"Well, I'm blessed!" said Norah, weakly.

"The mean little toad!" Wally's voice was full of scorn. "I'd like five quiet minutes with him with coats off when he comes back!"

"I guess he'll get that–or its equivalent," said Jim, grimly. "Which way did he go, Murty?"

"To the bush paddock, Masther Jim. He's that stupid, tin to one he's bushed in one av thim gullies."

"Or else Bobs has slung him; but in that case Bobs would be back at the gate," Jim said. "Perhaps he is."

"No, he ain't, Masther Jim, I wint over a bit an' had a look. There's no sign av either av thim."

"Well, I suppose we'd better go after them," Jim said. "What'll you ride, Nor? Would you care for Garryowen?"

Norah smiled at him.

"No, thanks, old man. I'll have Cirdar," she said. "Can you get him, Murty?"

"In two twos, Miss Norah," said the stockman, departing hastily.

"You're not worried, Norah, old girl?" Jim said.

"Why, not exactly; he can't hurt Bobs, of course, beyond a sore back," Norah answered. "I'm more cross than worried–it is such cheek, Jim, isn't it? All the same, I hope Cecil's all right."

"Him!" said Jim, with fine scorn. "That sort never comes to any harm. Well, hurry up, and get your habit on, old chap."

There was no need to tell Norah to hurry. She flew upstairs, Brownie plodding after; the news had flown round the house in a few moments, and there was a storm of indignation against the absent Cecil.

"If I'd knowed!" said Brownie, darkly, bringing Norah's linen coat out from the wardrobe, and seeking with vigour for a felt hat that already was on her head. "Me, givin' him tea and scones, an' talkin' about the pony, too, no less; little I guessed at the depths of him. Never mind, my dearie, Master Jim'll deal with him!"

"Oh, it'll be all right, if Bobs hasn't hurt him. Only there'll be an awful row when Jim gets him. I never saw Jim so angry," Norah said.

"A good thing, too!" said the warlike Mrs. Brown. "There you are, dearie, an' there's your 'unting-crop. Off you go!" and Norah ran downstairs, finding Jim and Wally waiting, boots and leggings on. They set off, Murty muttering dark threats against Cecil as he shut the gate of the stable yard after them.

Wally had recovered his cheerfulness, never long absent from him, and was, besides, not unpleasantly excited at the thought of war ahead. He chattered gaily as they rode through the first two paddocks. But Jim remained quiet. As Norah said, she had never seen him so angry. Anxiety in his mind warred with hot anger against the insult to Norah and to them all. He swept the bush paddock with his eye as they came up to it, seeing nothing but the scattered bullocks here and there.

"Wonder which way he'd go," he said. "Suppose you and Wally cut over to the right, Norah, and see if you can find any trace. I'll go over this way. We'll coo-ee to each other if we come across him." They separated, and Jim put Garryowen at a canter across the plain.

Here and there he could see a track—and something made him wish to go on alone.

He was nearly at the foot of the hills when a figure came out from their shadow. Jim gave a sudden little sound in his throat as he saw that it was Cecil—and alone. He was limping a little, and had evidently been down. Relief that he was safe was the first thought; then, anxiety being done with, there was no room for anything but anger. Jim rode towards him. At the sight of his approach Cecil started a little, and cast a glance round as if looking for a hiding place; then he came on doggedly, his head down.

"I've been looking for you," Jim said, controlling his voice with difficulty. "Where's Bobs?"

"Over there." Cecil jerked his hand backwards.

"Where?"

"Back there."

"What do you mean? did he get away from you?"

"He bolted," Cecil said.

"And threw you?"

Cecil nodded. "Yes—can't you see I'm limping?"

"Well, did he clear out again?"

"No—he's over there."

Jim's face went grim. "Do you mean—you don't mean the pony's hurt?"

"He won't get up," said Cecil, sullenly. "I've tried my best."

For a moment they faced each other, and then Cecil quailed under the younger boy's look. His eyes fell.

Jim jumped off. "Go on."

"Where?"

"Back to Bobs, of course. Hurry up!"

"I can't go back there," Cecil said, angrily. "I'm limping, and—"

"Do you think your limp matters an atom just now?" Jim said, through his teeth. "Hurry up."

He followed Cecil, not trusting himself to speak. A dull despair lay on his heart, and above everything a great wave of pity for the little sister across the paddock. If he could spare Norah—!

Then they were in the gully, and he saw Bobs above him, and knew in that instant that he could spare her nothing. The bay pony lay where he had fallen, his head flung outwards; helplessness in every line of the frame that had been a model of strength and beauty an hour ago. As Jim looked Bobs beat his head three times against the ground, and then lay still. The boy flung round, sick with horror.

"Why, you vile little wretch—you've killed him!"

He had Cecil in a grip of iron, shaking him as a dog shakes a rat—not knowing what he did in the sick fury that possessed him. Then

135

suddenly he stopped and hurled him from him into the bracken. He ran down the gully.

"Go back, Norah dear—don't come."

Norah and Wally had come cantering quickly round the shoulder of the hill. She was laughing at something Wally had said as they rode into the gully, and the laugh was still on her lips as she looked at Jim. Then she saw his face, and it died away.

"What is it, Jim?"

"Don't come, kiddie," the boy said, wretchedly. "Wally, you take her home."

"Why?" said Norah. "We saw Cecil—where's Bobs?" Her eyes were wandering round the gully. They passed Cecil, lying on his face in the bracken, and travelled further up the hill. Then she turned suddenly white, and flung herself off Sirdar.

Jim caught her as she came blindly past him.

"Kiddie—it's no good—you mustn't!"

"I must," she said, and broke from him, running up the hillside. Jim followed her with a long stride, his arm round her as she stumbled through the ferns and boulders. When they came to Bobs he held her back for a moment.

The pony was nearly done. As they looked his head beat the ground again unavailingly, and at the piteous sight a dry sob broke from Norah, and she went on her knees by him.

"Norah—dear little chap—you mustn't." Jim's voice was choking. "He doesn't know what he's doing, poor old boy—it isn't safe."

"He wants me," she said. "Bobs—dear Bobs!"

At the voice he knew the pony quivered and struggled to rise. It was no use—he fell back, though the beautiful head lifted itself, and the brown eyes tried to find her. She sat down and took his head on her knee, stroking his neck and speaking to him... broken, pitiful words. Presently she put her cheek down to him, and crouched there above him. Something of his agony died out of Bobs' eyes. He did not struggle any more. After a little he gave a long shiver, straightening out; and so died, gently.

* * * * *

"Come on home, old kiddie."

It seemed a long time after, Norah could not think of a time when she had done anything but sit with that quiet head on her knee. She shuddered all over.

"I can't leave him."

"You must come, dear." Jim's hands were lifting Bobs' head as

136

tenderly as she herself could have done it. He picked her up and held her as though she had been a baby, and she clung to him, shaking.

"If I could help you!" he said, and there were tears in his eyes. "Oh, Nor.—you know, don't you?"

He felt her hand tighten on his arm. Then he carried her down the hill, where Garryowen stood waiting.

"The others have gone," he said. "I sent them home—Wally and— that brute! I've told him to go—I'll kill him if I see him again!" He lifted her into his saddle, and keeping his arms round her, walked beside the bay horse down the gully and out upon the plain.

"Jim," she whispered—somewhere her voice had gone away—"you can't go home like that. Let me walk." His arm tightened.

"I'm all right," he said—"poor little mate!"

They did not speak again until they were nearly home—where, ahead, Brownie waited, her kind eyes red; while every man about the homestead was near the gate, a stern-faced, angry group that talked in savage undertones. Murty came forward as Jim lifted Norah down.

"Miss Norah," he said. "Miss Norah, dear—sure I'd sooner—"

The tall fellow's voice broke as he looked at the white, childish face.

"Thanks, Murty," Norah said steadily.

"And—all of you." She turned from the pitying faces, and ran indoors.

"Oh, Brownie, don't let any one see me!"

Then came a dazed time, when she did not know anything clearly. Once, lying on her bed, with her face pressed into the pillow, trying not to see a lean head that beat on the ground, she heard a dull sound that rose to an angry shout from the men; and immediately the buggy drove away quickly, as Wally took Cecil away from Billabong. She only shivered, pressing her face harder. Jim was always near at first; the touch of his hand made her calm when dreadful, shuddering fits came over her. All through the night he sat by her bed, watching ceaselessly.

Then there was a longer time when she was alone, and there seemed much going to and fro. But no sounds touched her nearly. She could only think of Bobs, lying in the bracken, and calling silently to her with his pain-filled eyes.

Then, late on, the second evening, Jim came back with a troubled face and sat on the bed.

"Norah," he said, "I want you."

"Yes, Jim?"

137

"I want you to be brave, old chap," he said slowly. Something in his tone made her start and scan his tired face.

"What is it?" she asked.

"It may be all right," Jim said, "but—but I thought I'd better tell you, Norah, they—we can't find Dad!"

CHAPTER XVIII

BROTHER AND SISTER

We were mates together,
And I shall not forget.

W. H. Ogilvie.

Jim had not wanted to tell Norah. It had been Brownie who had counselled differently.

"I think she's got enough to bear," the boy had said, sitting on the edge of the kitchen table, and flicking his boots mechanically with his whip. He had been riding hard almost all day, but anxiety, not fatigue, had put the lines into his face. "What's the good of giving her any more?"

"I do believe it'd be best for her, the poor lamb!" Brownie had said. "She's there all day, not speaking–it'll wear her out. An' you know, Master Jim, dear, she'd never forgive us for keepin' anything back from her about the master."

"No–but we've nothing definite. And it may make her really ill, coming on top of the other."

"I don't think Miss Norah's the sort to let herself get ill when there was need of her. It may take her poor mind off the other–she can't help that now, an' he was only a pony–"

"Only a pony! By George, Brownie–!"

"Any horse is only a pony when compared to your Pa," said Brownie, unconscious of anything peculiar in her remark. "I don't know that real anxiety mayn't help her, Master Jim. And any'ow, it don't seem to me we've the right to keep it from her, them bein', as it were, that partickler much to each other. Take my tip, an' you tell her."

"What do you think, Wally?"

"I'm with Brownie," said Wally, unexpectedly. "It's awful to see Norah lying there all day, never saying a word, and this'll rouse her up when nothing else would." So Jim had yielded to the weight of advice, and had gone slowly up to tell Norah they could not find David Linton.

"Can't find him?" she echoed. "but isn't he at Killybeg?"

"He left there yesterday morning," Jim answered. "A telegram came from him last night, and it was important–something about

139

cattle—so I sent Burton into Cunjee with it—Killybeg's on the telephone now, you know, and Burton could ring him up from the post office. But the Darrells were astonished, and said he'd left there quite early, and meant to come straight home."

"Well?" Norah was white enough now.

"Well, I got worried, and so did Murty; because you know there isn't any stopping place between here and Killybeg when you come across the ranges. And Monarch's pretty uncertain—in rough country, especially. So I got Murty and Wally to go out at daylight this morning, taking the straight line to the Darrells, and they picked up his tracks pointing homewards about five miles from the Billabong boundary. Murty made Monarch's shoes himself, and he could swear to them anywhere. They followed them awhile, and they came to a place where the ground was beaten down a lot, as if he'd had trouble with Monarch; I expect something scared him, and he played the fool. But after that the tracks led on to some stony rises, and they lost them; the ground was too hard. They could only tell he'd gone right off the line to Billabong."

"Jim! Do you think—? Oh, he couldn't be hurt! Monarch would never get rid of him."

"He'd stick to Monarch as long as the girth held and Monarch stood up," Jim said. "but it's rough country, and a young horse isn't handy on those sidings. Of course it may be all right; but if so, why wasn't he home twenty-four hours ago?"

"Have you done anything?"

"Been out all day," Jim said. "Murty sent Wal. straight home while he went on looking, and we went back with three of the men. But you know what that country is, all hills and gullies, and the scrub's so thick you can scarcely get through it in places. We found one or two hoof marks, but that was all. If he's not home to-night we're going out at daybreak with every hand on the place."

"I'm coming."

"I knew you'd want to," Jim said, anxiety in his tone. "But I don't think you're fit to, old girl."

"Jimmy, I'd go mad if I stayed behind."

"Oh, I know that, too. But you'll have to stay near me, Norah. and if you're coming you've got to eat now; Brownie says you've touched nothing all day."

Norah shivered a little. "I'm not hungry."

"No, but you've sense, old chap. You'd be the first to say one of us couldn't go out without proper food. Try, won't you?"

"I'll try," Norah said, obediently.

"Brownie's got dinner for Wally and me in the breakfast-room," Jim said. "Wouldn't you come down, old girl? It's only old Wal., you

140

know, and—and he's so awfully sorry for you, Nor. He's been such a brick. I think it would cheer him up a bit if you came down."

"All right," Norah said, hesitating a moment. "But I'm bad company, Jim."

"We're none of us lively," said the boy. "But we've got to help each other." And Norah looked at him gently, and came.

Dinner was quiet, for the shadow hung upon them all. Wally tried to talk cheerfully, checked by a lump that would rise in his throat whenever he looked at Norah, who was "playing the game" manfully, trying hard to eat and to be, as she would have said, "ordinary." They talked of the plans for the next day, when a systematic search was to be made through the scrub near where the tracks had been found.

"Each of us is to take a revolver," Jim said; "there are five altogether, and the men who haven't got them will have to use their stockwhips as signals if they find anything. Three shots to be fired in the air if help is wanted. And Brownie has flasks ready for every one, and little packets of food with some chocolate; if he's come to grief it'll be nearly forty-eight hours since he had anything to eat. Two of the men are to take the express wagon out as far as it can go, with everything to make him comfortable, if—if he's hurt. Then they can ride the horses on to help us search." Jim forced a sorry smile. "Won't he grin at us if he turns up all right? We'll never hear the end of it!" Then he got up abruptly and walked to the window, looking out across the moonlit flats; and they were all silent.

"I keep thinking all the time I hear him coming," Jim said, turning back into the room. "If you keep still, you can almost swear you can hear old Monarch's hoofs coming up the track—and half a dozen times I've been certain I caught the crack of his stockwhip. Of course, it's—it's all imagination. My word! it's hard to loaf about here and go to bed comfortably when you want to be hunting out there."

"You couldn't do any good, though?" asked Wally.

"No—it would be madness to go straying round those gullies in the moonlight; it's not even full moon, and there the timber's so thick that very little light can get through. There's nothing for it but to wait until daylight."

"It's hard waiting," Norah said.

"Yes, it is. But you ought to go to bed, old woman; you had precious little sleep last night, and the big bell is to ring at daylight."

"Then won't you boys go, too?"

"Yes, I guess we'd better," Jim said. "I'll come in and say good-night to you, Norah." A look passed between them; the boy knew his father never failed to pay a good-night visit to Norah's room. She smiled at him gratefully.

141

It was very lonely and quiet up there, undressing, with her heart like lead within her. She hurried over her preparations, so that she might not keep Jim waiting when he came; she knew he needed sleep–"a big boy outgrowing his strength like that," thought Norah, with the quaint little touch of motherliness that she always felt towards Jim. Once she caught sight of something on the end of the couch; the white rug that had been Jim's Christmas present, with the scarlet B standing out sharply in the corner–the rug Bobs would never use. Shivering a little, she put it away in her wardrobe. Just now she could only think of that most dear one–perhaps lying out there in the cold shadows of the bush night. She crept into bed.

Jim came in in his shirt sleeves.

"Comfy, little chap?"

"Yes, thanks, old man. Jim–shall I ride Sirdar tomorrow?"

"You needn't have asked," the boy said–"he's yours. And, Norah–I know Dad wouldn't mind. I'd like you to have Garryowen. He's a bit big, but he'll suit you quite well. I know he won't make up, but you'd get fond of him in time, dear."

"Jim!" she said–knowing all that the carelessly spoken words meant–"Jimmy, boy." And then Jim was frightened, for Norah, who had not cried at all, broke into a passion of crying. He held her tightly, stroking her, not knowing what to say; murmuring broken, awkward words of affection, while she sobbed against him. After a while she grew quiet, and was desperately ashamed.

"I didn't mean to make an ass of myself," she said, contritely. "I'm awfully sorry, and you were such a brick to me, Jimmy. I won't ever forget it; only I couldn't take your horse. I love you for it. But Sirdar will do for me quite well." And no arguments could shake her from that decision.

Jim put the light out after some time. Then he came back and sat down on the bed.

"I wanted to tell you, dear little chap," he said, gently. "I sent Mick out with Boone to-day, and–and they buried him under that big tree where he fell, and heaped up stones so that nothing could get at him." He stopped, his voice uncertain as Norah's hand tightened in his.

"Mick said there couldn't have been any hope for him, kiddie," he went on, presently. "His back was broken; no one could have done anything." He would not tell her of other things Mick had seen–the spur wounds from hip to shoulder and the marks of the stick that Cecil had thrown down beside the pony he had ridden to his death. "They carved his name on the tree in great big letters. Some time– whenever you feel you can–I'll take you out there. At least"–his hand gripped hers almost painfully–"Dad and I will take you."

142

Norah put her face against him, not speaking. They stayed so, her breath coming and going unevenly, while Jim stroked her shoulder. Presently he slipped to his knees by the bed, one arm across her, not moving until her head nestled closer, and he knew she was asleep. Then the big, tired fellow put his own head down and went to sleep as he knelt, waking, stiff and sore, in the grey half light that just precedes the dawn. He crept away noiselessly, going out on the balcony for a breath of the chill air.

Below him, against the stockyard fence, a black shadow stood and whinnied faintly. Jim's heart came into his throat, and he swung himself over the edge of the balcony, using his old "fire escape" to slide to the gravel below. He ran wildly across to the yard.

A moment later the big bell of the station clanged out furiously.

Norah, fastening her habit with swift fingers, ran to open the door in answer to Jim's voice.

"Hurry all you know, little chap," he said. "I'm off in a few minutes—breakfast's ready. Wally's going into Cunjee with a telegram to Melbourne for the black trackers, as hard as he can ride."

"Jim—there's something you know!"

He hesitated.

"I'd better tell you," he said. "Monarch's come home alone, Norah!"

143

CHAPTER XIX

THE LONG QUEST

The creek went down with a broken song,
'Neath the she oaks high;
The waters carried the song along,
And the oaks a sigh.

Henry Lawson.

The big black thoroughbred still stood by the rails as they rode away. He had got rid of the saddle, and the broken bridle trailed from his head. No one had time to see to him.

Billabong was humming with activity. Men were running down to the yards, bridle in hand; others leading their horses up to be saddled; while those who were ready had raced over to the quarters for a snatched breakfast. Sirdar and the boys' horses had been stabled all night, so that they were quickly saddled. Jim was riding Nan; Wally, on Garryowen, was already a speck in the distance.

"You'll be quicker if you take him," Jim had said. Then he and Norah had cantered away together.

"Monarch wasn't hurt, Jim?"

"He'd been down, I think," Jim said; "His knees look like it. But he's all right—why, he must have jumped three fences?"

After that for a long time they did not speak. Grim fear was knocking at both their hearts, for with the return of the black horse without his rider, their worst dread was practically confirmed. It was fairly certain that Mr. Linton was helpless, somewhere in the bush, and that meant that he had been so for nearly two days, since it was almost that time since he had ridden away from Killybeg.

Two days! They had been days of steady, relentless heat, untempered by any breeze—when the cattle had sought the shade of the gum trees, and the dogs about the homestead had crept close in under the tree lucernes, with open mouths and tongues lolling. The men working on the run had left their tasks often to go down to the creek or the river for a drink; in the house, closely shuttered windows and lowered blinds on the verandahs had only served to make the heat bearable. And he had been out in it, somewhere, helpless, and perhaps in pain; with nothing to ease for him the hot hours or to save him from the chill of a Victorian night, which, even

144

in midsummer, may be sharply cold before the dawn. The thought gnawed at his children's hearts.

They passed through the billabong boundary and out into the rough country beyond, sharply undulating until it rose into the ranges David Linton had crossed on his way to and from Killybeg. They had been fairly certain that he had come through them safely on his way home, and the thought had been a comfort—for to seek a man in those hills was a hopeless task. But suddenly a sick fear came over Norah.

"Jim," she said, "we don't know where Monarch got rid of Dad, of course?"

"No; but I expect it was near where they picked up his tracks."

"You don't think it might have been in the ranges?"

Jim looked suddenly aghast; but his face cleared.

"No," he said, decidedly; "I don't. That place where Monarch had been playing up shows Dad must have been on him—a horse alone doesn't go to market as he seems to have done there. I guess you can put that notion out of your head, mate." He smiled at Norah, who answered him with a grateful look.

Five miles from the boundary they came upon the tracks—to see them gave Norah a queer sense of comfort, since in a way they brought her in touch with Dad. Then they separated, beating into the scrub that hemmed them round everywhere, except when low, stony hills rose naked out of the green undergrowth.

"We must shout to each other every few minutes to make sure we're not getting too far apart," Jim said. "Of course, it's not so risky when you're riding—if you gave old Sirdar his head anywhere I know he'd take you home. Still, you don't gain anything by going far apart. A systematic search is what's necessary in a place like this, where you might ride half a dozen yards from him and not see him. Keep Tait with you, Norah."

"All right," Norah nodded. "What about coo-eeing, Jim? He might hear a shout and answer it, even if he couldn't see us."

"Yes, but you can't keep coo-eeing all the time," said Jim, practically. "I'll tell you what—sing or whistle. You can do that easily, and it doesn't tire you. And of course, if you find him, fire the revolver—you're sure you've got it carefully?"

"Yes, it's all right," Norah replied, showing the revolver in its neat leather case. Jim and her father had taught her its use long ago, and she understood it quite well. Mr. Linton held the view that all women in the bush should know how to handle fire arms, since the bush is a place where no one ever knows exactly what may turn up, from burglars to tiger snakes. "Fire three times in the air, isn't it, Jim?"

145

"Yes, that's right. Go on then, kiddie, and do take care!" Jim's voice was strained with anxiety and wretchedness. While Norah was full of hope, and, indeed, could scarcely realize that they might not find Dad soon, the boy had the memory of the fruitless search all the previous day to dispirit him. As he looked at the forbidding wall of green scrub, his feeling was almost one of despair.

It did not take long for Norah to realize the difficulty of their task. She beat up and down among the trees, striving to keep an eye in every direction, since any one of the big stumps, any clump of brushwood, any old log or little knoll or grassy hollow might hide the one she sought—unable, perhaps, to see her or call to her even should she pass in his sight. She remembered Jim's advice, and began to sing; but the words died in her throat, and ended in something more like a sob. Whistling was more possible, and mechanically she took up a tune that Wally used to sing, and whistled it up and down the scrub as she went. Soon she did not know that she was doing so; but years after she used to shudder within herself if she heard that foolish little tune.

The men came out a little later, and soon the scrub was alive with voices and the noise of the searching. It was weary work, with many a flutter at the heart when a sudden call would bring Norah to attention, rigid and listening—forgetting for the moment that only the three signals agreed upon were to give evidence of success. Hour after hour went by.

They had settled a certain signal to meet for lunch, and when it finally summoned them the searchers struggled out of the bush one by one. Jim's heart smote him as he saw Norah's white face, and he begged her to cease; to stay resting during the hot afternoon, even if she would not go home. Norah shook her head dully. She could not do it; and Jim, knowing how he would have felt were he in her place, did not press her, although he was miserably anxious. They sat down together on an old log, finding a shred of comfort in each other's nearness.

It was a silent party that gathered round when black Billy had the big quart pots of tea ready. No one seemed to have anything to say. Norah thought, with a catch at her heart, of the last time they had picnicked in the scrub; the happy talk and laughter, the dear foolish jokes and merriment. This was indeed a strange picnic—each man eating rapidly and in silence, and everywhere stern preoccupied faces. There was no waiting afterwards for the usual "smoke oh"; the men sprang up as soon as the hurried meal was over, and lit their pipes as they strode away. Soon the temporary camp was deserted—black Billy, the last to leave, muttering miserably to himself, hurrying back into the bush. The search went on.

There was no riding in the afternoon; they were in country where the tangle of dogwood and undergrowth was so thick that to take a horse through it meant only lost time, and hindered the thoroughness of the quest. Norah fought her way through, keeping her line just as the men kept theirs; her white coat stained and torn now, her riding skirt showing a hundred rents, her boots cut through in many places. She did not know it; there was only room in her heart for one thought. When, while waiting for lunch, she had heard Dave Boone say something in an angry undertone about Bobs, she had wondered dully for a moment what he meant. She had forgotten even Bobs.

The hours went by, and the sun drooped towards evening. In the dark heart of the scrub the gloom came early, making each shadow a place of mystery that gave false hope to the searchers a hundred times. Gradually it was too dark to look any more; for that day also they must give it up—the third since Monarch had broken free from his master and left him lying somewhere in the green fastness about them. There scarcely seemed a yard of it left unsearched. Despair was written on most of the faces as the men came one by one to their horses and rode home, picking up on their way those who were still beating the bush as far as the Billabong boundary.

Jim and Norah were the last to leave. They came back to the horses together, Tait at their heels, his head and tail down. Norah was stumbling blindly as she walked, and Jim's arm was round her. He put her up, and turned silently to unfasten his own bridle.

"Jim," she said, and stopped. "Jim, do you think we'll find him in—in time?"

Jim hesitated, trying to bring himself to say what he dared no longer think. Then he gave way suddenly.

"No," he said, hoarsely, "I don't; I don't believe we ever will!" He put his head down on the saddle and sobbed terribly—dry, hard sobs that came from the bottom of his big heart. And Norah had no word of comfort. She sat still on Sirdar, staring in front of her.

Presently Jim stood up and climbed into the saddle, and the impatient horses moved off quickly towards home, Tait jogging at their heels. Once Jim turned towards his sister, saying, "Are you quite knocked up, old girl?" Norah only shook her head—she did not know that she was tired. Neither spoke again.

It was perhaps a mile further on that Norah pulled up sharply, and whistled to Tait. The collie had slipped off into the undergrowth—she could hear him moving on dry sticks that crackled beneath him. He whined a little, but did not come.

"Don't wait," Jim said. "He'll catch us up in a minute."

"He always comes if I whistle," Norah answered, her brow

147

puckering. "I don't understand. Wait a moment, Jim." She had slid off her pony and followed Tait almost before Jim realized that she was gone.

The dog was nosing along a big log, the ruff on his neck bristling. As Norah saw him he leaped upon it, and down on the other side. Then she heard him bark sharply, and flung herself over the log after him. He was licking something that lay in the shadows, almost invisible at first, until the dim light showed a white glimmer. It was instinct more than sight that told Norah it was her father's face.

"Daddy–oh, Dad!"

The wild cry turned Jim to stone for a moment–then he was off his horse and through the scrub like a madman to where Norah knelt beside the still form, sobbing and talking incoherently, and screwing blindly at the cap of the flask she carried. They forced a little of the stimulant between the set teeth, once a terrified examination had told them that he still breathed; then Jim struck match after match, trying to see the extent of his injuries–a hopeless task by the flickering light that lasted only an instant. He put the box in his pocket at last.

"It's no good," he said, "we can't see. Wonder if the men are out of hearing." Running to the horses, standing patiently with trailing bridles, he fired off all his revolver shots in quick succession, and coo-ed again and again. Then he went back to where Norah sat in the darkness and held her father's hand.

"Don't wait," she said. "I'm sure they're out of hearing, Jim, darling. And we couldn't dare to move him by ourselves. Tear in and bring the men–and send for the doctor."

"I don't like to leave you here alone," he said, anxiously.

"Alone!" Norah said, in amazement. "But I've got Dad!"

"Yes," he said, "but–"

"Oh, do fly, Jimmy!" she said. "Leave me the matches. I'm all right."

She heard him crash back to the horses, and then the swift thud of Nan's hoofs grew fainter and fainter as he spurred her madly over the rough ground, galloping off for help. The darkness seemed all at once to be more complete, and the scrub to come closer, like a curtain round them–round her and Dad, who was found again. She put her ear close to his mouth–the breathing was a little more distinct, and so far as she could tell his head was uninjured. One leg was doubled up beneath him in an ugly manner. Norah knew she must not try to move it; but even in the darkness she was sure that it was badly hurt, and the tears were falling on David Linton's face as Norah crept back after her examination. It was horrible to see Dad, of all people, helpless and still.

148

Perhaps it was the tears that woke him from his stupor. He stirred a little, and groaned. At the sound, Norah, on her knees beside him, trembled very exceedingly, with a mixture of joy and fear that almost took her breath. She spoke softly.

"Dad!"

"Is it—you?" said David Linton, weakly. The darkness hid his face, but to hear his voice again was wonderful; and Norah's hands shook as she wrestled with the flask.

"Yes, it's me," she said. "Oh, Dad, dear old Dad, are you much hurt?"

"I don't know." The voice was very faint. Her fears surged back.

"Try to drink some of this—it's weak, and you won't choke," she said. "Is your head hurt, Daddy? Could I lift it a little?"

"Not hurt," he managed to say. So she groped in the darkness to lift the heavy head, and together they made a sorry business of the flask, spilling far more than he drank. Still, some went the right way; and presently he spoke again, his voice stronger.

"I knew you'd come... mate."

"Tait found you," she said. "And Jim was here, but he's gone for the men. We'll take care of you, Daddy. Could I move you any way to help?"

"Better not," he said. "Just—be there." His hand closed on hers, and he seemed to slip off into unconsciousness again, for when she spoke to him he did not answer. So Norah sat and held his hand; and the night crept on.

"Coo-ee!" Far off a shout. She slipped her hand away gently, and ran a little way before answering, lest the cry should startle him. Then she shouted with all her strength; and soon the beat of hoofs came nearer and out of the darkness Jim came back, Murty galloping with him.

"He's spoken," said Norah; "but he's gone off again. And he's had some whisky."

"Did he know you?"

"Yes; but he's terribly weak." They were all beside Mr. Linton now, and Murty struck a match, and carefully shading it, scanned the fallen man's face by its glimmer. Norah saw his own change as he looked. Then the match went out, and for a moment it was darker than ever.

"They're bringing things," Jim said. He took off his coat and spread it over his father, and Murty did the same. "And the doctor's coming—it's wonderful luck—he came out from Cunjee with Wally." Jim put his hand on Norah's. "Were you all right, old kiddie?"

"Quite right," said she. Then they waited silently until a rattle of

149

wheels came as the express wagon clattered up. Murty went out to the track to bring the doctor in.

Dr. Anderson cast a glance at Norah by the light of the lanterns they had brought, and spoke to Jim.

"Take her away," he said. "I don't want you, either. Murty and Boone will help me." So the two who were only children wandered off into the scrub together, sitting on a log, silently, in sick anxiety, while the doctor was busy. A groan came to them once, and Norah shuddered and put her face into her hands, while Jim, who had himself shivered at the sound, put his arm round her, and tried to whisper something, only his voice would not come. Then—ages later, it seemed—the doctor's voice:

"Are you two there?"

They hurried to him.

"We'll get him home," the doctor said. "A risk, moving him; but it's worse to leave him lying under that log. The men are getting some of the dogwood down, so that we can carry him out better. He's badly knocked about, but his head's all right. The leg is the worst; it's fractured in two places. You'll have a patient for a good while, Norah."

"Then—then he won't die?"

"Die?" said the doctor. "Not a bit of it! He'll—ah, you poor child!" For Norah had turned and clung to Jim, and was sobbing, while the big fellow who bent over her and patted her was himself unable to speak. Little Dr. Anderson patted them both, and choked himself, though he hid it professionally with a cough. He remarked afterwards that he had not known that young Norah Linton could cry.

It was only for a minute, though. The men came back carrying a stretcher, and Norah and Jim sprang to help. Very gently they lifted David Linton's unconscious form, and the four bore him slowly to the wagon, Norah backing in front with two lanterns to light every step.

"Chancy work through them dorgwood spikes," said Dave Boone. But they came out safely, and got him into the wagon, where a mattress was in readiness. The doctor heaved a sigh of relief when the business was done. So they took him home, the grey horses pulled into a slow walk, while Jim and Norah rode ahead to find the smoothest track.

It was past midnight when the lights of the homestead came into view; but everywhere Billabong was up. The men were round the open gate of the yard, from Andy Ferguson, the tears running unheeded down his old face, to Lee Wing, for once without his wide benevolent smile, and in the background Lal Chunder's dark face.

150

Beyond them was Mrs. Brown, with the pale-faced girls behind her. There were a score of willing hands to bring David Linton into his home.

A little later Jim came out to where Norah waited in the hall, a little huddled figure in one corner of a leather armchair.

"He's quite comfortable," he said; "hasn't spoken, but the doctor says it's a natural sleep, and Brownie and he are going to sit with him. Old kiddie, are you awfully tired?"

"I'm not tired one bit!" said Norah, with no idea that she was not speaking the exact truth.

"H'm!" said Jim, looking at her. He went into the dining-room, returning a minute later with a glass of wine.

"You're to have this," he said authoritatively, "and then I'm going to put you to—"

He broke off, looking at her with a little smile on his tired face. Norah had put her head down on the arm of the big chair, and was fast asleep.

CHAPTER XX

MATES

The sleepy river murmurs low,
And far away one dimly sees,
Beyond the stretch of forest trees,
Beyond the foothills dusk and dun,
The ranges sleeping in the sun.

A. B. Paterson.

Autumn was late that year at Billabong, and the orchard trees were still green, though a yellow leaf showed here and there in the Virginia creeper, as David Linton lay on the verandah and looked out over the garden. From his couch he could see the paddock beyond, and here and there the roan hides of some of his Shorthorns. They did not generally graze there; but Jim had brought some into the paddock the day before, remarking that he was certain his father would recover much more quickly if he could see a bullock now and then. So they grazed, and lay about in the yellow grass, and David Linton watched them contentedly.

From time to time Mrs. Brown's comfortable face peeped out from door or window, with an inquiry as to her master's needs; but he was not an exacting patient, and usually met her with a smile and "Nothing, Brownie, thanks—don't trouble about me." Lee Wing came along, shouldering a great coil of rubber hose like an immense grey snake, and stopped for a cheerful conversation in his picturesque English; and Billy, arriving from some remote corner of the run, left his horse at the gate and came up to the verandah, standing a black statue in shirt, moleskins and leggings, his stockwhip over his arm, while Mr. Linton asked questions about the cattle he had been to see. Afterwards Mrs. Brown brought out tea, having met and routed with great slaughter Sarah, who was anxious to have the honour that up to to-day had been Norah's alone.

"It's dull for you, sir," she said. "No mistake, it do make a difference when that child's not in the house!"

"No doubt of that," Mr. Linton said. "But I'm getting on very well, Brownie, although I certainly miss my nurses."

"Oh, we can make you comferable an' all that," Brownie said, disparagingly. "But when it comes to a mate, we all know there ain't any one for you like Miss Norah—though I do say Master Jim's as handy in a sick-room as that high-flown nurse from Melbourne ever was—I'm glad to me bones she's gone!" said Brownie, in pious relief.

"So am I," agreed the squatter hastily. "Afraid I don't take kindly to the imported article—and I'm perfectly certain Norah and she nearly came to blows many times."

"An' small wonder," said Brownie, her nose uplifted. "Keepin' her out of your room, if you please—or tryin' to—till Miss Norah heard you callin' her, an' simply came in at the winder! An' callin' her 'ducksy bird.' I ask you, sir," said Brownie, indignantly, "is 'ducksy bird' the thing anybody with sense'd be likely to call Miss Norah?"

"Poor Norah!" said Mr. Linton, laughing. "She didn't tell me of that indignity."

"Many a trile Miss Norah had with that nurse as I'll dare be sworn, she'd never menshin to you, sir," Brownie answered. "She wouldn't let a breath of anything get near you that'd worry you. Why, it was three weeks and more before she'd let you be told about Bobs!"

David Linton's brow darkened.

"I couldn't have done any good, of course," he said. "But I'm sorry I couldn't have helped her at all over that bad business. Well, I hope Providence will keep that young man out of my path in future!"

"An' out of Billabong," said Brownie with fervour. "Mr. Cecil's safer away. I guess even now he'd have a rough time if the men caught him—an' serve him right!"

"He seems penitent," Mr. Linton said, "and even his mother wrote about him more in sorrow than in anger. The atmosphere of admiration in which he has always lived seems to have cooled, which should be an uncommonly good thing for Cecil. But I don't want to see him."

"Nor more don't any of us," Brownie said, wrathfully. "Billabong had enough of Mr. Cecil. Dear sakes!—when I think of him clearin' away from Miss Norah that night, an' what might have 'appened but for that blessed 'eathen, Lal Chunder, I don't feel 'ardly Christian, that I don't! Not as she ever made much of it—but—poor little lamb!"

Mr. Linton's face contracted, and Brownie left the topic hastily. It always agitated the invalid, who had indeed only been told of Norah's night adventure because of the risk of his hearing of it suddenly from outsiders or a newspaper. The district had seethed over the child's peril, and Lal Chunder had found himself in the embarrassing position of a hero—which by no means suited that usually mild-mannered Asiatic. He had developed a habit of paying Billabong frequent, if fleeting, calls; apparently for the sole purpose

153

of looking at Norah, for he rarely spoke. There was no guest more welcome.

Presently Murty O'Toole and Dave Boone came round the corner of the verandah.

"Masther Jim gev special insthructions not to be later'n half-past four in takin' y' in, sir," said the Irishman. "The chill do be comin' in the air afther that, says he. An' Miss Norah towld me to be stern wid ye!"

"Oh, did she?" said Norah's father, laughing. "Well, I suppose I'd better be meek, Murty, if the orders are so strict—though it's warm enough out here still."

"The cowld creeps up from thim flats," Murty said, judicially. "An' whin y' are takin' things aisy—well, y' are apt to take a cowld aisy as well."

"I'm certainly taking things far too easy for my taste," Mr. Linton said, smiling ruefully. "Five weeks on my back, Murty!—and goodness knows how much ahead. It doesn't suit me."

"I will admit there's some on the station 'twould suit betther," Murty answered. "Dave here, now—sure, he shines best whin he's on his back! an' I can do a bit av that same meself. ("You can that!" from the outraged Mr. Boone.) But y' had the drawback to be born widout a lazy bone in y'r body, so 'tis a hardship on y'. There is but wan thing that's good in it, as far as th' station sees."

"What's that, Murty?"

"Mrs. Brown here do be tellin' me Miss Norah's not to go away—an' there's not a man on the place but slung up his hat!" said the Irishman. "Billabong wouldn't be the same at all widout the little misthress—we had a grudge agin that foine school in Melbourne, so we had. However, it's all right now." He beamed on his master.

"Only a postponement, I'm afraid, Murty," said that gentleman, who beamed himself, quite unconsciously.

"Yerra, it's no good lookin' ahead—time enough to jump over the bridge when y' come to it," said Murty, cheerfully. "Annyhow, she'll not be lavin' on us yit. Well, if y' are ready, sir?" He nodded to Boone and took up his position at the head of Mr. Linton's couch.

"I'll go into the dining-room," the squatter said, as they carried him gently into the hall. "Put me near the window, boys—no, the one looking down the track. That's all right," as his couch came to anchor in the bay of a window that gave a clear view of the homestead paddock. He chatted to them awhile longer before wishing them good-night.

The stockmen tramped out, making violent efforts to be noiseless.

"Whisht, can't y'?" said Murty, indignantly, as Dave cannoned

154

into a chair in the hall. "Have y' not got anny manners at all, thin, Davy? wid' him lyin' there, an' good luck to him! Did y' see how he made us put his sofy in that square little winder?"

"Why?" asked the slower Mr. Boone.

"An' what but to see the first glimpse av them kids comin' home? Y' do be an ass, Davy!" said Murty, pleasantly. "Begob, 'tis somethin' f'r a man's eyes to see how Miss Norah handles that bay horse!"

Left to himself, David Linton made a pretence at reading a paper, but his eyes were weary, and presently the sheet crackled to the floor, and lay unheeded. Brownie, coming in softly, thought he had fallen asleep, and tiptoed to the couch with a light rug, which she drew over him. They handled him very carefully; although his clean, hard life had helped him to make a wonderful recovery, his injuries had been severe; and it would be many weeks yet before he could use his leg, even with crutches. The trained nurse from Melbourne, who had been more or less a necessary evil, or, as Jim put it, "an evil necessary," had been dispensed with a week before; and now he had as many attendants as there were inhabitants of Billabong, with Norah as head nurse and Brownie as superintendent, and Jim as right-hand man. Once there had been a plan that Jim should go North, for other experience, after leaving school. But it was never talked of now.

This was the first day, since they had brought her father home, that Norah had been induced to leave him; and then it had taken a command on his part to make her go. She was growing pale and hollow-eyed with the long watching.

Dr. Anderson, whose visits were becoming rarer, had prescribed a tonic, which Norah had taken meekly, and without apparent results.

"The tonic she wants is her own old life," Brownie had said. "Stickin' inside the house all day! it's no wonder she's peakin' and pinin'. Make her go out, sir." So David Linton had asserted himself from his couch; and Jim had taken Norah for a ride over the paddocks, and to call for the mail at the Cross Roads, where the Billabong loose bag was left by the coach three times a week.

He was lying with his eyes fixed on the track when they came out of the trees; both horses at a hand gallop and pulling double. Norah was on Garryowen, her face flushed and laughing, her head thrown back a little as the beautiful bay reefed and plunged forward, enjoying the speed as much as his rider. Jim was a length or so behind on Monarch, whose one ambition at that moment was, in Murty's words, "to get away on him." It was plain that the boy was exulting in the tussle. The sunlight gleamed on the black horse's splendid side as they dashed up the track.

155

As yet there had been no talk openly of a successor to Bobs–that wound was still too sore. For the present Norah was to ride Garryowen, since Monarch was far too frivolous to stand a long spell; Jim would handle him for the months that must elapse before his father was in the saddle again. Later on, Jim and Mr. Linton had great plans for something very special–a new pony that would not disgrace Bobs' memory, and that would fit the unused rug with the scarlet B that lay locked away in Norah's wardrobe. Other things were locked away in her heart; she never spoke of Bobs. But the two who were her mates knew.

The swift hoofs came thudding up the track and scattered the gravel by the gate; then there was silence for a moment, voices and laughter, and quick footsteps, and Jim and Norah came in together, their faces glowing.

"How did you get on, Dad? Were we long?"

"Long!" said David Linton, whose face had grown suddenly contented. "The conceit of some people! Why, I had so much attention paid me that I scarcely noticed you had gone." He put up one hand and took Norah's as she sat on the arm of his couch. "But I'm glad you're back," he added. They smiled at each other.

"Conceit's bad enough," said Jim, grinning, "but insanity's worse. Had the maddest ride of my life, Dad–my poor old Garryowen's absolutely cowed, and has no tail left to speak of!" He ducked to avoid a cushion from his sister. "It's a most disastrous experiment to keep Norah off a horse for five weeks!"

"We won't repeat it," said her father, "not that Garryowen seemed to be suffering from nervous prostration as he came up the paddock–or Monarch either! Any letters?"

"One from Wally," Norah cried, "poor old boy. He says school is horrid without Jim, and he's collar-proud, and they lost the match last Saturday–he carried out his bat for thirty-seven, though!–and he misses Billabong, and he sends his love and all sorts of messages to you, Dad. I guess Brownie and I will fix up a hamper for him," concluded Norah, pensively, weighing in her mind the attractions of plum or seed cake, and deciding on both. "And mince pies," she added, aloud.

"What?" said her father, staring. "Oh, I see. Any other mail?"

"Oh, the usual pile for you, Dad. Agents' letters and bills and things. Jim has them. We didn't bring the papers."

"I should think not!" returned her father. "If I catch either of you carrying loose papers on those horses–well, one broken leg is enough in a family of this size!"

"Too much respect for Monarch, to say nothing of my legs," said Jim, laconically, producing a handful of letters. "There you are,

Dad; that's all. Do you want anything? I'm going down to the little paddock for a lesson in bullock driving from Burton."

"How are you getting on in the art?" asked his father, smiling.

"Oh, slowly. My command of language doesn't seem to be sufficient, for so far the team looks on me with mild scorn." Jim grinned. "It's nervous work for Joe, too. I got him with the tail of the whip yesterday, when I'd every intention of correcting old Ranger! However, I plod on, and Joe keeps well out of the way now. He yells instructions at me from some way back in the landscape!"

"Prudent man, Burton," laughed his father. "A good tutor, too. I don't know that I ever saw a man handle bullocks better. Most people don't credit bullocks with souls, but I think Joe gets nearer to finding that attribute in his beasts than the average driver, and with less expenditure of energy and eloquence! He's like the man we were reading about, North:

"As to a team, over gully and hill,
He can travel with twelve on the breadth of a quill!"

"Oh, could he?" asked Jim, with much interest. "Well, the width of the paddock doesn't seem more than enough for me, so far. We wobble magnificently, the team and I! However, I keep hoping! I'd better be going. Sure you don't want me, Dad?"

"Not just now, old chap."

"Well, I'll be back before long." He smiled at his father and Norah, swinging out over the window ledge, and whistling cheerily until his long legs had carried him out of sight.

"He'll be a good man on the place, Norah."

"Why, of course," said Norah, a little surprised that statement should be made of so evident a fact. "Murty says he's 'takin' howld wid' both hands, an' 'tis the ould man over agin,' though it's like Murty's cheek to call you that. You won't be able to let him go away, I believe, Dad."

"I don't see myself sparing him to any other place now," said Mr. Linton. "Nor the head nurse either!"

Norah slipped down beside him.

"I've been thinking," she said, a little anxiously. "It's been so lovely to think of no old school until midwinter—but I'd go sooner—when you're quite well—if you're worried really, Dad. I don't want to be a duffer—and of course I don't know half that other girls know."

"Jim will be able to keep you from going back, I expect," her father said, watching the troubled face. "He won't be exactly a stern tutor, and possibly lessons may be free and easy; still, after all, Jim was a prefect, and the handling of unruly subjects is probably not unknown to him."

"If Jim attempts to be a prefect with me," said Norah, "things will

157

be mixed!" She laughed, but the line came back into her forehead. "It's not the lessons I was thinking of, Dad."

"Then what is it?"

"Oh, all the other things I don't know that other girls do. Do you think it really matters, Dad? I know perfectly well I don't do my hair properly—"

"I seem to like it."

"And I can't talk prettily—you know, like Cecil did; and I don't know a single blessed thing about fancywork! I'd—I'd hate you to be ashamed of me, Dad, dear!"

"Ashamed?" He held her close; and when he spoke again there was something in his voice that made Norah suddenly content.

"Little mate!" was all he said.

THE END